BEAUTIFUL DECEPTION

RETRIBUTION SERIES
BOOK 4

MORGAN JAMES

ONE

GIULIANA

I stood at the counter and peered out the kitchen window into the bright morning light reflecting off the heavy layer of snow that had fallen last night, turning the backyard into a winter wonderland. Without warning, a pair of strong arms slipped around my waist.

"Morning, beautiful."

I leaned into Eric's warm body and tipped my head to the side, allowing him to drop a kiss on the slope of my neck. "I missed you last night."

"I know." I could hear the regret in his voice. "The Johanssons were at it again."

As sheriff of the small town of Pine Ridge, Eric took his job seriously. He was often called out in the middle of the night and though he had several deputies beneath him, he'd told me once that he felt an obligation to personally see to the citizens' safety. There was no doubt in my mind that he knew every single resident of Pine Ridge by name, and his protective and caring nature was evident in the way he handled his duties.

"I'm sorry." I snuggled further into his embrace. "I'd say I hope they'd learned their lesson, but…"

He chuckled, and his warm breath wafted across my cheek. "If they haven't figured it out yet, I doubt they ever will."

I wiggled my hips against his and felt the hard ridge of his arousal pressing into my bottom. His hands left my waist and slid down to the curve of my hips, his fingers curling into my flesh and pulling me close. I glanced at the clock and bit my lip. "Don't start something you can't finish."

He growled low in my ear, then nipped the soft flesh, making me jump. "I always finish, and so do you."

"But I can't take time to appreciate it properly," I complained without heat. I shivered as his mouth moved downward, his teeth skimming the cords of my throat.

"Only because I want to make sure you're properly taken care of."

It was true; he was notorious for spending an inordinate amount of time ensuring I derived as much pleasure from our lovemaking as possible, as many times as possible—and I loved every second of it.

"I would," I said regretfully, "but I have a meeting with Tony and Mia this morning to go over plans."

I loved my job at Briarleigh Lodge and Resort, a beautiful retreat for vacationers situated at the top of Mount Washington in northern Montana. Jack and Mia Prescott, the owners, were amazing to work for. Barely ten years older than myself, they were more like friends than employers. When I'd suggested the addition of a spa a couple of months ago, they'd immediately hopped onboard. Since then, Mia and I had been working nonstop to get everything ready for its grand opening. It had taken a lot of research and the application of multiple licenses, but everything was finally starting to fall into place.

"What time will you be done?"

I shrugged. "Probably normal time, as long as nothing crazy happens between now and then."

"Tonight then." Eric spun me in his arms and stared down at me for a moment. "But I'm not letting you go without this."

He took my mouth in a hard kiss, his tongue sliding over mine, and my knees went weak like they did every time he touched me. I'd never felt so cherished, so loved, as I did with him. I would forever be grateful that he found me on the side of the road that day nearly three months ago.

Born into the Capaldi crime family, I was a mafia princess and only daughter of the capo of the Chicago outfit. When my father was killed three years ago, my uncle took over, and things changed drastically. In an attempt to align the Italian and Russian families, Uncle Massimo arranged my marriage to the Bratva captain, Nikolai. My uncle was abusive and cruel, often locking me away in the dark, stifling closet for hours at a time, but I'd heard the swirling rumors that Nikolai was worse; his first two wives had disappeared without a trace, and I refused to be another statistic. With little more than the clothes on my back, I ran and never looked back. As I stood in the circle of Eric's arms, I had never been more thankful for anything in my life.

He broke the kiss, and I stared up at him, studying his features. He was a hard man, stronger than anyone I knew, but he would never hurt me. He'd saved me more times than I could count, not only from external threats, but from myself as well. In those early days, I'd been tempted to flee at the first sign of trouble. Eric had slowly coaxed me out of my shell, urging me to believe in him. And I did—I trusted him with my life.

"You okay?"

His brows drew slightly together as he stared down at me, and a smile slowly spread over my face. "Perfect."

He stared at me dubiously, and I tightened my hold on his

shirt where it was still clenched in my fists. "I was just thinking about how lucky I am."

His expression softened, and he pulled me infinitesimally closer. "You've got that wrong, babe." He dipped his head and brushed his lips over mine, soft and sweet. "I'm the lucky one."

I leaned into him for a long moment, soaking up the heat and solace his large body offered. His touch was like a balm to my soul. Sometimes in the still darkness of night, when I found myself feeling lost and adrift, I would reach for him. The second my skin touched his, my heart calmed, and my mind relaxed, the connection between us potent and undeniable.

I'd never before believed people who said their partner completed them; now I knew what they meant. It was the physical closeness, that deep level of trust I'd never found with another person. Eric was everything to me, literally the other half I hadn't known I was missing.

Peeling myself away, I peered up at him. "I should get going."

"I know." He framed my face with his large hands and dropped another soft kiss on my lips. "Have fun. And don't forget about dinner tonight."

A grin spread over my face. It was our first real date, and I was more excited than I should be. Though we'd been dating for almost two months, things had been hectic and I was glad the holidays were over so we could focus more on our relationship. There was a restaurant at the resort, but Eric had decided we deserved something special, so tonight we were headed down to a steakhouse in Kalispell to relax and unwind.

"I can't wait."

I stretched up on my toes and stole one more kiss before pulling away and grabbing my keys from the small table near the front door. Eric's searing gaze watched me the entire way, sending tendrils of heat curling through me.

God, I loved that man more than anything.

A smile on my face, I hopped down the two wide porch steps and bounded through the powdery layer of snow to my car. The little Cavalier had served me well, but I'd recently considered upgrading to an SUV. Eric had tried to buy something for me a few weeks back, but I'd turned him down. It wasn't that I didn't appreciate the gesture—I did. But he'd already done so much for me, and I didn't want to feel indebted to him more than I already did. I wanted him to know that I was with him because I loved him, not because of what he could offer me. More than that, I wanted to prove to myself that I could do it on my own. For the first time in my life, I had a job—one that I loved and that paid well—and I was determined to forge my own path through life.

I hummed a happy little tune as I navigated the short drive down to the lodge, then pulled into the employee lot and put the car in park. For the past couple of months, ever since the incident at Eric's house, we'd been staying in a cabin that had once belonged to Mia's late father, Bruce. It was empty and they had offered it up, not wanting to part with it. It was one of only a handful of homes high up on the mountain, and Jack and Mia's place was only a few miles away. It was private and peaceful, and an added bonus was that it was only a few minutes' drive to the resort.

My gaze lifted and I froze in place as an Escalade slowly drove down the narrow lane of parked cars. The sight hit me with the force of a freight train, bringing with it a thousand memories I thought I'd buried. Horror replaced my earlier joy, turning my blood to ice in my veins. I grabbed the steering wheel, holding on for dear life, ready to throw the car in drive and race away. All black with tinted windows, the huge SUV was the same high-end vehicle my uncle had chosen for himself and his men.

Heart banging against my ribcage, the sound echoing in my ears, I resisted the urge to slump down in my seat and hide away. Had Uncle Massimo finally found me? I held my breath as I studied the driver through the darkened side window. Dressed in what appeared to be a casual long-sleeved shirt, it wasn't the pristine suit I was expecting of the soldiers who worked for my uncle. Sunglasses and a ballcap obscured most of his face, but he didn't look familiar.

Thank God.

The Escalade rolled past, and my eyes darted to the license plate affixed to the back of the vehicle. South Dakota. I relaxed my hold on the steering wheel and slowly let out a relieved sigh. I'd half expected to see an Illinois plate on the bumper, some indication that the man had come all the way from Chicago to find me.

I watched as the Escalade stopped at the end of the row. The driver hesitated for several interminable seconds, then turned left toward the visitor parking lot. He was just lost, then.

My lungs deflated as I let out the breath I'd been holding and I pressed one hand to my chest, willing my heart to slow its rapid pace. I briefly closed my eyes and swallowed down the last of my fear. Uncle hadn't found me yet; he wouldn't. I'd left literally everything behind—clothes, cell phone, credit cards. I was untraceable and living in a remote mountain town. My fear was unfounded; I was safe.

Shaking off the lingering chill that clung to my spine, I slipped the keys from the ignition then climbed from the car and headed inside. A glance at my watch told me I had approximately forty minutes until our meeting with the supervisor. I jingled the keys as I walked, and I opened the pro shop first.

The manager Jack and Mia had hired would be here shortly, but I enjoyed opening each morning, getting everything ready in the peace and quiet before the bustle of the day began. Once it started, it wouldn't stop again until after midnight when the restaurant bar closed down.

I booted up the computer and glanced through yesterday's sales, making quick note of anything that needed to be restocked or reordered.

"Good morning!"

Jenn's happy voice cut through the still air, and I smiled at her as she approached the desk. "Morning."

I moved out of the way so she could use the computer to clock in, then she turned to me. "How was it yesterday?"

I handed her the papers. "Pretty decent for a Tuesday." I checked the clock on the computer. "All right. I'm off."

With a smile and a little wave, I headed down the long hallway toward the spa. Tony, the supervisor for the addition, stood outside the large oak doors, and he threw a smile my way. Somewhere in his late sixties, he was still handsome, salt and pepper flecking his dark hair. I wasn't terribly comfortable around most men, but Tony put off a fatherly vibe that had immediately set me at ease.

Mia joined us and for the next two hours, we discussed the progress of the spa. Each room of the facility had been framed in and plumbing and electricity had already been run. They planned to start the drywall next week, then the flooring would go in. The tile we'd chosen for the salon was backordered, but it wasn't a huge concern, according to Tony. All of the other materials were in the back waiting to be installed, so they could finish the salon once everything else was done.

We thanked Tony, then Mia turned to me, her eyes bright. "I have a surprise for you."

"Okay…" I drew out the word, confused.

"Close your eyes." I did as she asked, then her hands landed on my shoulders. "Now turn around three times."

"What? Why?"

"So you won't know where we're going." Her tone was tinged with exasperation, and I let out a little laugh.

"How will that help? I could just open my eyes if I really wanted to know."

Mia paused, and her hands lifted away from me. I could just imagine her gesticulating wildly as she spoke. "Whatever. You know what I mean. Baby brain."

A low chuckle met my ears, and my eyes popped open as Jack approached. "Don't let her fool you. That started long before she got pregnant."

I pressed my lips together to hide my smile as Mia leveled a haughty glare at her husband. "Are you intentionally trying to pick a fight?"

"Never." His expression never changed, but I could see the teasing glint in his eyes as he stared at her.

Mia lifted one brow at him. "Mhmm."

He stepped close as if to pass us by, then dipped his head and spoke low in her ear. Mia's cheeks turned pink, and she licked her lips as Jack straightened. He took her chin between his thumb and forefinger, then looked deep into her eyes for several long seconds. Finally, he released her and nodded toward me.

"Try to keep her in line."

I shrugged helplessly, a smile pulling at the corners of my mouth. "No promises."

"You're telling me," he murmured. With one more meaningful look at Mia, he turned and strode down the hall. My gaze drifted toward Mia as she watched her husband, a hungry look of longing etched on her face.

It was always interesting watching those two interact. Mia was perpetually bubbly while Jack was so intense. And yet it just… worked. I could feel the desire, the love crackling between the two of them, despite the fact that they were rarely—if ever— affectionate in public. I knew part of that was Mia's choice. Since she was partial owner of her late father's company, Hamilton Construction, I knew she felt she had to try twice as hard to be taken seriously in what people still considered a man's role.

"If you'd rather wait…"

Mia's head snapped toward me, and her eyes cleared. "No! I've been waiting all day for this."

I barely suppressed a smile. "It's barely eleven o'clock."

Pretty blue eyes rife with mock condescension glared at me. "You know what I mean."

I laughed, and she cracked a smile. "Seriously, this kid's killing me. I'm tired and hungry all the time, and I swear I'd forget my head if it wasn't attached."

"I'm sure that's normal," I assured her. Playing along with whatever scheme she'd concocted, I turned around and closed my eyes. "All right. I'm game."

Her hands fell to my shoulders once more, and she guided me forward. "No peeking."

"Okay, okay." Curiosity tugged at me as we passed the kitchen, the sounds of clanging pans giving away our location. Another minute later, Mia pulled me to a stop. "Okay… Open!"

I blinked my eyes open and came face-to-face with… A door? "Ummm…"

Mia moved to my right side and tipped her head toward the plaque hanging on the wall which read "Special Events Coordinator."

I whirled toward her. "What is this?"

A huge smile lit her face. "Your new office."

I turned back toward the oak door, emotion clogging my throat.

"I know we haven't talked about it," Mia spoke up, "but I wanted it to be a surprise. Even if you don't want the position, the office is still yours."

I swallowed hard and blinked away the tears of gratitude

that had formed while she spoke. "Mia, I... I don't know what to say."

She lifted her hands and spread her fingers wide. "I'm not an expert, but "yes" seems as good a response as any."

I covered my face with my hands, grinning like a fool. "Yes!"

"Yay!" Mia's arms came around me in a huge hug, and I held on tight.

Never in my life had I felt happier, more accepted than I did here. Months ago I'd arrived in Pine Ridge alone and scared, and badly in need of funds to keep me going. Eric found me on the side of the road when my car ran out of gas, and he'd called in a favor to Jack to hire me on. Now I had a man who loved me and friends and coworkers whom I adored.

Life truly didn't get any better than this.

TWO

ERIC

Pulling open the top drawer of my desk, I fished deep in the back and extracted the little black box. Using my thumb, I flipped it open and gazed at the sparkly diamond inside.

"Finally going to ask?"

Lost in my thoughts, I hadn't heard Riley enter. Snapping the box closed, I dropped it back into the drawer and raked my hands over my face. "Fuck. I don't know."

Riley sank into one of the hard plastic chairs and stared at me across the desk between us. "How long have you been holding onto that thing now?"

Nearly a month. I'd lied to Jules and told her that I got called into work one day. Instead, I'd gone down to Kalispell and spent nearly six hours looking for the perfect ring.

"Too long," I responded, and Riley laughed.

"What the hell are you waiting for? Gotta lock your girl down before someone else does."

I knew he was just yanking my chain, but I couldn't help the sudden surge of jealousy. Jules was smart and beautiful, and I sure as hell didn't deserve her, but I wasn't about to give her up. She was mine and mine alone.

Falling for her was never the plan. When she showed up last December, she was cool and distant, hiding from a past she refused to reveal. Much too young and utterly vulnerable, she was completely off limits. But no other woman made me feel the way she did. She'd managed to worm her way into my heart with her sweet smiles and guileless green eyes, and I'd fallen hard and fast. She meant more to me than anything on earth, and I wanted her by my side forever. Though she still hadn't opened up to me about what had brought her here to Pine Ridge, I decided it wasn't important. I hoped that one day she would be comfortable enough to tell me the truth, but the past was the past, and now it was just Jules and me. Nothing else mattered.

"I'm taking her out to dinner tonight. I plan to ask her after that."

"Good luck, man," Riley said as he stretched one hand across the desk. "You deserve it."

I slipped my palm into his. "Thanks."

I wondered if Riley could feel my hand shaking, and I yanked it away. I was nervous as fuck. What if she said no? It was part of the reason I'd waited so long to ask. After everything she'd been through, I wanted to make sure she was making the right decision. Now that things had returned mostly to normal and we'd fallen into a kind of routine, I was a little more confident. Jules and I had begun as roommates and we soon became friends, then lovers. Each day with her was better than the last, and I wanted to see her beautiful face every morning until I took my dying breath.

"What are you waiting for? Get out of here." Riley hitched one thumb over his shoulder toward the door.

I grabbed the black box out of my drawer once more and shoved it into my pocket as I stood. With a nod to my deputy, I slid my arms into my jacket, then strode out the door and climbed into my cruiser. My thumbs tapped an impatient rhythm on the steering wheel as I drove home. The little black box burned a hole in my pocket, and I was a nervous wreck by the time I pulled up in front of the large log cabin that had once belonged to Mia Prescott's father. This house held memories too, but not like mine.

We still hadn't listed my house for sale, but I knew without a doubt we would never go back there. I'd never get the image of Jules's terrified face, the dark stain of blood saturating the bedroom carpet out of my mind. I felt like we needed a fresh start as a couple. If everything went well tonight, I would soon have a fiancée. The idea of starting a family with Jules turned my blood hot. I climbed out of my car and placed a hand on the hood of Jules's older blue Cavalier. Still warm. She must've only beat me home by minutes, and I went in search of her. Pushing the front door open, I saw her in the kitchen to my immediate left, and I automatically gravitated toward her.

She smiled up at me as I approached. "Hey. How was your day?"

Afraid to open my mouth, terrified that I would spill the secret if I did, I slipped my hands into her hair and crashed my mouth to hers. Her body melted against mine under the force of the kiss, her mouth hot and sweet. I loved the feel of her, the taste of her. I would never get enough. A few seconds later, I lifted my head, and Jules looked up at me, a tiny smile lifting the corners of her mouth. "That good, huh?"

"That good," I agreed as I dipped my head to kiss her once more. "Are you ready for dinner?"

Her hands splayed over my pecs, and she pouted playfully. "Or we could just stay here and finish what you started."

It was an easy out that I was tempted to take, but in the end I shook my head. "No, baby, you deserve this."

It had taken me weeks to convince her to go on a date

with me—a real date. Pine Ridge had exactly two restaurants, not counting the restaurant that had just opened at Briarleigh. Rosie's Café closed down daily at two o'clock, at which time the adjoining bar would open. I wasn't about to take her to a bar for our first date, and I sure as hell couldn't propose in front of a hundred people we knew and saw every day. Though she would've been happy enough to have dinner at the resort, I wanted to do something special for her and take her down to Kalispell.

I glanced at the clock. "Reservations are for an hour and a half from now, so get that cute ass in gear." I gave her bottom a little swat to get her moving, but it had the opposite effect—not that I was complaining. Her arms wound around my neck and she pulled me down for another long, slow kiss.

She broke away with a soft, sweet little sigh and spoke against my lips. "I love you."

Twining one arm around her tiny waist, I pulled her flush against me and brushed my nose against hers. "Love you, beautiful."

I'd almost lost her once, and I wasn't too proud to tell her every day what she meant to me. I'd do it every day for the rest of my life if she'd let me.

I growled as I gently pushed her away. "Go before I throw you over my shoulder and carry you to the car."

A broad smile curved her mouth, lighting her eyes, and the sight of it made me go weak in the knees. She slowly backed away, then flounced toward the loft so she could change. As soon as she'd disappeared up the stairs, my hand went to the box concealed in my coat pocket. I drew in a deep breath, trying desperately to calm my fraying nerves.

That look on her face told me everything I needed to know; she was the woman I wanted to spend the rest of my life with. I hung up my coat and jogged upstairs, then quickly shed my uniform. Twenty minutes later, I'd showered and shaved, and we made our way out the door.

During the ride to Kalispell, we chatted amiably, Jules telling me all the plans for Briarleigh's new spa. I was nervous as shit and feeling more tongue-tied than ever, so I gladly let her fill the silence. As soon as we were seated and had a bottle of wine delivered and poured, Jules folded her hands and placed them in front of her on the table. She tipped her head slightly to one side, a mischievous glint in her eyes as she peered at me.

"So, we have something else to celebrate tonight."

I felt the blood drain from my face. How the hell had she found out? I decided to do what I did best: play dumb.

"Oh? What's that?"

"Well..." Jules dragged out the word, and I found myself holding my breath. "You're looking at Briarleigh's new Special Events Coordinator."

I blinked, so totally consumed by relief that it took me a moment to respond. "God, babe, that's awesome. I'm so happy for you."

I reached across the table and took her hand in mine. It was her left hand, and I eyed her ring finger for a minute before giving her a gentle squeeze. I wouldn't do this now; I wanted her to revel in this special moment, about her and her alone. "I'm so glad it's worked out for you. You deserve it."

That smile I loved so much lit her face again, full of pure joy and happiness, and it served only to reinforce my decision. This was her time. But later... later she would be mine.

THREE

GIULIANA

My heart beat nervously as I stared across the room at Eric. He'd been acting strange the whole evening, and he'd barely spoken a word during dinner. He'd congratulated me, of course, and seemed to be truly happy for me. Yet... something seemed off.

I rolled the hem of my shirt between my fingers as Eric built up a fire in the large stone fireplace. He stood and wiped his palms on his thighs, a movement to me that appeared agitated, nervous.

His gaze shot to me, the green of his hazel eyes boring into me. "Will you help me grab some firewood?"

"Sure." Pushing down my anxiety, I stood from the couch and approached him. I stepped into my boots, and Eric held the door for me as we moved out on the porch. The cold air hit me like a punch to the gut, freezing the air in my lungs. I briskly rubbed my arms as Eric looped an arm around my shoulders and pulled me close.

Tipping my head up, I gazed at the stars shining brightly in the winter sky, only two tiny wisps of clouds marring the endless black expanse. Once upon a time we had a discussion about thermal energy, and the memory brought a smile to my lips.

I tilted my face toward his. "Going to be cold tonight," I said teasingly.

Eric looked at me, but he didn't smile. His expression was solemn, and it kicked my pulse into a rapid tempo.

"What's wrong?" I whispered. A thousand thoughts flooded my mind, none of them good. My breaths came stilted and shallow, my lungs threatening to hyperventilate as I contemplated his reaction. Eric was serious, but this... I'd never seen him so stoic before. Fear flashed, rendering me motionless. Was he leaving me?

Eric turned to face me more fully, an emotion in his eyes that I didn't recognize. He lifted his hands and cupped my face, his long, strong fingers cradling my neck and jaw. His head moved in a jerky motion as he stared intently at me, and he tenderly brushed his thumbs over my cheeks. "You are everything right with the world."

Relief cascaded over me, pushing away the fear as I took in the love in his eyes. His hands slid down my neck, over my shoulders, and coasted along the length of my arms until he took my hands in his. "I love you more than anything, and I want to spend every day making you happy."

Even when he bent to one knee in front of me, it didn't fully click until he began to speak. "I had a whole speech prepared." He let out a self-deprecating little laugh. "I recited it to myself a thousand times over dinner, and now I can't remember a damn word."

My lips parted into a little 'O', but no sound came out. My eyes misted over, and I pressed my hands to my lips as Eric released me to withdraw a little black box from the inside pocket of his jacket.

"I'm no good at this, so I'm just going to ask. Jules... Will you marry me?"

Eyes wide, I opened and closed my mouth, but nothing came out. It was literally the last thing I had expected, and surprise halted the words on my tongue. Finally, I managed a shaky nod.

Eric stared up at me and quirked a brow. "Is that a yes?"

"Yes," I whispered, my voice breaking on the word.

Eric grasped my left hand where it still covered my mouth and brought it to his lips. He pressed a kiss to the back of my fingers before slipping the ring on. Still holding my hand, he climbed to his feet and pulled me into his arms. "You sure about this?"

His quiet words jerked me from my stupor and I threw my arms around his neck, a huge grin overtaking my face. "Yes!"

Eric caught me as I threw myself at him and wrapped my legs around his waist. Our mouths fused together in a heart stopping kiss, and I felt him moving toward the front door. Without breaking the kiss, he shifted me in his arms to open the door, then kicked it closed behind us.

His hands slipped beneath my bottom, his long fingers stretching down and brushing my center through the material of my pants. His hair was too short to pull, so I settled for raking my nails across the base of his scalp. I wiggled against him, and his low growl rumbled across my lips. His arousal between us seemed to grow impossibly thick and hard, and I rocked my hips against his.

He nipped my bottom lip and carried me up to the loft bedroom without another word. As soon as we reached the foot of the bed, he set me on my feet. His hands grasped the hem of my sweater dress and drew it hastily over my head. It landed on the floor with a whisper, but I didn't even notice as he dropped to his knees.

His hands went to one boot and he tugged it off before moving to the other. They, too, landed in a heap by the closet, and he began to attack my leggings. He delved inside the waistband then drew them down my hips, trailing kisses over my flesh as it was revealed to him. I pulled one leg free, then the other, and stood before him in only my bra and underwear.

"Turn." His voice was husky as he made a circle motion with his finger, and I bit back a smile as I followed his instructions. I made a full circle, then faced him again.

He loved sexy underwear, and I hadn't yet had a chance to surprise him with these. The red lace panties had ties on each side, much like a bikini. Three little bows ran vertically, like a ladder, connecting the material of the front to the back. As each bow came untied, the panties became looser, just like unwrapping a Christmas present.

His eyes were hot and dark as they moved to the laces on one hip. "New?"

"Mhmm..." I hummed out a response as he leaned forward and pressed an open-mouthed kiss to my hip bone. He trailed lower and took the tie of one bow between his teeth, then pulled. My hands moved to his head as he loosened the second, then kissed his way across my stomach and performed the same actions on the other side.

His fingers trailed up the backs of my legs, and I shivered as goosebumps rose in their wake. It wasn't from the cold— oh, no. Everything about Eric was hot and hard, and he made me feel things I'd never experienced. I was a virgin when I showed up three months ago, and I'd dreaded ever being with a man. But Eric... He was so much more than I could have ever asked for. He was my first lover—and he would be my last.

He glanced up at me as the remaining two ties pulled loose, and the fabric slowly slid from my body. My bottom bumped the bed as he gave me a gentle shove, and I collapsed backward as he'd intended. Propping myself up on my elbows, I watched him pull my hips toward him so I was suspended just over the edge of the mattress.

One eyebrow ratcheted toward his hairline, and the corner of his mouth lifted in a sexy smirk. It was a look I loved on him, because it meant he was about to get his way. It also almost always led to an immense amount of pleasure for me.

He pushed my knees apart, and I bit my lip as his hands coasted up the inside of my thighs. He stroked and massaged his way upward until he finally found my folds. His tongue darted out, and I jumped as he flicked the sensitive nub, now completely exposed.

Eric let out a rusty chuckle. "So sexy."

One thumb slid through my slick entrance, then his mouth was on me again. Fisting my hands in the bedspread, I braced myself against his onslaught. I closed my eyes against the sensation and let myself drift in the sheer ecstasy of the sensation.

His hands roamed my body, over my stomach and ribs, then upward to cup my breasts. Pulling the cup of my bra down, he circled my nipple. I arched into him as he tweaked the tip, teasing me until I writhed beneath him. An electric current shot from my breast all the way down to my core, and each stroke of his tongue stoked the fire within until wildfire roared through my veins.

He knew I was getting close. I let out a whimper and sank my teeth into my lower lip as he slipped two fingers inside me. He withdrew, then thrust deeply. The motion sent me over the edge, and a keening cry ripped from my throat as pleasure slammed into me, exploding in a shower of stars.

He rubbed gently through the slick folds, drawing out my orgasm until I collapsed, boneless and sated. I felt his fingers leave me, and he slowly prowled over me, kissing and licking his way up my body. His mouth landed hard on mine, and I tasted myself on him as his tongue slid between my lips.

I pulled my knees up to grip his hips as he settled his weight over me, his erection prodding my entrance. Flattening my hands on his chest, I pushed him away—no easy feat, considering he weighed damn near twice what I did.

He pulled back and arched a brow. My only answer was a gentle shove to his shoulder, and he fell to his back, pulling me with him. I slithered my way down his body until I was settled between his legs, and I smiled up at him. "Your turn."

FOUR

ERIC

That sexy little smirk would be the death of me. It made me want to dominate her, bury myself so deep inside her that she would feel me for weeks. I'd been her first—and I would damn well be her last. No other man would ever touch her; I would never give her up.

Eyes locked on mine, she slithered down onto her belly and propped her feet in the air behind her, suspending them over that gorgeous ass of hers. It was sexy as hell, and the little tease knew it got to me every time. I shoved a second pillow behind my shoulders and laced my fingers together behind my head as I settled in to watch her.

Her tongue darted out and flicked against the head of my cock, making it jump. Her plump lips opened and slid over the rounded head, taking in just the first inch before releasing it. She fisted my shaft, and the ring on her finger sparkled as she ran her left hand up and down my cock in a firm stroke. The sight of it sent a thrill of possession through me.

I watched as she ran her tongue from base to tip, and my hips jerked upward. There were times when Jules was still so shy, so reserved. But in bed... Fuck. She was free and uninhibited and more than I could have ever dreamed of. She opened herself to me fully and gave as much as she took. She reveled in the pleasure we drew from one another's bodies with insatiable need. Though we routinely had sex once a day —if not more—it wasn't enough. My sweet, innocent girl was a nymphomaniac, and I loved the hell out of it.

Her mouth felt like heaven, but I needed to be inside her. I needed to feel her muscles contracting and holding me close as her heat flooded my cock.

I lifted her away and guided her over me. "Get your sexy ass up here."

Hands braced on my pecs, she moved over my hips and positioned herself over me. Jules let out a sexy little moan as I speared up into her, and I tangled my tongue with hers. I tasted my lust on her, and the erotic sensation spurred me on. Her inner muscles were tight, still slightly swollen from her earlier release; it felt like coming home.

I curled my fingers into her hips as she began to move, slowly at first, then faster. The walls of her core constricted around me, spurring me on, and together we raced toward completion. She came first with a cry, and her head fell into the crook of my neck as her arms tightened around my shoulders.

Wrapping one arm around her waist, I flipped her over. She stared up at me, those gorgeous green eyes so full of lust and love and everything in between. I pulled out and thrust deep. Her back arched, and I laced our fingers together over her head. Eyes locked on hers, I took her hard and fast.

My blood went hot, and my dick turned rock-hard every time I saw her. It was an exercise in restraint trying to hold myself back. A tingling sensation shot through my stomach, then lower, and Jules let out a little sigh of ecstasy as my shaft swelled with my impending release. I wanted nothing more than to come inside her—but not yet.

Over the past two months, I'd mastered the pull-out method. She was sensitive to condoms, and we never talked about birth control. I knew she didn't want to use it, but I wasn't sure if it had more to do with the fact that she refused to put her name on anything or if she was against it due to personal or religious reasons. I felt like we were gambling every time we had sex, but I couldn't bring myself to care. I wanted so fucking badly to fill her up with my seed so she'd grow round with my children. It sounded archaic and primitive, but I didn't give a damn.

With a ragged groan, I pulled out. Jules's torso lifted and fell on rapid breaths, my desire glistening against her pale flesh. I slid my free hand to the back of her neck and squeezed. I couldn't resist. "One of these days I'm going to come inside you, really make you mine."

She nodded silently, and I took her mouth in a hard kiss before pushing off her. Reaching toward the nightstand, I swiped a handful of tissues from the box and cleaned up our lovemaking. I tossed them in the trash can beside the bed, then slid in next to her and pulled her close.

She curled onto her side, resting her head on my chest, and I dropped a kiss on the top of her head as she held up her left hand to examine the ring. It was the first time she'd really looked at it, and anxiety churned in my gut. I hoped she liked it. "What do you think?"

"I can't believe this is really happening," she said, her tone saturated with incredulity.

I captured her hand in one of mine, enjoying the way the diamond looked on her finger. "If you don't like the style, we—"

"No!" She snatched her hand away and turned her head to look up at me. "I love this one."

She turned her gaze back to the ring, and I pulled her closer, smiling against her silky hair.

I'd agonized over which ring to buy for hours, and I'd

damn near driven the saleswoman crazy, asking to see hundreds of different rings. Finally, I'd settled on a vintage-looking band with a single carat diamond in the middle. It was feminine and pretty, and it reminded me of Jules. "I'm glad you like it."

Her head nodded against my shoulder. "It's perfect."

Turning my head, I brushed my lips over the top of her head. She had that wrong; she was perfect. And I was never letting her go.

FIVE

GIULIANA

I practically skipped into Briarleigh the following morning, my heart swollen with love, my head in the clouds. The whole way to work, I kept glancing at my left hand where it rested on the steering wheel. The diamond glinted in the morning sunlight, sending tiny rainbows over the interior of the car. I held my hand up in front of me once more, and an elated grin lifted my lips.

I hadn't felt this happy in a long time. Maybe ever, if I was being entirely honest. Eric made me feel things I'd never experienced, and joy this pure was just one of them. He loved me for who I was, not who I could be. He'd accepted me wholly and without question when I showed up several months ago. Every day since then had been better than the last, and I looked forward to what our future might bring.

Yanking open the employee door, I hummed softly to myself as I strolled down the hallway to my new office. A huge grin split my face as I unlocked it and stepped inside. The walls were bare, and the only decoration was a small, fake potted plant that Mia had put in here, but I didn't care.

It was a space of my very own, a reminder of how much things had changed in just a few short months. No longer was I under my uncle's watchful gaze, kept locked away in my bedroom until he could marry me off. I had a job I adored, amazing friends and coworkers, and a man I loved more than anything. What could be better than that?

I still couldn't believe they'd done this for me. I glanced around the sparse space, debating how I wanted to decorate it. I sank into my chair, my gaze sliding over the sleek wooden desk, and I suddenly realized the most important thing it was missing. I needed a picture of Eric in here.

We'd only actually been dating for a little over two months, but it felt like we'd known each other forever. I'd have to rectify the picture situation here soon. Eric would probably fight me on it; judging from the scant number of photos he had, I figured he wasn't a fan of having his picture taken. Well, that was just too bad. I looked forward to whatever fight he would put up before he finally—inevitably—gave in. Mostly, though, I looked forward to the making up part of it.

It felt as if a smile had taken up permanent residence on my face today, and my cheeks ached from having been forced into the same position for so long. I massaged my jaw, grateful that I was in my own office where no one could see me. I probably looked like a deranged lunatic, but whatever. I couldn't bring myself to care. Life was too good right now to let anyone get me down. I did, however, have work to do.

I dug my keys out as I stowed my purse in the bottom drawer of the desk, then I locked up my office and headed toward the pro shop. I unlocked the doors and propped them open, then moved over to the bank of lights to switch them on. Bright light flooded the room, and pride filled me as I looked around. Though I didn't personally own the shop, I had done most of the work to get it up and running. My days now consisted mostly of making preparations for the spa, but one of my responsibilities was to manage the pro shop.

Most mornings, I would open the shop in preparation of customers and double check inventory. I liked to personally look over the new merchandise catalogs and select what I thought would sell best. Several catalogs lay on the desk, left out by whomever had closed last night. I picked one up and thumbed through it. I dogeared a few pages with apparel I liked so I could run it by Mia later. As if my thoughts conjured the woman, she strode through the double set of oak doors, looking harried.

"Hey. Thought I might find you in here. Sorry I'm late, I... overslept."

She was the boss here, and she had no need to apologize to me, but it was one of the things I appreciated most about her. Despite co-owning a multi-million-dollar company, as well as Briarleigh, Mia was one of the most down to earth people I'd ever known. She always gave 110%, expecting more of herself than others.

My eyes narrowed as I stared at her. Her cheeks were flushed pink, and her hair was slightly disheveled, but I recognized the look in her eyes. I tried to bite back my smile but failed miserably. "Your shirt's inside out."

"Damn it," she hissed, and I laughed.

"I think it's cute that you guys can't keep your hands off each other, even after all these years."

Mia spoke as she moved past me to one of the fitting rooms so she could adjust her shirt. "I swear, my hormones are crazy right now. I want to have sex all the time."

I laughed. "I can't imagine Jack is complaining about that."

Mia didn't answer one way or the other, but her satisfied little smile when she exited the fitting room gave me my answer. "So what do we have on the agenda today? I told

Carter we would have final figures for him by the end of the day."

I passed her the magazine that I'd flipped through earlier. "Take a look at these and let me know what you think. I'd like to fill out a purchase request for some new stuff."

She slipped the catalog from my fingers and began to flick through the pages I'd marked. "Oh," she breathed. "I like this one."

I peeked over the edge of the magazine and smiled when she complimented my favorite choice. Intentionally using my left hand, I pointed at it. "While we're talking about new things…" I allowed my words to trail off.

"What's…?" Her gaze slowly made its way up my pointer finger and across my knuckles to the sparkly diamond.

"Oh, my God!" She dropped the magazine, and it landed with the splat at our feet as she grabbed my hand. "Is this what I think it is?"

"Yes!" I cried as I bounced on my toes, unable to contain my excitement any longer. She let out a squeal then threw her arms around me in a fierce embrace. I hugged her back just as hard, elation filling me.

"Did I miss something?"

Mia and I pulled apart at the sound of Jack's deep voice, and she squeezed my arm. "He finally proposed!"

The corner of Jack's mouth lifted. "About damn time."

My gaze bounced between them. "You guys knew?"

"Not for sure," Mia assured me, "but I hoped he would."

Jack inclined his head at me. "Congratulations."

I couldn't keep the smile off my face. "Thank you."

Mia turned to me. "Guess we'll put that special events room to good use. I have a great idea!" Her eyes lit up as she rushed on. "We can have a spring-themed ceremony, and I can photograph it for the website. It'll be amazing. We'll have Lily do the flowers and Rosie can cater—as long as you don't mind." She seemed to catch herself and bit her lower lip. "Sorry, I kind of got ahead of myself."

As a professional photographer, Mia loved landscapes most of all, but she never passed up an opportunity to get good shots. She was responsible for all the photographs of Briarleigh, including aerial photos from a helicopter they'd rented one afternoon. She rode with Jack and Carter, the VP of Operations for the resort, who had heliskied down the mountain in celebration of the lodge opening. Her pictures now graced the website, drawing in customers from all over with images that showed how warm and inviting Briarleigh was.

She was amazing at what she did, there was no question about it. I was thrilled and so very grateful that she was willing to help set this up, but I still had to defer to Eric.

"Honestly," I replied, "we haven't even talked about it. I don't know if he'll want to have a ceremony or anything."

As a child, I thought occasionally of what my wedding would be like. I always pictured myself walking down the aisle of the old stone church where I'd been baptized, the pews filled with family and friends as sunlight streamed through the stained glass windows. When my uncle had arranged my betrothal to a Bratva captain, that dream had soured. As long as Eric was the man beside me, I didn't care how or where we tied the knot.

"Well, anything you want or need, just let me know." Mia smiled softly. "I'm so glad you're happy."

I returned the sentiment. "Me, too."

A sliver of guilt stabbed into my heart. I'd put it off for so long, but now it was time to open up. Eric deserved to know everything about his future wife, and I resolved to tell him— soon.

After work, I headed home, and I smiled when I saw Eric's cruiser parked out front already. He often worked long hours, but he made it a point to try to spend as much time with me as possible.

I made my way inside, expecting to see him in the kitchen or living room, but both rooms were empty and dim. I toed off my boots, leaving them in the tray next to the door to dry, then dropped my keys in the bowl on the side table. A soft creak drew my attention to the hallway just off the kitchen, and I headed that direction. A small office was situated diagonally from the kitchen, and I quietly stepped up to the door.

Eric sat with his elbows propped on the desk as he stared intently at the sheaf of papers in front of him. I smiled. He got that way sometimes; he had an almost single-minded focus that wouldn't allow him to rest until every detail had been sorted and catalogued.

"You gonna stand there and stare at me all night?"

Eric didn't bother to lift his head when he spoke, and my grin grew wider. "Maybe."

Though I'd been hovering just off to the side, almost out of sight, he was acutely aware of everything around him at all times. I rounded the doorjamb and entered the office. "Are you hungry?"

He shoved his chair back and opened his arms, his eyes darkening with desire as he pulled me into his lap. "Starving."

His mouth took mine in a brutal kiss, his hands already roaming over my back and sides. His fingers slipped beneath the hem of my sweater, and I lifted my arms, allowing him to draw it up and off. Deftly, he unsnapped my bra and pulled it off, then tossed it to the floor.

His eyes took on a heated quality as he palmed my breasts, his rough thumbs brushing the sensitive peaks. I sucked in a breath as he took one between his lips, and a bolt of lightning shot straight to my core. His erection swelled beneath me, and I ground against it.

He let out a rough chuckle. "Not yet, pretty girl. Not until I get a taste of you. We've got all night, and I plan to make the most of every minute."

SIX

ERIC

Shifting her to my forearm, I swept the papers on the desk out of the way and set her on the edge of the cool wood. She blinked sensually at me, then fell to her back when I gave her shoulder a gentle shove.

I moved my hands to her waistband, and her hips lifted as I unsnapped the button, then peeled them down her slender legs. My gaze roved over her gorgeous body, bare except for a tiny pair of teal panties with butterflies all over them.

My sweet, sexy little butterfly.

I grinned at the image that popped into my head. Gone was the naïve young woman I'd found on the side of the road months ago. Just like a caterpillar morphing into a gorgeous, uninhibited butterfly, she'd come completely out of her shell for me and spread her wings.

Sliding my hands under her legs, I reveled in the feel of her ass cheeks filling my palms. I fucking loved her ass. Round and muscular and so goddamn sexy, I was pretty sure it was my favorite part of her.

I coasted my hands up her inner thighs until I reached her

core, then nudged the material aside. My gaze flicked to her face, and I watched her eyes flutter closed, her teeth sinking into her lower lip as I swiped through her slit.

I'd felt her eyes on me the moment she approached the office. She rarely, if ever, entered what she considered my domain, but I was glad she'd chosen to do so tonight. The fantasy of fucking her right here on this desk had come to life with surprising force, and I couldn't wait one more second to be inside her.

Using one foot to push the chair backward, I kissed my way up her body. I claimed her mouth again, and her arms twined around my shoulders, holding me close. Reaching between us, I flicked the button on my pants and used one hand to work them down over my hips.

My erection jumped to attention, brushing the inside of her thigh as it sprang from its confines. I pressed the head to her entrance, then froze. Jules's breathing changed, coming faster and harder, the rapid tempo spurred by anticipation and excitement, the way it did every time just before I slid deep inside her.

Part of me wanted to prolong it, to break down every single reaction frame by frame so I could fully enjoy the way I turned her on. Vindication flashed in my heart and mind as her nails cut into my shoulders, her hips arching toward me desperately.

God, I loved how responsive she was. I held on to that feeling, reveling in it for a fraction of a second before thrusting deep.

Her soft mewl of pleasure rolled over my tongue, and I swallowed the heady sound. Unable to hold back, I plunged into her over and over, hard and relentless, and a stifled scream ripped from her throat as she shattered in my arms.

Her silky flesh constricted around me, heightening the sensation, and I gritted my teeth as heat swept up my back and shoulders. I rammed deep twice more, then dropped my head against her shoulder as I pulled free and spilled my seed over her stomach.

Forcing my muscles to cooperate, I lifted my head and kissed her one last time, demanding and possessive, marking her as mine before I levered myself away from her. She pushed herself into a sitting position on the desk, and my gaze swept over her as she grabbed a tissue from the box on the corner of the desk and cleaned herself.

I knew it was depraved, but the sight of her sitting on the desk cleaning up the evidence of our lovemaking turned my blood hot with lust. I swore I would never get enough of this woman, taking her anywhere and everywhere I possibly could. Reality had more than lived up to the dreams; we would definitely have to revisit this particular fantasy later.

I bent and picked up her sweater and pants, then passed them to her. She dressed quickly, and I did the same, both of us working in comfortable silence. Jules wasn't chatty like typical women her age. She said whatever needed to be said in as few words as possible; otherwise she stayed silent. I knew from experience, though, that the woman didn't miss a damn thing. She was used to looking over her shoulder, and no detail escaped her attention.

I loved touching her, and I brushed one hand over her lower back as we made our way to the kitchen. She broke away from me then, moving toward the sink to load the dishwasher while I pulled out ingredients for tonight's meal. Jules joined me as I placed pork chops in the pan to sear, watching me intently.

In moments like these, I couldn't help but wonder exactly where Jules had come from. The woman could practically burn water when she'd first shown up, and we'd spent the last couple of months studying recipes and experimenting together. I was used to cooking for myself, so it didn't bother me one bit to do most of the work. Just having Jules by my side was enough.

She'd been awfully quiet this evening, and I surreptitiously studied her across the table. After we made love she seemed to retreat mentally, her mind a thousand miles away. Was she thinking about the wedding, or was it something else? "Have you thought about what you might like to do?"

Her head jerked up, and she blinked uncomprehendingly at me. "For what?"

Guess that answered my question. I fought down the mixture of apprehension and concern churning in my gut, praying to God she wasn't already second-guessing it. "The wedding."

Jules's eyes cleared, and a sardonic smile twisted her pretty lips. "Mia is already planning the whole thing."

I let out a little laugh. "That doesn't surprise me at all."

Jack and Mia had just recently married, and under Mia's direction, she and Jules had thrown everything together in only a couple of weeks. It'd been classy and understated, but I wondered if that was enough for Jules.

"Their wedding was nice," I offered. "Do you want to keep it small or do something more lavish?"

Personally, I thought weddings were a waste of time and money. My first marriage had been a sham of epic proportions. We'd spent thousands of dollars we didn't have to put on a show for hundreds of people, only to get divorced less than two years later. I didn't care whether we married in a courtroom or in some ostentatious ballroom somewhere; all I wanted was Jules.

Jules lifted one shoulder. "What do you think?"

Did she really not care, or was she dragging her feet? "I'll go along with whatever you decide. All I want is for you to take my last name."

Jules froze, her fork suspended in midair, her stare fixed on her plate. I held my breath, waiting to see how she'd react. It was a small test of sorts, and the fact that she still hadn't spoken of her past hovered over me like a black cloud. She'd come a long way since she'd first shown up here, and I knew she loved me, trusted me.

I was going to find out sooner or later; she had to know that. Whether she was penniless or the heiress to a fortune didn't matter one bit to me. So why wouldn't she tell me what happened to her?

Finally, she lowered her fork and met my gaze. "I want your name..." Her voice was soft but sure, the solemnity in her eyes almost overwhelming. "More than anything."

Pride infused me, and the frustration that'd been building in my chest immediately dissipated as I took in her sincerity. I couldn't come up with any other words at the moment. It bothered me that she wouldn't tell me her story, but it didn't change the facts—Jules was here with me, and in a few short months, she would be my wife. Forever.

I tipped my head at her plate. "You almost done?"

She let out a slow breath and smiled shakily. "Yep. I'm going to clean up a bit, then I'll be up."

I studied her from beneath my lashes for a long moment, a hundred emotions roiling inside me. She still seemed on edge, and though my mind wanted to drag forth every detail, my heart told me not to push. She would come to me in her own time—hopefully sooner rather than later.

"Okay." I pushed my chair back and stood, picking up my plate as I did so. I paused by her chair as I passed, then leaned down to cup the back of her head. She tilted her face up, and her gaze met mine, something swirling in the emerald depths. Worry? Fear? I couldn't be sure, but whatever it was, I wanted to push it away.

I brushed my lips over hers. "I'll be waiting for you."

She seemed to read the dual meaning of my statement, because her tongue darted out to wet her lips in a nervous gesture I'd seen a hundred times.

I released her and set my plate by the sink, then headed

upstairs to shower and get ready for bed. Jules followed half an hour later, and I flipped off the bedside lamp as she slid in next to me. Tangling her legs with mine, she pillowed her head on my shoulder as she snuggled in close to my body and laid one hand on my chest.

A shaft of silvery moonlight spilled into the room, and it picked up the refraction of the diamond, making it sparkle. The sight of my ring on her finger marking her as mine sent a thrill of possession through me.

Jules was strong and smart and independent, very much her own person—but her heart belonged to me as mine belonged to her. I knew deep down that there was no one else in the world for me; our souls were entwined like old friends, as if we'd known each other forever.

I captured her tiny fingers, sealing them between my hand and my heart, wondering if she could feel every strong, rapid beat. I'd felt cold and lonely before Jules arrived, and she filled a space in my life and in my heart that had long been empty. I was so glad I'd given in to the attraction between us; she was the woman I'd been waiting for my whole life.

I lightly drew my fingers over hers and traced the ring, the metal warm from her body. Turning my head, I brushed a kiss across her brow. So many emotions were conveyed in the silence between us. I felt every breath, every beat of her heart that thudded in time with mine. She let out a muffled little sound of contentment and turned her face into my neck.

Her chest rose on an inhale, and I knew she was getting ready to speak. "Can I ask you something?"

"Of course." I stroked my hand over her head, tangling in my fingers in her long mane of silky, dark hair.

Her hand coasted up my chest and fingered the silvery scar at the base of my throat. My gut clenched, and every muscle in my body tensed. Most days, I could block it from my mind, push down the pain of loss. It was something I never wanted Jules to know about, but I couldn't keep it from her forever.

"This looks dangerous," she remarked softly.

I directed my attention to a spot on the ceiling. "It was," I replied, memories of that night flooding my mind.

"Will you tell me what happened?" Her soft voice, so full of love and understanding, twined around my heart and gave me the courage to continue.

Aside from the men who'd fought beside me, I'd never told anyone the truth of what happened that awful night three years ago. "Ever since I was a kid, I wanted to be a cop. I saw some bad shit in the neighborhood where I grew up, and all I ever wanted to do was help people, protect them. As soon as I graduated, I went into the Academy. My ex-wife hated it, but—"

Jules jerked upward, balanced on one elbow as she stared down at me with wide eyes. "You were married?"

I couldn't tell if that was disbelief or jealousy pinching her tone, but I hoped it was the latter. "Briefly," I responded, hoping she would let it go. My first marriage was something I preferred to leave in the past and pretend had never happened.

Her brows drew slightly together as she studied me. "Did you love her?"

I turned my head slightly so I could see her better. "I thought so at the time. But it's not even close to the way I feel about you."

Seeming to accept my answer, she allowed me to pull her back down into my arms. I stroked one hand down the expanse of her back and cupped her bottom where she lay partially draped over me. "I'll never love anyone the way I do you."

It sounded cheesy, but it was the truth. I could feel her smile against my chest, and some of the tension left her body.

I drew in a deep breath, resigned to telling her the tale of how I'd earned the scar that stretched across the base of my throat.

"After I put in a few years on the force, I applied for a promotion. I ended up qualifying for a position with a SWAT team, and I took it. I loved the rush of it, the adrenaline high after each assignment." I paused, unable to form the next words.

Jules's hand stroked lovingly over my chest, and she turned her head to place a kiss over my heart. With my free hand, I lifted a tendril of hair that lay on my chest and curled it around my finger.

"We worked primarily with the police, but also any government agency that needed us. There was a crime syndicate, a branch of the mafia, that the FBI had been watching for a long time. They caught wind of an incoming shipment of illegal firearms and set up a sting to intercept them."

Jules's entire body went rigid, and guilt slammed into me. So innocent, almost naïve, I hated to sully her with details of the darker parts of life. My hand left her bottom and traced soothing circles over her back as I continued. "The weapons were set to be delivered to a warehouse just outside of town, and we all got into place as soon as the trucks arrived."

I shook my head. "I still don't know what went wrong. But the second we stepped inside, it turned into a nightmare. All I remember is the rapid fire of pistols and assault rifles discharging, echoing in my ears. My partner, Ric, was beside me and, all of a sudden, he dropped, and I knew he'd been hit."

I swallowed hard, the past unfolding before my eyes. "The shooting seemed to go on forever, but it couldn't have been more than a minute or two. As soon as we had them neutralized, I focused on Ric. We were partially concealed behind a pillar, so I set down my rifle to start chest compressions until the medic could get to him.

"I never heard the guy behind me—he just came out of nowhere—and slipped the blade beneath my helmet. Ric must've seen him coming, because he whipped my rifle over my shoulder and fired before I even knew he was there. The pain was excruciating, like fire ripping across my skin. I couldn't move, couldn't think..."

It was a stroke of luck that I'd turned my head just at that moment. He'd come so damn close to the artery; a few millimeters to the left and I would've bled out. I tried not to choke on my next words. "Ric saved my life, but... he didn't make it."

Jules trembled in my arms, and her hand curled into a tiny fist where it rested on my chest. "Did you find out who it was?"

I let out a little sigh. "The boss of the crime family, the head of the Chicago outfit. Ric's shot had met its mark, and I was told he died instantly. The Feds arrested everyone else, but only a few were charged. Things were quiet for a while, but I'm sure someone took over operations."

"I'm sure," Jules parroted from beside me, her voice high and thin.

I pushed on, wanting to lighten the mood. "After that, I just needed some peace and quiet. I'd heard about this place from a friend, so I packed up and moved out. Somehow, the people here in town managed to coerce me into running for sheriff, and I got elected almost two years ago."

Her head nodded against my chest before she slithered off my body and rolled so her back was facing me. I knew it was a hard story to digest, and though I wanted to give her space to process everything, I needed to feel her in my arms. I turned on my side and spooned her, draping one arm over her stomach.

I felt lighter after telling her the story, and I was glad to get the weight of it off my chest. It was one less thing between us. I smiled, remembering her reaction when I'd told her I was married. I liked that she was possessive and protective, but she had nothing to worry about. I wasn't going anywhere.

The trembling of her body next to me drew my attention, and I heard a slight hitch in her breathing. Suddenly, it hit me —she was crying. "Jules, what's wrong?"

Her hair tickled my cheek as she shook her head, and I lifted onto one elbow. The sight of silvery tears coasting down her cheeks threatened to rip my insides to shreds. Fuck, I hated to see her cry. "Talk to me, babe."

She shook her head again, eyes clenched tightly closed, and I sighed. "I'm sorry, I shouldn't have said anything—"

"It's…" Her chest rose on a shuddering sob as she tried to rein in her tears. "Thanks for telling me."

I nodded, though I still felt like an asshole as I lay down next to her again. For several long minutes we remained silent while I trailed my fingers up and down her arm, unable to sever the connection between us just yet. I paused my movement as she spoke.

"Eric?"

I lifted my head, my hand slipping down to the indent in her waist. "Yeah?"

I could hear her swallow hard. "I'm glad you're okay."

"Me, too." I settled back down next to her. "Love you."

After a long moment, her hand moved to mine and laced our fingers together. Her chest rose and fell, then she squeezed my fingers where they rested on her stomach. She hadn't said the words, but she didn't have to; I knew she loved me just as much as I loved her.

Burying my nose against the back of her neck, I dropped a gentle kiss there, then allowed myself to drift off to sleep.

SEVEN

GIULIANA

I felt the soft brush of Eric's lips across my forehead, but I kept my eyes clenched closed, feigning sleep. His footsteps moved away from the bed, then down the stairs and out the door.

As soon as I heard the tell-tale snick of the lock snapping into place, my eyes popped open. I flopped onto my back and stared at the pinewood ceiling.

I'd almost told Eric about my past last night, but I'd chickened out at the last moment. Instead, I'd asked about his. Now I almost wished I hadn't.

I'd lain awake half the night, trying to process everything he'd told me. Strangely, the first thing that popped into my mind was the fact that, somewhere out there, was a woman who'd loved him first. Irrational jealousy roared through my blood, turning my body hot.

For some odd reason, I couldn't picture Eric being married. Maybe it was because I didn't want to; I wanted to believe that he was meant for me alone, and no one else. My gaze strayed to the ring on my left hand, and I brushed my thumb over the warm metal. My heart broke a little bit as my thoughts turned to the second part of our conversation.

Eric was good. Noble. Everything right in this world. He was also partially responsible for my father's death.

I'd found a man I loved with my whole heart, but at what price? It wasn't fair that Eric had survived while Daddy hadn't. I remembered those days just after his death when my world had been shrouded in sadness and pain.

Mama and I were never particularly close, and I'd lost the only person who'd truly loved me in the warehouse that night. Daddy had been barely cold in the ground when Mama pawned me off on Uncle Massimo. It was for my own good, she'd told me. I was the boss's daughter, and Massimo would keep me safe.

She'd lied. I would've been better off alone in the streets than enduring the physical and mental abuse I was subjected to under my uncle's supervision. I was starved, locked away in my bedroom, unable to leave the house.

Then there was the closet. I hated the dark confine of that tiny room most of all. When I spoke up or acted out, Uncle would lock me in the closet for hours at a time. My hand flew to my throat just thinking about the thick, humid air clogging my lungs as I tried to breathe.

I hated that they'd taken my father away from me. If Daddy hadn't died, none of that would have happened. I was furious with the man who'd taken that shot and changed my life forever. I hated all of them. As soon as the thought crossed my mind, regret burned in my stomach like acid. Eric was a good man and a good cop who'd been in the wrong place at the wrong time. Just like Daddy.

My emotions ping-ponged all over the place, and I didn't know what to think, what to feel. Eric wasn't directly responsible; he hadn't been the one to shoot my father. Both men had walked into the warehouse that night knowing the consequences of their actions.

I couldn't delude myself—my father wasn't a good man. Although Eric's story had stunned me, it made sense. My father was known for his expertise with knives. I shuddered at the thought of the long scar along the base of Eric's throat. In my mind, I could hear his raspy, roughened voice. He'd been hurt—badly—because of my father. He was damn lucky to even be alive. It just hurt that Daddy couldn't be here, too.

I covered my face with my hands and let out a groan. I needed to stop thinking about it. How, I had no idea. I would have to tell Eric the truth. And I dreaded that more than anything. My father had tried to kill him. How would he react to that? And how the hell could I tell him without losing him forever?

Oh, God. This was going to be so bad. I didn't want to do it, but I had no choice in the matter. If we got married, he'd learn my real name. Capaldi wasn't exactly a common surname, and I had a feeling he already suspected I was from Chicago. It wouldn't take a genius to put two and two together.

Oh God, oh God, oh God.

I threw the covers off and stumbled from the bed as I headed toward the bathroom. Bile churned in my stomach, burning my esophagus. I closed the lid of the toilet and sat down, then dropped my head between my knees. Several long, deep breaths later, I lifted my head and forced the nausea away. I needed to get ready for work, but my body refused to cooperate. My legs trembled as I turned on the shower and stepped beneath the spray. The shaking intensified, and I slumped to the floor, pulling my knees to my chest.

I didn't know how long I stayed like that, but the cooling water jerked me back to reality. I was soaked but hadn't made any attempt to wash up. I used the last bit of tepid water to quickly wash and rinse, then I toweled off. I felt numb as I dressed and pulled my hair up into a messy bun without even bothering to dry it first.

The drive to Briarleigh passed in a blur, and the rest of the day was just as bad. I couldn't focus; my mind was a blank void filled with white noise and memories of the past that played on loop. Happy times. Then the bad times.

Thankfully, Jack and Mia were both absent today, so I didn't have to worry about running into them. I knew my face revealed every emotion, and Mia would've known immediately that something was wrong. She'd told me yesterday that they were driving back to Spokane to meet with their lawyer over some business matter.

She didn't offer any more information, and I didn't pry, but I assumed it had something to do with Hamilton Construction. Mia's late father, Bruce Hamilton, had started the company decades ago, then partnered with Jack during the recession when things had gotten tough. Mia had received her father's share when he passed, though I knew there had been stipulations to his will that she'd had to fulfill in order to do so. It was actually the reason she'd ended up here in Pine Ridge and had reconnected with Jack after spending years apart.

I walked into the cabin that night completely drained. Eric wasn't home yet, and I was grateful that I had a few minutes to myself. Not bothering to turn on any lights, I made my way to the couch where I sank down in the corner and cradled my head in my hands. I couldn't put it off any longer. Especially not now. I was going to have to tell Eric the truth—all of it.

Despair settled over me, and I popped up from the couch, needing to do something to take my mind off the conversation that could possibly change my life. I meandered into the kitchen, but my stomach turned over at the thought of food. My gaze strayed over the countertop to the doorway of the darkened office, and I moved in that direction.

I'd be lying if I said I hadn't wondered how things were back home. Were they still looking for me? The obvious answer to that question was yes. The fact that I'd escaped must have infuriated my uncle. A tiny smile curved my mouth. I hoped the Bratva brought hell down on him for failing to "deliver me" as promised.

Just days before I was supposed to marry Nikolai, the captain of the local Bratva, I had wheedled my way into leaving the house to go shopping. I'd made friends with the owner of a little boutique, and over the course of several months, Lila had helped me ferret away cash in the event I ever needed to escape. When I showed up that day, she knew.

While Lila distracted my bodyguards, I'd skipped out the back entrance and into a car that her boyfriend, Jake, had secured for me. I'd tossed my cell out the window a hundred miles south, then I turned west and finally north. A week later, I'd ended up broken down on the side of the road right outside of Pine Ridge. And that was exactly how Eric had found me.

No license, a car that wasn't legal—he'd had every reason to haul me into jail that night. Instead, he'd taken me to his place. It probably sounded creepy to the average person, and I did have my doubts initially. But Briarleigh was still under construction, and the closest hotel was more than an hour away in Kalispell. I'd taken my chances, and I thanked God every day that I had.

He'd quickly proved himself trustworthy, and he was the one who'd gotten me the job at Briarleigh. I fell fast and hard for him over those first few weeks. Though he'd tried to push me away to maintain a professional distance, he quickly gave in to the undeniable attraction between us. He told me every day how much he cared for me; I could only pray that what he said was true, because his love for me was about to be tested in ways we never imagined.

I took a seat in the leather chair, and butterflies kicked up in my stomach as I turned my attention to the computer in front of me. I pressed the button to power it up, and several minutes later the home screen appeared. I maneuvered the mouse up to the search bar and typed in the name of the local paper back home. The Tribune's main page popped up, and I started a new search. Typing in my last name, I held my breath while results filled the page.

I scrolled through the headlines, dread settling like a stone in my stomach as I read of the recent unrest. Tensions between *la Cosa Nostra* and the Bratva had escalated, leaving destruction in their wake. Arrests and even deaths of men with connections to the various syndicates were detailed in each article.

Uncle Massimo, however, seemed wholly unaffected. He'd been photographed out and about several times, once even with the mayor at a ribbon cutting ceremony for a new hospital wing. It was almost as if he was untouchable. He used donations to cover up his crimes and keep politicians, judges, and members of law enforcement in his pocket. Anger simmered in my gut. I hated him for that. I wanted him to be held responsible for his actions, but I knew it would never happen.

Asshole.

I closed out the search window and sat there for a long moment, just staring at the screen. I hadn't read anything about Matteo. That was good and bad, I guessed. Was he safe? I prayed he was. I knew he would one day fill Uncle Massimo's shoes, and I hoped he would be a better boss—a more compassionate and just leader—than his father.

I bit my lower lip and guided the mouse back to the search engine to pull up my email. I held my breath as it loaded, and disappointment slammed into me when I found the inbox full of junk. I didn't know what I'd been expecting. Some sort of communication, maybe? I'd considered reaching out to

Matteo a hundred times to let him know that I was safe. Instead, I'd been too afraid.

Tears crowded my eyes at the thought. Now I wished there was something. But as I quickly scrolled through, waiting for a familiar name to jump out at me, it remained infuriatingly absent. Maybe he'd given up on me.

Just as I was about to give up on the email as well, something caught my eye. Received a little over two months ago from an unknown sender, one message had a video file attached. Apprehension filled me as I clicked on the video and it began to play.

Black and white, the image was grainy—but I knew exactly what it was. Or, rather, who it was. Me.

From high up, I watched my profile as I slipped from the back entrance of the mall, then cut across the parking lot and climbed into the little Cavalier that Jake had left in the back of the lot for me. I couldn't see the plate—thank God—and I hoped that meant Uncle Massimo hadn't been able to discern the number, either. It was possible that he'd been able to obtain it from another camera across the city, but all the video proved was that he knew I'd escaped. He could track the car all he wanted, but it would never come back to me.

Other than offering to buy me a new vehicle, Eric hadn't said a word about it. He watched me sometimes when he thought I wasn't paying attention, and I knew he was wondering if I would feel the need to flee again. That was how much he cared about me—he wanted me to be safe and secure, no matter what. But I was tired of running. The only thing I feared now was never having Eric by my side. I couldn't imagine life without him.

The thought brought tears to my eyes. I'd already lost one man I loved. What if the truth cost me the other?

The video stopped playing as the car turned out of the lot and onto the main road. With a sigh, I closed out the message and scrolled through the unread messages again, more slowly this time. Another unknown sender—different than the last—jumped off the screen, and a shiver stole down my spine. The time-stamp showed it'd been sent only two weeks ago.

The mouse trembled in my shaky hands as I clicked on the file to open it. The feed on this tape was in color and startlingly vivid—unfortunately. My stomach clenched as a familiar face came into view, and I recognized Lila, the woman who owned the boutique I'd snuck away from. On the screen, I watched my worst nightmare unfold.

Lila and a man, who I assumed was her boyfriend, knelt on the floor facing the camera. Their hands were bound in front of them, fear etched deep into their faces. Tears streamed from Lila's eyes, tearing a hole deep into my soul.

I began to hyperventilate, my lungs rising and falling rapidly with each shallow breath. I knew what was going to happen, though I prayed with every fiber of my being that I would be wrong.

"Do you know this woman?"

Bile churned in my stomach as a man off to the side held up a photo, first toward the camera, then turned it toward Lila.

She nodded shakily as her eyes scanned my picture. "I remember her. She used to come into the shop from time to time."

There was a slight movement off to the left, just out of view of the camera, and the second man made a soft scoffing sound in the back of his throat. Was that Uncle Massimo? My ears perked up, listening intently for any discernible tone or phrase.

The first man spoke again. "When was the last time you saw her?"

Lila's whole body shook. "I—I don't know. Before Christmas?"

It came out like a question, and the man pressed forward. "Are you sure about that?"

"I—" She paused and licked her lips. "Y-yes. I'm sure."

"She left your shop through the back door." Lila trembled, but didn't speak, and the man continued. "Did you help her?"

Lila's eyes darted off to one side before going back to the man. "S-she asked for some clothes. I didn't know what she had planned."

That was the truth; I'd never told Lila any details for fear of what might happen—that this very thing might happen. My throat constricted, and I fought to swallow down the dread choking me.

"Yet you helped her anyway."

A tear slid down Lila's cheek. "She was my friend."

Oh, God. My hand flew to the base of my neck as a soft gasp left my throat. She had no idea what she'd just done. Uncle Massimo had kept me sequestered in my room, isolated and alone. I wasn't even allowed to speak privately with the staff who worked with him. I knew it was because they'd witnessed his treatment of me, and he worried that they would help me escape.

"Where is she now?"

Lila shook her head. "I—I'm sorry, I don't know."

"Just tell me," the man urged. "We just want to bring her home."

"I promise, I don't know!"

For a long moment, everything was silent. Then, without a single word, the man off to the left gestured impatiently toward the couple. The gun in the foreground moved to the boyfriend, and I jumped in my seat as a crack filled the air. I slapped my hands over my mouth, my head shaking frantically back and forth, my stomach pitching violently.

No.

No, no, no, no, no.

This couldn't be real. This could not be happening. Yet I knew from the dark stains and his limp body that this wasn't staged. Lila screamed and reached for the man, her body contorting as she threw herself toward him. For several long seconds she sobbed, cries mingling incoherently with muttered words. Finally, she lunged upward and glared at the man behind the camera. Tears streaked her pretty face, and her mouth twisted as she shrieked at him.

"You killed him! You fucking asshole! Why are you doing this?"

The gun moved swiftly back to her, and her voice broke over the curses pouring from her mouth.

"Tell me what you know."

"Nothing! I don't know anything! Please, just let me go."

She began to plead for life, and I found myself begging along with her. Tears filled my eyes and slipped over as the man spoke up again.

"Are you sure you don't have anything else to tell me?"

"Please," she begged. "I told you everything I kno—"

The gun went off midsentence, and Lila's body slumped to the side, landing partially over her boyfriend.

I closed out the window, my entire body shaking. I shut down the computer and sat frozen for a moment. It took me three attempts to stand, my knees weak and wobbly, my head woozy. My heart raced in my chest, and I felt faint. This was all my fault. In a daze, I made my way to the living room and sank down into the corner of the couch. I felt cold all over, my fingers numb as I tried to draw the blanket over me. I curled into a ball as if to make myself as small and inconspicuous as possible, then closed my eyes and cried.

EIGHT

ERIC

I stepped inside and quietly closed the door behind me, a grimace pulling at my mouth. It was late; I'd missed dinner, and I wondered from the darkened state of the cabin if Jules was already asleep.

I toed off my boots, then left them in the tray by the door to dry and cut across the living room. I'd made it four steps when I saw her. Huddled in the corner of the couch, knees pulled up to her chest, Jules slept deeply. Long, dark curls tumbled over the arm of the couch, and I reached out to touch the silky soft strands.

A smile lifted my lips, and I dropped to one knee in front of her. My gaze slid over her pretty features. She looked younger than her twenty years, like a porcelain doll. She would hate it if she heard me say that, but it was true. Her features were Italian perfection, from the soft olive tone of her skin to her symmetrical bone structure. God, she was gorgeous. And all mine. How I'd ever gotten so lucky, I had no idea. But I wasn't about to let her go, not ever.

She seemed distressed, her brows pulled slightly together,

and I wondered if she was dreaming. She did often, sometimes crying out in her sleep. She played it off each time, telling me it was nothing, but it bothered me immensely. I hoped that she would open up to me soon. She was about to be my wife, and I wanted to know everything about her.

I reached out and smoothed the tiny ridge over her nose, and her lashes fluttered as she came awake. Sleepy emerald eyes landed on me, then blinked once before she bolted upright.

"Eric!"

Thank God I was already on the floor, because the force of her body slamming into mine would've knocked me on my ass.

"Babe, wha—"

Her mouth landed on mine, frantic and needy, and I twined one hand in her hair, holding her close. Small hands roamed over my shoulders and through the short hairs at the back of my neck as her kisses grew to a fevered pitch. Our tongues tangled together, and I fell backward to the floor, pulling her with me.

She ripped her mouth away from mine and kissed her way over my cheeks and jaw, teeth scraping along my throat as her hand snaked between us to unfasten my pants. Not that I was complaining, but...

"Jules? Honey, what's wrong?"

She shook her head as she tore at my clothes. I lifted my hips, and she shoved my pants down just far enough so my cock sprang free. She slithered between my legs and ripped the shirt off over her head, then shucked her pants. All the while, I watched silently. Her face was a mask of concentration, and... something else I couldn't quite put my finger on.

Clambering over me, she straddled my hips and began to lower herself onto me. I caught her hips just as the head of my cock prodded her pussy, and her head jerked upward.

"Jules." She blinked owlishly at my stern tone, and I waited a beat. "Eyes on me, baby. I'm right here. You with me?"

She blinked again, and this time, the hysteria was gone, replaced instead by love and lust. She gave a little nod. "I… I need you." Her voice fell to a whisper. "I want to feel close to you."

I knew exactly how she felt. Eyes locked on hers, I thrust upward and impaled her. Our mingled breaths filled the air as she moved over me, her hips lifting and falling as she found her rhythm. She bit her lip as if fighting the urge to come, and I gritted my teeth against the fire burning low in my belly.

Fuck. I couldn't hold back anymore. "Jules… Goddamn it, baby, I'm gonna come."

Her eyes closed for a moment, then blinked open to meet mine. "Let go."

What the hell did that mean?

I grasped the back of her neck. "Last chance before I come inside you. Tell me to stop."

With a little shake of her head she ground down, and the last of my control slipped away. Clutching tightly to her, I pounded upward, my balls tightening as electricity zipped down my spine. I let out a feral groan as cum spurted deep inside her, and Jules cried out at the same time, her pussy clenching around my cock. The effect drew out my orgasm, and I rode the high before crashing to the ground, literally and figuratively. I collapsed, boneless, and Jules followed, her head landing in the crook of my neck.

Panting breaths filled the air, and the rush of blood thrummed in my ears. As things slowly returned to normal, I dipped my chin and brushed my lips across her forehead. "We're gambling hard."

She took a long moment to respond. "I know."

I palmed the small of her back, enjoying the feel of her

splayed over my body, my shaft still buried deep inside her sheath. I could feel literally every inch of her, inside and out, her heart beating in time with mine. I never wanted to let her go.

———

I stared at Jules as I paused with my hand on the door handle. "You okay?"

The wind whipped around us, lifting the strands of brown hair around her face. Standing in the parking lot adjacent to Rosie's, I hated being in front of so many prying eyes. Ever since last night, things between us had felt… off. Something was bothering her, and I wanted to know what it was.

She gave a halting little nod. "I'm fine."

She was lying. She could pretend that she was fine on the surface, but she couldn't hide the worry etched deep into her features. Those green eyes held a mixture of fear and apprehension, though I couldn't begin to determine why. Everything seemed to be going so well. Was she having second thoughts about sticking around? She was antsy and jumpy, and she'd appeared startled when I came up behind her in the kitchen this morning.

We'd decided to grab breakfast in town, our first foray into public as an engaged couple. She'd smiled and said all the right things when people congratulated us, yet there was a darkness hovering in her eyes that refused to lift. I'd held her until she'd fallen into a restless sleep, tossing and turning all night long. I hadn't asked what was bothering her, and she hadn't offered an explanation as to why she reacted the way she had.

I walked a fine line with her sometimes. I wished I knew what was going through her mind, but I didn't want to press and risk pushing her away. She needed to know that I would be here for her regardless. Though I needed to get to work,

Jules had the day off. Worry congealed in my stomach at the thought of what might transpire during those few hours apart.

I slipped a hand around the back of her neck and pulled her close. "Will I see you after work?"

She dropped her gaze to the ground before tipping her face up to meet mine. Tears sparkled in her eyes, and her teeth sank into her lower lip as she fought to keep them from falling.

"Sweetheart, is everything okay?" She nodded but didn't say a damn word. Helplessness raged through me. I wanted to be there for her, but I needed her to trust me, to open up and tell me what was bothering her, because I didn't believe for a damn second that it was nothing. "You know you can tell me anything, right?"

"I know." She leaned her head on my chest and I wrapped my arms around her, an irrational fear haunting me. Suddenly I was terrified that this might be one of the last times I ever got to do this. I couldn't tell why the sensation came over me, but with the way Jules was acting, I couldn't write anything off. I squeezed her tight one more time then released her, my heart heavy in my chest. I didn't know what I would do if she walked away from me.

Jules peeled away and gave me a sad little smile that didn't quite reach her eyes. "I don't want you to be late."

Barely managing to hold my tongue, I closed the door behind her as she slid inside, then made my way around the truck. A heavy silence lay between us as I pulled onto the main drag, turning toward the cabin so I could drop her off before I headed into the department.

We could have driven separately since I was already dressed and ready for work, but she'd specifically asked me to drive, which worried me all the more. She'd been here for months, yet now she refused to drive her car. Was she concerned someone was actively looking for her? And what had spurred that thought?

She knew she was safe with me, and I was sure that was the only reason she'd agreed to go for breakfast this morning. I hated the thought of leaving her alone in the cabin all day. It would be difficult to find if you weren't familiar with the area, but still…

I snuck glances at her from the corners of my eyes as we drove down the main street back toward the house. All the while, Jules stared pensively out the window.

"Eric?" Her sweet voice washed over me like a silky caress.

"Yeah, baby?"

"I…" She trailed off, looking more worried than I've ever seen, and dread sat in my stomach like a stone. "Can I tell you something?"

"Anything." I both anticipated and dreaded what I was about to hear.

"I think I need help," she whispered.

The vulnerability in her voice nearly tore me to shreds. "You know I'll always do anything in my power to help you," I replied forcefully.

She drew a deep breath. "Before I came here, I… I was supposed to be married."

At the word 'married,' I snapped my head toward her. It was a fatal mistake. From the corner of my eye, I saw a SUV come barreling through the stop sign at the cross street. Instinctively, I threw my right arm across Jules to protect her as I braced for the impact. The black SUV slammed into my front fender, narrowly missing the driver side door. I heard a soft intake of breath as the sound of glass shattering and the airbag deploying filled my ears. The truck spun under the impact, and I watched the trees fly past in a green and white blur as I fought to regain control. With a jolt, the back end slammed into the ditch, and I pitched forward, my head slamming into the steering wheel. Everything went black.

A loud buzzing filled my ears, and I blinked in and out of consciousness as I heard voices approach. I couldn't make my body respond, and I stared up helplessly into a pair of dark eyes as the man fisted his hand in my hair and lifted my head.

"Don't come after her." He paused then, sounding remorseful. "I'm sorry."

Sorry for—?

The sound of a gunshot filled the air, and my vision went black once more as I collapsed in a boneless heap.

NINE

GIULIANA

My body felt hot all over, almost feverishly so, and sore—so sore.

A dark, dense fog shrouded my mind, and I clawed my way through it. Finally I broke the surface and dragged in a deep breath. My eyes felt heavy and tired, and I blinked them open for a fraction of a second before letting them slide closed again. A flash of bright light strobed overhead, hurting my eyes and sending my mind spinning.

Where was I? And why did everything hurt so much?

Though I lay on my back, my neck was cocked at an unnatural angle, and I kicked out my legs in an effort to stretch. Half a second later my feet encountered something hard, halting my progress. I drew my knees upward again, curling into myself as panic set in.

Somewhere in the deep recesses of my mind, memories swirled and though I desperately grabbed at them, they remained elusive and out of reach. My mind remained a blank void, and a soft buzzing filled my ears. As my heart rate increased, the rapid pounding of my heart replaced the white noise, and my lungs rose and fell rapidly, threatening to hyperventilate.

What was happening? Why couldn't I remember anything?

I kept my eyes clenched closed, and forced several long, deep breaths into my lungs. Panicking was the worst thing I could do. Drawing on instincts deeply conditioned over the past few years, I shoved the fear aside. Instead, I focused on the sounds around me as they came to me in pieces: A low humming sound. Soft music playing from somewhere that seemed far away.

My brows drew together. It all seemed so familiar, even the faint rocking motion beneath me, as if I was hovering in midair. At the strange thought, my eyes popped open. I blinked several times and squinted into the dim light, trying to discern where exactly I was. Another bright yellow glow flashed overhead, then was gone a second later. My brain throbbed as I stared into the darkness once more, blinking the pain away.

Flash.

The light came again, and I grimaced. On and on it went, the bright flashes coming at even intervals every few seconds. I closed my eyes against the dizzying sensation. What were they? It seemed so obvious, yet still so out of reach, and I willed myself to open my eyes again. I redirected my gaze away from the bright blaze of light and studied the dark gray fabric above me. As I focused again on my surroundings, my brain finally made the connection. I was in a vehicle.

My gaze sluggishly moved away from the gray fabric, then lower, and I looked out the window. All I could see was inky blackness. I couldn't make out anything in the near-dark —no trees, no signs overhead, nothing. Where was I? And who was driving?

I closed my eyes again and lifted one hand to my head. Despite the darkness of the sky, the frequent flashes of the street lights overhead sent pain spiking through my skull. It was so acute that I couldn't formulate a single thought; I just lay there and massaged my temple, praying that it would go away. Gradually, it began to fade and I tried to open my eyes once more. It was a mistake.

The car hit a bump, and my stomach revolted. It clenched tightly, and bile burned the back of my throat as it rose up, hot and fierce. I rolled quickly to my side and ejected the contents on the floor of the car. I heard cursing in the background, but blood thrummed through my veins, rushing in my ears, drowning out my surroundings. I pressed one hand to my stomach as it coiled and released once more.

Drained, both mentally and physically, I flopped to my back and closed my eyes against the pain and humiliation.

"Drink." A strong hand holding a water bottle moved to my mouth.

The voice was smooth and cultured. Familiar. Mind still muddled, I tried to place it but failed as my brain threw up another blank wall. I couldn't focus; memories lurked just out of reach, on the periphery of reality. The one thing I knew with certainty was that it didn't belong to Eric. I ached to hear the raspy roughness of his voice like a caress sliding over my skin.

Tears pricked my eyes. Why wasn't he here with me?

I choked on the tiny sip of water and began to cough. Pain burst across the back of my skull, and stars danced in front of my eyelids.

The man tipped the water bottle up again, and I forced my throat to swallow. A second hand moved to the back of my head, holding me still as he urged me to drink more.

Through it all, I kept my eyes closed. I feared that if I opened them again, the water I'd just drunk would end up on the floor, too.

My stomach had seemed to settle, thankfully. I didn't

want to think, didn't want to feel. I curled one arm around my waist, pretending that it was Eric's as he held me close.

A hand brushed gently across my brow. "Sleep."

That voice again. It was so familiar; who was it?

There was a sudden, sharp pinch in my upper arm, and I cried out as liquid fire seemed to burn through my body. I opened my mouth, tried to formulate words but failed. My tongue, thick and unwieldy, refused to cooperate. My body began to relax, and a blessed calm descended over me, pulling me under.

TEN

ERIC

A familiar voice came from somewhere around me, and I fought to open my eyes. My entire body hurt, and my head ached worst of all. I tried to focus on the voice as it spoke again.

"Donahue. Can you hear me?"

I tried to formulate words, but nothing came out. I could barely hear my own thoughts over the pounding in my ears, but I listened again as the person spoke.

"Shit. Hang in there, man."

The accident. Jules. Was she okay? I tried to stretch a hand toward her seat, but it refused to cooperate. The voice bled away as the darkness consumed me, dragging me into the abyss once more.

A persistent hum filled the air, punctuated every so often by a low beep. Through sheer force of will, I managed to crack my eyes open. The light was dim, but it felt abrasive, and I closed my eyes almost immediately. I blinked once more and took in as much of my surroundings as possible before closing them against the pain again.

White ceiling. Industrial-style lights that were currently—blessedly—turned off. The room was dark and unfamiliar. I took quick stock of my body, finding my muscles stiff and sore, especially in my upper back near my ribs. The third time I tried to open my eyes, I managed to keep them open. I rolled my head left and right, taking in the strange machines on either side of the bed. A hospital. God knew I'd spent enough time in a room just like this back in Chicago after the incident in the warehouse. Was I dreaming? I tugged against the IV threaded through the back of my hand. The tight pinch of skin told me I was wide awake. That meant…

I drew back and searched my memory, trying to remember the last thing that happened. I remembered Jules this morning —God, I hoped it was this morning—acting strangely on the drive to Briarleigh. She'd been just about to tell me something before the car had come out of nowhere. Through my mind's eyes, I watched the accident unfold with startling clarity. The black SUV had run the stop sign to my left and plowed into the left front fender of the truck, sending us into a crazy spin. I saw the white powder fill the air as the airbag deployed, tasted it on my tongue as it filled my mouth and nose. The next few details were sketchy. I remembered reaching for Jules, finding the door wrenched open, the passenger seat empty.

Jules. I had to find Jules. I pushed myself up in bed just as the door opened, and a pair of familiar brown eyes met mine.

Jack's expression registered surprise as they landed on me, and he quickly crossed the room. "Hey. How are you holding up?"

"Like shit," I replied. "How is Jules?"

His face twisted with regret. "I'm not sure. I haven't heard from her."

What? That didn't make sense. "I need to see her. Right now."

Jack made a little shrugging motion, his face contorting with regret. "We haven't been able to get ahold of her."

"What the fuck are you talking about? She was in the car. She has to be here!" Panic made my voice rise several octaves, and Jack's eyes grew round with worry, sending my heart into overdrive.

"I didn't know she was with you. We didn't see anyone else."

Motherfucker. I grimaced as I ripped the IV from my hand, sending the machine into a beeping frenzy.

"Hey." Jack held up a hand in my direction. "You need to stay. Your wrist is fucked up and you look like shit."

I glanced down at the bandage around my left wrist. Well that explained why my arm wouldn't cooperate. I struggled from the confines of the bed.

"Are you sure she didn't leave?" he asked softly.

I turned an angry glare on him. "Don't even fucking think it. She wouldn't leave me."

Jack rested a hand on my shoulder to steady me as I stumbled. "I didn't say that. Maybe she just—"

"No." My voice was hard as I cut him off. I stared at him for several long seconds before releasing a heavy sigh. "Someone took her, Jack. I've gotta find her."

"Who took her?"

"I don't know." My tone was hard and too loud, driven by desperation and worry.

"Okay," Jack said. "Let's think this through. What do you remember?"

Not enough. I closed my eyes and tried to focus. As soon as I'd registered that Jules was gone, my door had been wrenched open. I saw a man in my mind's eye, but the features were blurry and incomplete. He'd said something before slamming my face into the steering wheel. What the hell was it?

"I don't know. Dark hair, dark eyes I think?" Jack just stared at me.

"I was fucking half conscious," I snapped. "What the hell do you want from me?"

"Just trying to help," Jack offered.

"Want to do my job while you're at it?"

Jack stared impassively back at me, and I raked one hand through my hair. "Fuck. I'm sorry. I'm just—"

My words were cut off by a nurse entering the room. She eyed me where I stood beside the bed. "Sir, you—"

"I'm officially checking myself out," I cut her off. "Give me whatever paperwork you need signed. I'm leaving."

Pain exploded behind my eyes as I stood, and the nurse rushed over to me. "Let me at least get some painkillers for you and get you dressed," she offered.

"No," I responded immediately to both.

Jack spoke up. "I'll help him from here."

The nurse reluctantly let go of me and was out the door a moment later, presumably to get whatever discharge papers she needed to have on file.

Jack's fingers curled into my shoulder, and I grimaced at the pain. He gazed down at me. "Unless you plan to walk out there with your bare ass hanging out, I suggest you put some clothes on."

Fuck. Had I been in the right frame of mind, I would've felt the slight breeze on my back a few minutes ago. As it was, the only thing I could think about was Jules and bringing her back to me safely.

"Fine." I waved a hand at Jack. "But hurry up."

He made a low sound in his throat as he dug my bag of clothes out of the bottom drawer of the dresser nearby. He passed them to me without another word, and I began to dress when something occurred to me. "What day is it? How long have I been here?"

"They brought you in yesterday morning," Jack responded.

My eyes widened in disbelief. "You let me stay here for a whole goddamn day?"

"Jesus Christ," Jack quipped. "You're a fucking nightmare. How the hell does Jules put up with your shit?"

I flipped Jack off and resumed dressing as quickly as I could, my body still sluggish and uncoordinated. "We need to check around town, see if anyone has seen her during the past twenty-four hours."

Jack remained silent, and I searched his questioning gaze before blowing out a hard breath. "She was with me in the car. I'm not crazy. We had breakfast at Rosie's, then I headed back to Bruce's place to drop her off. I think she was finally going to open up…"

I tensed at the reminder. I couldn't believe she'd been engaged at one point. Jealousy curdled in my stomach like acid, but I forced it down. She'd reacted the same way when I told her I'd been married before, but it felt different somehow. Maybe because she was so young. Perhaps it was because I suspected she'd been running from a man when she first showed up three months ago, sporting a collection of dark bruises. I debated whether to tell Jack what she'd said but held my tongue.

"A car ran the stop sign at the intersection of I-93 from the south and slammed into us—black, I think. The next thing I remember—"

The gunshot. The thought made me pause, and I ran my hands over my body, checking for any bandages. Jack watched me with a combination of concern and interest, and my brows drew together as I pieced together the events. My back was sore which meant he'd hit the plate, but the bullet hadn't penetrated. "He didn't shoot me."

One dark brow lifted toward his hairline. "Isn't that a good thing?"

My mind spun furiously. Why hadn't he killed me when he had the chance? He was too close to have missed. If Jules's fiancé had come to take her back, wouldn't he have killed me on the spot instead of just warning me away? "When I reached over to check on Jules, she was gone. He said something like, 'don't come after her.' There was a gunshot, and I blacked out."

Jack swore, and I met his dark gaze. "I need to find her."

"All right," he acquiesced. "Let's get you out of here."

Three minutes later, Jack returned with the nurse holding a clipboard and a wheelchair. I eyed the contraption with no small amount of animosity. "No fucking way."

"Hospital rules," he replied. I swore I could hear the laughter in his voice though he concealed his smirk.

As if losing my fiancée hadn't been enough of a blow to my pride. I scowled. "Jesus Christ. Let's get this over with."

I scrawled my signature over the papers the nurse presented in front of me then reluctantly climbed into the wheelchair, Jack at the helm. "If you dump me out of this thing, I'll murder you," I bit out.

This time, Jack couldn't contain his laugh. "Tempting as that sounds, I wouldn't do that to you. Gotta be in one piece to bring Jules home."

His words triggered something else. The only personal effects in the hospital room were my clothes. I assumed that my cell, my wallet, everything else was still in my truck.

"Can I borrow your phone?" I asked as soon as we were settled in Jack's Tahoe. "I'm guessing mine was forgotten at the scene."

Jack nodded. "I don't remember seeing it, but I'm sure it's there. Maybe one of your deputies grabbed it."

I turned surprised eyes on him. "You were there?"

He nodded, his face serious. "I was the one who found you."

"Jesus," I muttered. "Thanks for your help."

He offered a little nod as he passed his phone to me. I stared out the window as I dialed the number.

I'm coming for you, Jules.

ELEVEN

GIULIANA

I blinked my eyes open and stretched, my muscles aching with the effort. My whole body hurt, from the top of my head to the tips of my toes. I felt sluggish and slow, like I was still half asleep. I closed my eyes again as I yawned, and fatigue pulled at me, along with another sensation I couldn't identify.

What the hell had happened?

Memories came to me, like clips on an old-fashioned movie reel flickering frantically. Waking up in the car. The pain shooting through every cell of my body. Getting violently ill and throwing up in the back seat. Someone forcing me to drink, then… blessed darkness.

My brows drew together. There was something before that, though… Eric had convinced me to go to breakfast this morning; we'd eaten at Rosie's, then—

Oh, God. *The accident.*

My eyes flew open as I bolted upright—or tried to. My muscles refused to cooperate, and I flopped like a fish as pain spiderwebbed across my brain. I grasped my head, willing it to recede. The vehicle had slammed into Eric's truck, and the impact sent us spinning. My head had hit the passenger side window, and everything after that seemed fuzzy.

There was a voice in the car. It had been familiar, yet I knew with certainty that it wasn't Eric's. The man had given me water, then… The thought of that sharp prick to my arm came back. *I'd been drugged.*

It was almost too unbelievable to contemplate. Who the hell would do that? And why?

I took quick stock of my body. Most of the pain seemed to be centralized in the back of my head. Did I have a concussion? I thought protocol dictated you keep someone awake if they had brain trauma, not put them to sleep. Unease spread through me.

Darkness shrouded the room, and it took me several moments to register what I was seeing. The ceiling, the walls, everything was familiar but… not. Was I dreaming?

I swallowed hard and tried to sit up, but my body wouldn't cooperate. Sinking back down into the mountain of pillows, I closed my eyes again. When I next opened them, a body occupied the chair next to my bed. Startled, I drew back until the man's face came into focus.

"Matteo!"

His face pulled into an expression of worry, he stretched one hand across the white sheets and enveloped my fingers in his. "How are you feeling?"

I lifted my free hand to my head, where the blood pulsing through my veins throbbed against the backs of my eyes. "My head hurts. What happened?" My gaze flew around the room, and my heartbeat accelerated as it made the connection. The walls were now bare, devoid of any decoration, but it was the same room I'd been confined to for years.

No, no, no.

I gripped Matteo's hand, my fingers digging into his skin. "I can't be here. Please, I have to leave. If I don't, Uncle will—"

Matteo adjusted our hands and smiled soothingly at me. "The deal is off. You don't have to worry about Nikolai now."

I flopped back against the pillows. That was a small consolation. Matteo had to know that. My uncle had brought me back here for a reason. If not to sell me to Nikolai, then to someone else. I had to get out of here. "Matteo, please," I pleaded with him. "They'll kill me."

"No, *principessa*." Matteo shook his head. "Everything will work out the way it's supposed to. Trust me."

I didn't believe him, but I didn't want to hurt Matteo's feelings by disrespecting him. In our family, it was the men's job to protect their women; if Matteo thought he was in control, I wasn't going to argue. Yet.

Damn it. I'd tried so hard to hide in plain sight. I paid for everything in cash and refused to put my name on anything. "How did you even find me?"

He closed his eyes briefly before meeting my gaze. "We—"

"Good. You're awake." I jumped as the door to my room slammed open and my uncle bustled through. He gestured to me. "Right here."

Yanking the covers up to my neck, I cowered against the headboard as a second man entered the room. Older with graying hair, he offered me a kindly smile. "Good morning, miss."

I eyed him warily. Who the hell was this? "Hello."

Uncle Massimo jerked his chin toward him. "Get on with it."

My brows drew together as the man slowly made his way toward me. "What are you doing?"

"My name is Dr. Hinckle," he said as he set a small bag on the pristine white quilt covering the bed. He unzipped it and pulled out several instruments. "I'm here to examine you."

I relaxed a fraction as he leaned close and took my head in his weathered hands, gently tilting it from side to side. "You were in an accident, yes?"

I nodded as he released me. "Yes. I—" My gaze shot to Uncle Massimo, and the words froze on the tip of my tongue.

The doctor made a little sound. "A few abrasions, but I'll get those cleaned up. What I'm going to do now is check you for a concussion."

He did so, checking my eyes and hearing, then moving lower to inspect my arms and torso for any injury.

"Mild concussion," Dr. Hinckle directed toward my uncle. "But some rest over the next few days will fix that."

Curling my fingers into the sheets, I nodded. I didn't have a couple days—I didn't have a couple hours. I needed to get the hell out of here and back home to Eric.

"Well?" Uncle Massimo snapped, dragging my attention back to him. "What are you waiting for?"

The doctor turned back to me, and his lips turned up in an apologetic smile. "I'll need you to lower the sheet, please, miss."

"Why?"

Uncle Massimo glared at me. "Do as he asks."

I clenched my thighs tightly together, a sick sense of dread curdling in my stomach. I asked the question, though I already knew. "W-why?"

My uncle reached down and snatched the corner of the fabric, ripping it away. I let out a soft cry as I tried to cover myself. "Hey—!"

"Lie down."

I trembled as I stared up at him. "N-no."

My uncle's searing dark gaze bore into mine. "Do not test me, Giuliana."

I shook my head, a terrible sick feeling coming over me. "I won't do it."

I screamed as he grabbed one ankle and tugged. Matteo jumped from his seat, swearing at Massimo.

"No!" I begged, my eyes clouded with tears. "Please don't!"

Shame and humiliation coursed through me, and I could feel the men's gazes, hot and intent on my bare legs. I refused to expose myself to them. I couldn't do it.

My uncle whipped a knife from a sheath in his waistband and pressed it against my stomach. "Spread your legs like the whore you are, or I'll spill your blood all over this bed."

The tip of the blade dug into the cavity of my stomach, and a dark bead of red appeared as I twitched under its sharp point.

Sobs wracked my body, and I covered my face as I allowed my knees to fall open. I tried to shut it out of my mind as someone—the doctor, I hoped—pulled my panties down my legs. Fresh tears leaked from my eyes as he inserted an instrument inside me. It was cold, and every touch felt like an invasion of my body.

Over the pounding in my ears, I barely heard the low hum of voices, then a door slammed. My panties were pulled back up into place, and the door opened then closed again, much softer this time.

Alone and completely ashamed, I curled up on my side under the covers and cried. Great, heaving sobs shook my body as I vented my frustration. My rage. My humiliation.

I stiffened as a warm body lay next to me, and Matteo pulled me into his arms, covers and all. "I'm sorry, *principessa*. I'm so sorry."

Several long minutes later, exhausted from my outburst, I turned into his arms and bowed my head. "I hate him," I whispered.

Matteo's chest rose and fell beneath my cheek. "Me, too."

"Does he still plan to give me to Nikolai?"

I felt Matteo's chin brush over my hair as he shook his head. "No. The Russians retaliated after you..." He paused, then seemed to change direction. "It's worse than before. We've been embroiled in a war for the past several months, and Nikolai has aligned himself with the Irish. Their numbers are small, but they're dangerously unpredictable."

I didn't know if I should feel relieved or not. So why the hell did Uncle Massimo bring me back here if he didn't plan to get rid of me? Was this just a power play to wield his control over me?

Matteo drew a deep breath. "Have you ever heard of Fox?"

I stiffened, horror washing over me. Oh, God. Even I'd heard of the man who went only by Fox because of his cunning and ruthless nature. Nikolai seemed like an infant next to Fox. Though he was an independent, he'd made a name for himself over the past several years. If Uncle wanted to screw the Russians, Fox was the ally to use. Matteo had told me that he tolerated nothing, and I'd heard that he once sawed off a man's head with a box cutter just to prove a point.

A shiver racked my body, and my stomach rolled. "Matteo…"

"I would never let anything happen to you."

"You can't save me," I lamented. If Uncle was negotiating with Fox… "It's already done."

Matteo's jaw clenched. "Won't stop me from trying."

"What is he like?" What I really wanted to know was if I would have any chance of eluding him.

"Dangerous," came Matteo's response, low and gruff. "Do you remember when Elle Masterson disappeared?"

Daughter of the mayor of Chicago and wife of a state senator, her disappearance had been big news nearly a year ago. Right before I'd left home, they'd found her remains—what little was left of her, anyway—in the woods outside of town. "Was Fox… Did he…?"

Matteo nodded, but didn't say anything else, and my body went cold. Those were two of the most powerful men in the state. How in the hell had Fox gotten away with it? That alone was a testament to his power. "I can't stay here."

"Trust me, Giuliana." One heavy hand cupped the back of my head and held me close. "I'll take care of you."

I nodded, but I didn't mean it. The only person I could trust was myself. One last tear squeezed from my eye, and I hastily brushed it away. Tears were for the weak; I was stronger than that. I wouldn't let them break me. I wouldn't bow to anyone. And I was going to get the hell out of here if it was the last thing I did.

TWELVE

ERIC

My deputies stood assembled around me in a semicircle, and I met each of their solemn gazes before I spoke. "Thank you all for coming in. As many of you know, I was involved in a car accident yesterday morning."

"Glad you're okay," Riley spoke up.

Murmurs of agreement rose from the others, and I nodded appreciatively. "Thank you. Head still hurts like a bitch, and I'm sore as fuck, but we need to hit the ground running."

From their mildly curious stares, I could tell they hadn't heard the news yet. "I wasn't the only one in the car yesterday. Jules was with me, but..." I drew a harsh breath before continuing. "When I came to, she was gone."

My deputies stiffened, wariness and anger entering their eyes. I relayed everything that had happened, including the man's last words to me before I blacked out again. It still didn't feel real. My mind had replayed the memory thousands of times, and I'd begun to wonder if it was all a figment of my imagination, just some terrible dream that I'd concocted.

I shook the thought from my head. No. There had definitely been another person there, and he'd taken her from me. Jules and I had been on the verge of a breakthrough, but she hadn't had time to tell me what was bothering her. She'd told me she was supposed to have been married, and I wondered if it was somehow related to her abduction. Was it him? Was that who'd kidnapped her? I cursed the fact that we'd been in my personal vehicle, because at least the cruiser had a dash cam.

I turned my focus back to the men in front of me. "Have any of you been to the scene yet?"

Hawkins tipped his head toward O'Neill. "We were up yesterday when McBride towed your truck back to the shop."

"Did you see anything?"

He shook his head. "Nothing out of the ordinary. Some broken glass, some orange plastic from what I'm assuming was a marker light."

I nodded thoughtfully as I processed the information. Whoever was driving the vehicle had hit me damn hard. The impact would've been severe enough to do more damage to the front end than just busting out part of a headlight.

I drew back on my memory from the following morning. The vehicle had been a dark blur as it plowed through the stop sign and into my fender, but I was positive the shape had been an SUV. There more than likely wouldn't have been much time to clean up any debris before someone would've stumbled on them. That left me with one other option—the vehicle that hit me was armored. That in a way helped to narrow it down a little bit. It was outrageously expensive to outfit a vehicle like that, and few people could afford it. Definitely no one around here, that was for certain.

I glanced up at my men. "We need to get back up to the scene and see if we can find any other distinguishing marks or evidence," I said as I pulled my phone from my back pocket, which O'Neill had returned to me as soon as I'd arrived this afternoon. "You guys head on up and I'll meet you there. O'Neill," I turned to the man as I addressed him. "You'll stay here and hold down the fort."

He gave me one concise nod, and I strode back to my office, dialing as I went. There was really only one way out of Pine Ridge, and the main road went through Kalispell.

After three rings, Tom Rooney, the sheriff down in Kalispell, answered. "Donahue. What can I do for you?"

I looped behind my desk and wiggled my mouse to wake the computer monitor. "Need a favor. We have a missing persons here."

My voice cracked as I said it, and I steeled my spine. I was determined to stay positive and not let myself think about the alternative. I quickly walked him through the events of yesterday morning, telling him about her recent change in behavior and her last words to me.

"My vehicle was struck at the intersection of Main and I-93, and a passenger was taken from the scene."

He remained stoically silent as I gave him Jules's description and told him my suspicions about the armored SUV. After a long pause, he finally spoke. "BOLO?"

I grimaced. "I didn't catch the plate number, and no one seems to have seen anything."

A deep breath filled the other end of the line, then— "You know I've got to ask," he said haltingly. "No license, no way to trace her... you sure she didn't leave willingly?"

It was a good question, but I was getting fucking tired of hearing it. "Positive," I bit out.

Rooney sighed resignedly. "Send me a picture and I'll circulate it, see what I can turn up."

With that, he hung up. I stared at the phone for a minute, dozens of emotions swirling inside me. Fury that someone had taken her from me. Guilt that I hadn't been able to stop them. Irrational anger that anyone thought she would willingly leave. The emotions bubbled to the surface, and I lashed out, swiping the contents of my desk onto the floor.

"Goddamn it!"

I was angry with her for not opening up sooner. I was angry with myself for not trying harder to convince her to trust me. And I was absolutely furious with the person who had the fucking balls to take her from me in broad daylight. When I found him—and I knew with absolute certainty that it was a *him*—I would make the rest of his days on this earth, what few of them there may be left, absolutely miserable.

I stood there breathing hard, my chest rapidly rising and falling with each breath. The wave of rage that rose within my chest threatened to consume me. By sheer force of will, I tamped it down and scrubbed my good hand over my face. I opened my eyes and caught O'Neill standing in the doorway silently, just watching me. I was ashamed that he had seen my outburst, seen my weakness. I opened my mouth to lash out at him, but he spoke before I had the chance.

"Give me her information, and I'll start running it through the databases. Something's bound to turn up."

I clenched my fists and swallowed hard, gratitude for his offer overwhelming. "We need to question everyone in town, see if they've seen anything. Find a witness."

I had a feeling I knew the place to start. Since Jack had dropped me off in town, my cruiser was still at home. I stormed out of the station and settled in the extra cruiser out back. It was an older style sedan, and it felt uncomfortable as fuck. I fumbled the seat belt with my left hand, still in a splint from the hospital, and my arm got tangled in the fabric.

"Fucking son of a bitch!"

The clasp made a loud clank as it smacked off the window, and I dropped my chin to my chest, my hands going to my head. I needed to lock down my emotions, I knew it, but it was so fucking hard to separate myself from the situation. I felt fucking impotent, useless. Where the hell was Jules while

I was in the hospital? How was she holding up? Was she scared? Hurt? That made me feel even worse. I couldn't believe I'd let my guard down. A second was all it took, and she'd been ripped from my life without a trace.

I started the cruiser and drove the six blocks back into town and parked in front of Rosie's Café.

"Lordy be!" Rosie's honeyed voice called out as I walked through the front door. "We heard you were in an accident. Sit down, Sheriff, and relax."

I waved her off and approached the counter that separated the dining area from the kitchen. "Thank you, ma'am, but I just stopped in to ask a couple questions."

Her expression turned teasing, and she winked. "You want me to make your favorite chicken for the wedding?"

A jolt shot through me, and my heart twisted in pain. Over twenty-four hours had passed already. Would there even be a wedding?

No. I wouldn't let myself think like that. I had to find her and bring her home where she belonged. She meant everything to me, and I couldn't imagine life without her.

"No, ma'am. I, uh…" Emotion rose up, threatening to choke me. "I need to ask you something."

Immediately her mirth vanished, replaced with concern. "What's wrong?"

Only everything. "Did you happen to see anyone strange come through town yesterday?"

She looked contemplative for a moment. "We had a family stop in for breakfast, said they were headed up to the resort."

Fuck. "I'm looking for a loner. Dark hair, dark eyes. Could've been with someone else, probably another man."

"No one like that." She eyed me speculatively. "What happened?"

I aimed my stare over her shoulder, unable to meet her eyes. "When Jules and I left here yesterday morning, someone ran the stop sign at the intersection of I-93. The impact knocked me out, and when I woke up... Jules was gone."

Rosie was quiet so long that I finally dropped my gaze to meet hers. There was something so fierce, so intent there, I couldn't make out exactly what it was.

"We'll find her," Rosie said firmly. "Whatever you need, Sheriff, you let me know. I'll let everyone know to contact you if they've seen anything."

"Thanks, Rosie."

She nodded perfunctorily. "People don't just disappear. We'll find her," she reiterated.

I offered a small smile I didn't feel, then turned and trudged out the door. It was nothing I hadn't expected. If someone had put that much effort into kidnapping Jules, I was sure he'd taken care to conceal himself until he was ready to make his move. I needed to get up to Briarleigh to see if anyone Jules worked with had heard or seen anything.

Ten minutes later, I walked in the side door, despair tugging at me. I stopped by Jack's office first. He'd dropped me off at the station a couple of hours ago and told me he'd be here if I needed anything.

I paused in the open doorway when I heard voices. One I recognized as Jack's; the other belonged to Mia. Their heads snapped toward me, and my gaze collided with Mia's. She looked distraught, her eyes red as if she'd been crying.

"I'm so sorry, I never thought..." Her hand fluttered to her mouth, and Jack looped one arm around her shoulders.

I tried to smile but failed. "It's not your fault."

I knew from Jack that they'd been in Spokane with their lawyer the day before Jules had disappeared. Yesterday was Jules's day off, so Mia had no reason to check in on her.

"Would you mind if I questioned some of the employees, see if they noticed anything?"

"Of course." Jack nodded. "Check with Jenn first. She

leaves in about an hour, and I don't want you to miss her. She's in the pro shop."

"Thanks."

I moved that direction and waited not-so-patiently off to the side while the young brunette finished up with a customer. She offered me a worried smile as I stepped up to the counter. "Can I help you?"

I introduced myself, then launched into my reason for being there. "I'm investigating a disappearance." I almost choked on the words, unable to believe I had to say them. Fuck, this was the hardest thing I'd ever had to do. I swallowed hard and continued. "Jules has been missing for twenty-four hours, and we suspect she may not have left on her own."

Jenn's eyes grew wide. "Oh, my God! I—I..." She stuttered and trailed off, looking disturbed.

I couldn't bear to see the worry and pity evident in everyone's eyes, so I did what I'd done for years: I pushed it down, pretended it wasn't there, and focused on the job at hand. I poised my pen over the notebook in my hand. "Was she involved in any recent altercations that you're aware of?"

"N-no. Everyone loved her."

Jenn's voice trembled, and I took pity on her. "I believe the man who took her had dark hair and eyes. Have you seen anyone like that?"

She shook her head. "During the week it's pretty slow still. No one has come in here, and I don't remember seeing her with anyone except Tony."

I remembered the man; he was the supervisor she and Mia were working with for the spa. "If you think of anything else, please let me know."

I handed her a card and left, then stopped to speak with several more employees. Two hours later, I had exactly nothing to show for my time and effort. No one had seen a man matching the suspect's description, nor had they heard of her being involved in any kind of disagreement. It was just as Jenn had said; everyone loved Jules and watched out for her.

I stopped by Jack's office, and he retrieved a copy of her office key for me. I entered and glanced around the nearly bare space. Though there were a few papers scattered over the desk, I found nothing in any of the drawers or cupboards. I sifted through the files on her computer, but nothing jumped out at me. I locked up her office as I left, and worry came back full-force as I exited into the dark, cold evening air. It was literally as if she'd disappeared without a trace.

She'd never told me her full name or where she'd come from, and the knowledge that I might not be able to find her finally started to sink in. After all, how the hell did one go about finding a ghost?

THIRTEEN

GIULIANA

A hard knock came from my bedroom door, and I turned as it swung open.

"Your uncle would like to see you."

I scanned Johnny's face before glancing at the man next to him. I'd never seen him before. My gaze jumped back to Johnny, and I jerked my chin at the new guy. "Where's Tommy?"

For as long as I'd been with my uncle, Johnny and Tommy had been assigned to watch over me. I wasn't sure how long they'd been with Uncle Massimo, exactly, but I figured it wasn't terribly long. Glorified babysitting was a position low on the totem pole with little responsibility.

"Gone," he responded.

His response was abrupt. *Gone?* I knew what that meant, but... "How?"

"Nikolai," he spat.

I knew things with the Russians had not gone well since I'd run away, but it was almost a blow to the heart to know we lost someone I knew so well. He wasn't a good man, but he was part of the family and I couldn't help but mourn his loss. I focused on Johnny again as he turned slightly, and my eyes narrowed as I studied him.

In the light, a fresh scar cut across his cheek, and my heart jumped into my throat. It was a knife wound—I knew it from the shape. I swallowed hard at the sight of the thin, raised red line that ran from his temple to his jaw, unable to tear my eyes away. He'd been punished for my leaving, and guilt sat heavily in my stomach. He'd been marked for everyone to see, and it was my fault. I thanked God my uncle had shown him some mercy at least, because Massimo could easily have cleaved off a hand or killed him.

Johnny must have seen the remorse in my eyes, because he gave his head a little shake. I pressed my lips together to stem my apology, though tears burned the backs of my eyes as I averted my gaze.

Knowing that it wouldn't do me any good to fight with them, I stood and they flanked me as we fell into step on the way to my uncle's office. Johnny knocked on the door, and Uncle Massimo's response came a moment later, swift and abrupt.

"Enter."

Johnny turned the knob and opened the door, allowing me to enter. As soon as I was inside, he immediately closed it again. I regarded my uncle, who had yet to acknowledge me. The sight of him sent loathing, hot and furious, streaming through my blood. I hated him for what he'd done. I wouldn't go down without a fight. I'd escaped once; I would do it again. He would surely be expecting me to try something, so I had to be on guard and choose precisely the right moment. I knew that, even though *la famiglia* had lost several men, surveillance around the house had been tightened. No one would get in or out without his knowledge, and I knew he wouldn't be stupid enough to let me go outside without a valid excuse. I needed to come up with a plan and quick. I knew that Eric would be looking for me, but he didn't even know my real name. How would he ever find me?

"Sit." My uncle nodded to the chair on the opposite side of the desk.

Swallowing down the retort on my tongue, I placidly approached and sank down onto the edge of the leather chair. Like the good little doll I was supposed to be, I folded my hands in my lap, the picture of propriety. My uncle's gaze dropped to my hands, and he lifted one brow. I knew exactly what he was thinking. During my three years of captivity with him, anxiety had caused me to pick and bite at my nails, sometimes until they were ragged and bloody. Now they were long and smooth and healthy, a result of my time spent with Eric, where I'd felt safe and comfortable.

His frigid gaze swept over my body before meeting mine. "You gained weight."

His voice was rife with derision and disapproval, and I notched my chin up. It was true—I'd gained almost ten pounds since living in Pine Ridge. While my weight hadn't been healthy before, my body now felt softer and more rounded, with curves instead of angles. Uncle had practically starved me in order to achieve what he deemed perfection; in his eyes, along with my virtue, it would have made me the perfect bride. Too bad I'd ruined his plans on that score. I fought to keep the smirk from forming on my lips but lost the battle.

His lip curled in disgust when I refused to rise to his bait. "Disgusting. See if you can find something that will fit."

"For what purpose?"

He took in my challenging tone and blinked once, hard. "We are going to dinner."

I had no desire to eat, too stressed out to even contemplate it. "No, thank you."

Sparks of fire shot through his eyes. "It wasn't a request."

"I don't care if it was a request or not. I'm not going."

Uncle slowly uncoiled from his chair, his dark eyes never leaving mine. "You should care very much what happens next. No one will save you now."

God, I loathed him so much. Anger made me bold, and I glared at him. "He'll find me."

A cold smile lifted my uncle's lips. "I wouldn't count on that."

Ice sluiced through my veins as fear seized my heart. "Why?"

Uncle waved a hand dismissively. "You don't have to worry about your cop anymore."

"What did you do?" I whispered.

He stared at me, those cold, dark eyes unblinking. "You know how much I despise loose ends."

"No." My fingers curled into the arms of the chair, and I shook my head, unwilling to fathom never seeing Eric again. It couldn't be true; it just couldn't. "You didn't."

My uncle ignored my words and glanced at his watch before sinking back down into his chair. "You have one hour to be ready."

I shot from my chair and leaned over the desk, my palms splayed over the cool wood. "Tell me!" I screamed. "I want the truth! Tell me, damn it!"

My uncle's hand shot out and wrapped around my throat, cutting off my hysterical screams. "You want the truth?" His fingers tightened as he glared at me. Papers scattered, and something fell to the floor with a crash as he dragged me across the desk. "He's right where he belongs. Just like your father."

I clawed at him, kicking, biting, trying to tear the skin from his body for what he'd done. He threw me to the side, and I hit the floor hard, the impact making my teeth clack together and sending a shooting pain through my skull. One hand fisted in my hair, and I fought to get my feet under me for leverage as he pulled me across the room. I screamed at the sting of pain exploding across my scalp, but I continued to fight as hard as I could. The closet came into view, and I let out an ear-shattering shriek as he shoved me toward it.

No. I wouldn't spend one more second in that awful place. I braced myself against the doorjamb, and I felt the bones in my arms flex as he put more pressure on them. Another howl of pain ripped from my throat, and I pulled them in just in time to keep them from breaking. I landed hard on the floor of the closet, my arm twisted beneath me at an awkward angle, and he slammed the door behind me.

Pushing down the agony shooting through my body, I clambered to my feet and pounded on the door. "I hate you! You won't get away with this!"

A cold laugh filled the air, muted by the thick wood separating us. "I already have."

I backed up a step and kicked at the door. It rattled but didn't splinter, and I grunted with frustration. Backing up as far as I could, I took two running steps and threw my entire weight against the door. It didn't move.

I grasped the handle and shook, but the solid wood held steady. Tears of rage filled my eyes, and I screamed, long and loud.

A sharp retort filled the air, immediately followed by the sound of a bullet striking wood. *What the hell?* Rendered motionless with shock, I lifted my chin and stared in horror at the small pinhole of light coming through the door. Holy shit. Someone was shooting at the door!

Another shot followed the first, a second circle of light appearing a few inches above my head, and I sucked in a breath, unable to scream. I threw myself to the floor and curled up in a ball, trying to make myself as small as possible. Clenching my eyes closed, I covered my head and prayed for it to stop. Fear snaked through me, stealing my composure, and I felt my bladder release. My pulse thrummed in my ears and my lungs heaved with shallow breaths, threatening to make me hyperventilate. Fifteen rounds later, silence reigned. My ears still rang from the sound of the staccato blasts, but I forced myself to open my eyes. The vibration of heavy footsteps striking the hardwood floor rolled through my body as they neared the closet.

My uncle wrenched open the door and stared at me, his expression a picture of disgust as he took in my position on the floor. Still unable to get a full breath, I couldn't cry out, couldn't scream as he curled his fingers into the material of my shirt and dragged me out. I saw another figure in the room, and hope filled me as I recognized my cousin. My arms flailed out in an attempt to catch myself as Uncle Massimo deposited me at Matteo's feet.

"You beg for her life?" My uncle sneered at me, though his words were directed at Matteo. "This worthless, vile excuse for a human being?"

Silently, Matteo extended one hand and helped me to stand. He opened his mouth to speak, then slammed it closed again, and I could practically feel the disappointment rolling off him. Tears stained my cheeks and the scent of urine clung to me as he led me down the hall and back to my room.

He paused in the doorway but released me and gestured with his chin for me to go inside. "Shower and get dressed."

"Matteo—"

The rest of my words were cut off by a hard shake of his head. "Go."

Tears burned my eyes as I started to close the door, but his hand shot out and stopped its progress. My startled gaze jumped to his, then over his shoulder to Johnny as he took up guard by my room. His dark eyes watched me intently as Matteo stepped back into the hallway.

"It stays open. Bring her down when she's done."

Johnny tipped his head without looking away from me. "Yes, sir."

My chin trembled, but I refused to cry. I spun on a heel and made my way toward the bathroom. Johnny hovered just inside the doorway to the bedroom, and I wondered if I'd have time to slam and lock the bathroom door before he made it across the room.

My gaze slid to his and, as if reading my mind, he gave a slow shake of his head. "It will only make it worse."

Anger coursed through me. I hated that he was right. Storming into the bathroom, I turned on the shower and stripped off my clothes, then stepped under the hot spray. Though I couldn't close the door, at least I was concealed from his view in here. I soaped off, shame filling me once more as I cleaned the stickiness off my legs.

The scene in the office replayed through my mind in vivid color, and it sent a shudder down my spine. What if he'd accidentally shot me? Would he have cared? Probably not, though I knew his intention wasn't to end my life. He'd wanted to scare me—and he'd succeeded. The bullets had all been over my head, carefully placed, and I'd reacted exactly the way he'd wanted. He derived great pleasure from my fear, and I hated myself for showing my weakness.

Uncle Massimo's words came back to me. *"You don't have to worry about your cop anymore. You know how much I despise loose ends."*

Was Eric really gone? Despair assailed me. My heart wanted to believe that Eric was still alive, but I knew better. Uncle had no reason to lie. My back hit the cold tile, and I slid down until I was seated. The water beat down on my back as I pulled my knees to my chest and curled into a tiny ball. Then the tears came.

I cried for myself. For Eric. For the future that had been so ruthlessly ripped away. I couldn't imagine life without him. It was like my heart had been torn to shreds, and all that remained was a gaping, aching hole.

I don't know how long I sat there, but the feel of cold

water pouring over me finally jerked me back to reality. I felt numb, dead inside. Slowly, I pushed to my feet, the motion seeming to take the last reserve of energy I had. My motions were slow and labored as I toweled off.

Anger and sadness swirled inside, battling for dominance. Anger won out. The pain of loss was still there, a sharp, aching reminder of everything I'd lost. It served to fan the flames of my fury. I would find a way to avenge Eric's death if it was the last thing I did.

Not bothering with the towel, I dropped it to the floor and turned to leave. The motion in the mirror caught my attention, and I paused. I leaned against the vanity and stared at my reflection. My face was pale, dotted with blotchy patches, and dark circles had bloomed beneath my eyes, reddened from my tears. Dark hair. Green eyes. I was my father's daughter, through and through. I lifted my chin and steeled my spine. Ignacio Capaldi wouldn't have gone down without a fight, and neither would I.

I hated Uncle Massimo. He'd stripped me of my innocence, taken away my confidence and the one person I'd loved more than anything. Never again would I allow him control over me. As much as I despised the idea, perhaps marrying was for the best.

I wasn't stupid; Uncle would never relax his guard around me. My new husband, though… he would never see it coming. I would play the perfect, obedient wife. I would win him over, make him trust me. Then I would find a way to bring them both down.

Deciding to leave my face bare and my hair to dry on its own, I left the bathroom. I refused to doll myself up for whatever my uncle had planned. While I was in the shower, someone had set a tiny black dress on the bed. Keeping my back to Johnny, I covered my breasts with one arm as I scooped up the dress and stepped into it, then tugged it into place. I struggled to pull the zipper along the side but finally managed to get it closed. With the weight I'd gained, the dress now hugged every curve, acting almost like a corset and making it hard to draw in a full breath. A tiny pair of panties had been set out, but no bra, and I quickly shimmied into them. A pair of ridiculously high stilettos that I'd once adored sat in their box on the bed; now I eyed them with loathing as I slipped them onto my feet.

I could feel Johnny's attention focused acutely on me, I glanced over my shoulder at him. "Enjoy the show?"

He blinked once, completely unaffected by my bitter tone. His voice was soft, almost inaudible when he spoke. "Dissociate."

I jerked back at the single word and swallowed hard. It was he who, after witnessing my uncle's cruel punishments, told me to retreat to a fantasy within my mind to escape my dismal reality. I swallowed hard and straightened my spine.

He studied me, his expression unreadable. "Stay strong."

Easier said than done, but I was sure he knew that. I choked back the tears, pushing down the pain. My gaze fell once more to the scar on his cheek as I neared him, and I met his eyes. "I'm sorry," I whispered.

He stared for a moment, then tipped his chin infinitesimally, apparently accepting my apology. He fell into step beside me as I made my way downstairs, to whatever fresh hell awaited me tonight.

FOURTEEN

ERIC

I sighed and scrubbed at my tired eyes. It'd been fifty-six hours since she'd disappeared, and each minute that ticked by without answers was more excruciating than the last. I'd wasted an entire fucking day stuck in the hospital, and our questioning yesterday and today hadn't yielded a damn thing. I swore we'd spoken with every single person in Pine Ridge and the valley beyond, but no one admitted to seeing anything or anyone out of the ordinary. There were only so many databases I could access, only so many threads I could pull before I hit a dead end. I wasn't too proud to admit it—I needed help.

Something deep in my gut told me I needed to focus around the Chicago area. Thankfully, it was where I'd grown up, and I still retained some contacts there. I knew several of my former SWAT teammates still lived in the area, even if they weren't still active on the force. A glance at the clock on the wall told me it was just after six p.m.

Picking up my phone, I dialed a number I hadn't used in more than three years. My stomach dipped with disappointment when it went unanswered and rolled over to Frankie's voicemail. I left him a quick message asking him to call me when he got a chance. I gave no other details before I hung up, and I prayed that he would take the time to get back to me.

Leaning back in my chair, I stared at the decades-old water stain on the ceiling. Two months ago, I'd sat here on Christmas Day, staring at that same goddamn broken heart-shaped stain, thinking of her. Everything reminded me of her; I couldn't get Jules off my mind. I'd asked myself a million times what I'd missed. What was she going to tell me in the car?

"Before I came here, I… I was supposed to be married."

I could only surmise that it was her fiancé she'd fled from months ago. She'd been terrified of men when she first arrived, and she constantly had one eye over her shoulder, waiting for the other shoe to drop. During her time with me, she'd begun to relax. But all that had changed the day before she'd disappeared. Why? Had she suspected he'd found her? She didn't keep in contact with anyone from her previous life that I was aware of, so what had tipped her off? I wondered if she'd seen him somewhere, either in town or at Briarleigh.

Jack was reviewing camera footage from around the resort to see if Jules had come into contact with anyone matching the man's description. I hoped he found something—anything—because we had less than nothing to go on.

Whoever the hell had kidnapped her must have some serious resources at their disposal to track her down; she practically lived off the grid. If he were wealthy, it would explain the armored vehicle and ability to find her. I suspected long ago that she'd come from money, yet she didn't have a single thing to her name. She refused to keep a bank account, didn't have a valid driver's license, and the car she was currently driving was unregistered. I'd strongly considered putting it in my name, but if the person hunting her had the kind of connections I speculated, then doing so would have pointed right to her location.

Goddamn, I wished she'd been able to tell me before everything went down. The worst part was, there wasn't a single damn thing to give me any indication of where she might be or with whom. My phone rang and I picked it up. "Donahue."

"Hey, man, how's it goin'?" Frankie sounded winded, like he'd just gotten done running ten miles. Knowing him, it was a good possibility.

"Good. What's up with you?"

After some obligatory small talk, I cut to the chase. "Need your help with something. You still have friends in the bureau?"

"Whatcha need?"

Steeling my heart and voice, I told him about Jules, reciting the facts as I would any case.

Frankie's tone was hard when he spoke. "Let me put out some feelers, and I'll let you know what I come up with."

I thanked him and hung up, frustrated. I felt like all I'd done over the past two days was hurry up and wait. Each thread I pulled raised a hundred more questions I didn't have the answers to. I knew she was twenty, and I knew her height and weight, the color of her eyes and hair. Beyond that, her past was a blank slate. I didn't know her last name, her heritage, her hometown. I could guess, but I didn't have the resources to even begin to accurately narrow it down. I needed someone with computer experience who could access databases across the government channels. She had to be in there somewhere; I just needed to find the person who could help me with that.

It was frustrating as fuck being stuck in limbo like this, with no answers and no leads to follow. While my deputies were covering the daily shit that popped up, I'd been focused entirely on Jules. It wasn't fair to them, but they understood.

This was personal, and they hadn't hesitated to help one of their own. I would burn down the world to find her, and I would never give up on her.

All I knew was I couldn't sit here any longer, and I pushed out of my chair. O'Neill nodded to me as I left, and I knew he was still dedicating his spare time to finding Jules, leaving no stone unturned. I climbed into the cruiser and headed toward my house. I kept putting off going to the cabin, unable to bear the thought of going home and not seeing her there. I'd seen every article of clothing she'd brought with her. There was no cell phone, no laptop or tablet—not even a fucking journal.

I parked in the garage, then entered my house for the first time in more than a month. I'd left the heat on low so the pipes wouldn't freeze, but most everything else had been moved into the cabin. It felt dark and empty and lifeless. There was no fucking way I was going anywhere near the bedroom. Instead, I collapsed on the couch, propping one foot over the armrest so I could stretch out. It was the first time I'd lain down since I was released from the hospital. I'd gotten a total of about six hours of rest over the past couple of days, catching short naps in my office when my body refused to stay awake any longer. My eyes burned, but I refused to admit that it was anything more than lack of sleep causing the moisture there. I threw one arm over my face and tried to turn my brain off. I just needed a few minutes, then I'd get up and get back to work.

The vibrating of my phone jarred me from sleep, and I bolted upright, grabbing for the phone that rested on my stomach. My body's internal clock told me I'd slept for about an hour, and I felt more exhausted than I had when I laid down. I fumbled it for a moment before sliding my thumb across the screen and lifting it to my ear. My voice was scratchy with sleep and rougher than normal. "Donahue."

"Hey, man. Sorry, didn't mean to wake you."

I scrubbed a hand over my face and shook my head as I

pushed to a sitting position. "No, no. You're good. What's up?"

"I reached out to a friend of mine from the bureau and told him your story. He's retired now and working for a private firm in Texas, but I think he's the man you need."

"That'd be great," I replied.

"I'll shoot you his contact information now. He's expecting your call."

Almost as soon as he said it my phone pinged with a notification, and I saw Jason Doyle's phone number pop up on my screen. On the other end, Frankie continued to speak. "I've got some friends here on the force who might be able to help too. If we can get Doyle to narrow down her ID and possible location, they may be able to track her down for you."

"I really appreciate this," I said softly.

Frankie cleared his throat uncomfortably. "Let me know how it works out, and don't hesitate to call if you need anything."

I hung up with the promise to do so, then tapped the contact information he'd sent my way. A man answered seconds later, as if he had been waiting for my call. "Doyle."

"Sir, this is Sheriff Eric Donahue from Pine Ridge, Montana," I introduced myself.

"I figured that was you," the man spoke. "Heard you need my help with something."

"Yes, sir. I need the full name and possible location of a young woman—my fiancée," I added.

If he thought my request odd, Doyle didn't say a word. "The more I know, the better I'll be able to help you. Start at the beginning."

I drew back to two months ago, and relayed everything that had happened since her arrival. I told him my suspicions that she had once lived in or around the Chicago area from a conversation we'd once had.

"Physical description?" he asked.

"Five-foot-two, approximately one hundred fifteen pounds. Dark brown hair, green eyes. Twenty years old." Jules had celebrated her birthday right before Christmas, and I gave him the date. She had no reason to lie about that, so I assumed December twenty-first was her true birthdate.

He made a thoughtful sound. "Anything else you can think of?"

I shook my head. What I really knew about her was pitifully little. "No, sir. I just… I'll appreciate anything you can dig up for me."

"Give me some time and I'll get back to you."

I fucking hated waiting for answers. But more than that, I hated not having her here with me. I wanted her back in my arms, her skin pressed to mine, right where she belonged. I prayed that I'd have another chance to hold her, because a future without her wasn't worth living.

FIFTEEN

GIULIANA

Guards flanked us in a diamond shape as we exited the car and made our way into the restaurant. Two more soldiers were posted outside the doors, and one held the door open as we approached. I threw him a beseeching glance, but he pointedly ignored me.

Desperation crawled up my throat as we stepped into Richie's, the small Italian bistro that my family had owned for decades. Surrounded by so many of my uncle's men, there was no way I could even make a break for it. They hadn't let me out of their sight during the two days I'd been home, and I knew my uncle had insisted on their vigilance. A combination of humiliation and anger coursed through my veins. If he thought I would go down without a fight, he was dead wrong. I just needed to wait for the right moment to act.

Uncle still hadn't given me any details about tonight's outing. All he had said on the ride over was that we were meeting someone for dinner. Matteo had been less than pleased, but I couldn't tell if it was the idea of the dinner itself or the fact that Uncle had dressed me up like a whore to be auctioned off to the highest bidder.

The skimpy black dress bared most of my breasts, and it clung to my ass, riding high on my thighs as I walked. I could feel the men's eyes on me as we filed through the back door of the restaurant, and I discreetly tried to tug the fabric back down into place. I swallowed hard, forcing down my humiliation. I felt… dirty. Part of me was amazed that I could feel anything but grief. Every inch of my body ached with it, and my blood felt thick and heavy as it flowed through my veins, like my heart was loath to continue beating.

I blinked away the tears burning my eyes as I glanced around the familiar space. Richie's was separated into two areas; the front was designated for patrons only. This portion —the back—was reserved for family only. For *business*.

A handful of men I didn't recognize stood inside the entrance, their vigilance palpable. I knew they didn't belong to *la famiglia* by their features, but they didn't appear to be Russian either. I didn't know if that was a good thing or bad. As far as I knew, my betrothal to Nikolai had been declared null after my disappearance—but that didn't mean it couldn't be resurrected. If Uncle Massimo handed me over to him, I would appeal to my new husband. But if he was truly as awful as the stories made him out to be, I might be forced to stand up against him. My stomach roiled at the thought. Could I kill him if need be? If it came down to my life or his, I wouldn't have a choice in the matter; I would have to.

Uncle gripped my biceps and practically dragged me along to a table in the middle of the restaurant. I stumbled in the five-inch heels that had been selected for me, and I began to tumble forward. Digging his fingers into my skin, he drew me up and pulled me roughly to my feet. In a flash, his arm drew back and he delivered a slap to my cheek that made my head spin. Without waiting for me to recover, he forced me forward until we reached a table in the middle of the room.

I blinked several times to clear the stars dotting my vision before my gaze fell on the man seated across from us. In a deliberate show of entitled defiance, he didn't bother to rise for our arrival. His eyes were deep as the depths of hell and just as dark. The absolute absence of emotion I saw there sent a chill down my spine. If this wasn't Nikolai, then who…?

My uncle shot the man a winning smile. "Good evening, Fox. Thank you for joining us."

I felt the blood drain from my body as the man's name registered. My stomach dropped to my toes and clenched so tightly that I thought I might throw up on my shoes.

Those emotionless black eyes flicked to me, and one dark brow arched toward his hairline before he turned his gaze back to my uncle. "It's a pleasure."

Uncle moved his grip to my shoulder and shoved roughly. "Show some respect. Kneel for the gentleman."

I hit my knees hard under the force of the movement, and pain shot through my kneecaps and up my spine. Uncle pulled out a chair and seated himself at the table, and Matteo followed suit. "And how do you find your accommodations so far?"

Uncle waved one hand around to emulate the restaurant, but Fox's expression never changed. "Fine, thank you."

My uncle's lips flattened at his response. He was used to people bowing and scraping to him, and he didn't like this man's impassivity. Without having to be asked, a waiter approached and poured red wine into three glasses, then disappeared once more, quick and silent as a specter.

Adopting a submissive pose, I bowed my head slightly and studied Fox from beneath lowered lashes. He didn't look like the cold-blooded killer Matteo had described. Then again, they never did. Impeccably dressed in a three-piece suit and shoes polished to a high shine, he looked more like a businessman. It was an apt description, except for one little detail—instead of dealing with investments and returns,

Fox's currency of choice was drugs, illegal arms, and other incomprehensible forms of payment.

"I'd like to propose a toast," my uncle said with a huge smile as he lifted his glass. "To the promise of a new future."

Fox didn't respond but raised his goblet in kind, then drank deeply. Niceties aside, Uncle Massimo launched into the reason for the meeting.

"The Russians have been encroaching on our territory for years," Massimo hissed with a sneer. "It is time for us to take back what is rightfully ours. We have tried reasoning with them, but our… *arrangement*"—he shot me a dark look—"fell through. Now they have aligned themselves with the Irish, and I find myself in need of an ally with which to stop them."

Fox studied my uncle. "I have had my own issues with them. What is your proposal?"

"We split the profits—sixty/forty. In addition, I'll give you the girl." Uncle Massimo tipped his head toward me, and my heart stuttered to a stop in my chest as Fox's cool eyes drank me in. Goosebumps swept up my arms as his gaze lingered on my breasts, the rosy tops of my nipples exposed by the low cut of the too-tight dress. My cheeks burned with mortification and fear.

Long, lean fingers played with the stem of his glass; I could easily imagine them snapping it in two. I envisioned him wrapping those fingers around my neck and squeezing until I submitted. My chest rose and fell rapidly, unable to draw in enough oxygen as unease turned to panic.

Fox's eyes met mine before sliding back to my uncle. He leaned back in his chair a bit more, adopting a casual pose. "That's quite a sacrifice for my men. I have to ensure that this will be worth my effort, you understand."

My uncle's jaw worked, and my entire body trembled. I didn't want to go with Fox, but I was terrified of what my uncle would do if Fox turned him down. "Firearms as well, then. We provide the best."

Fox stroked his chin. "Perhaps. And the girl…?"

Matteo spoke, his voice tight. "She is an innocent in all of this. Surely we can come to some other agreement."

Uncle Massimo made a derisive sound. "She is unpure, and she deserves far worse."

Matteo's face turned a mottled red, and he jumped to his feet. "Your hate controls you. There is a better—smarter—way to go about this without sacrificing her."

No one ever spoke back to my uncle—ever. I watched in horror as Massimo slowly pushed his chair back and stood. Fox settled back in his chair, his face a cool mask as he watched the scene unfold.

Massimo regarded Matteo. "You would fight for her—this whore?" Matteo was silent for a long moment, and Massimo chuckled as he resumed his seat. "You are a fucking coward. Just like your mother."

In the blink of an eye, Matteo pulled a pistol from his shoulder holster and extended it across the table. His finger pulled back on the trigger, and a loud report filled the room as the gun went off.

SIXTEEN

ERIC

Pushing off the couch, I pocketed my phone and strode toward the front door. My stomach growled, and I tried to remember the last time I'd eaten. Yesterday, maybe? I didn't know. Every hour, every second of the day, had been consumed by thoughts of Jules and trying to trace her whereabouts. I didn't have time to eat; I barely had time to sleep. But I could do all of those things later. Right now, I needed to put all of my time and energy into finding her and bringing her home.

The house was still dark, and I moved from memory as I exited into the garage and slipped into the cruiser. Though I'd questioned her coworkers and searched her desk, something kept nagging at me. I decided to go back up to Briarleigh and take another look around.

Even this late at night, it was still well-lit now that operations were in full swing. I pulled into the side lot where the employees parked, then headed for the staff entrance. The office doors along the hallway were closed up for the night, and I assumed everyone had gone home. Retrieving the key Jack had given me, I strode toward Jules's office.

I unlocked the door, then stepped inside, once more taking in the sparse furnishings. She hadn't had time to decorate, and the only pieces of furniture were a sturdy oak desk and two chairs—one for Jules, and one for a guest. Winding my way around the desk, I sank into her chair and glanced around.

Everything was exactly the same as yesterday; I don't know why I expected anything different. Her desktop computer hummed in sleep mode, and I jiggled the mouse to bring up the main screen. Though I'd searched all of the files yesterday, I did so again just to make sure I hadn't missed anything.

Each document I opened revealed carefully researched notes regarding the new spa: licenses, restrictions, and other business-related information. There were photos of Briarleigh in a separate folder labeled "website" that I assumed Mia had taken. I casually flipped through them, looking for anything that jumped out at me.

I stopped at one in particular, a tiny smile curving my face. In the new addition for the spa, Jules stood off to the side of the photograph, pointing at something. Only her profile was visible, and most people wouldn't have even been able to tell it was her. Except I knew every line of her body, every curve of her pretty face. Even from this position, I could see the smile lighting her expression, the joy in her eyes. The sight made my heart hurt. She'd been so happy here. She wouldn't have just left—I refused to even entertain the possibility.

I propped my elbows on the desk and looked around. The room smelled like her, and I drew the scent into my lungs, holding onto it, storing it in my memory until I saw her again. I reached out to touch the notepad sitting to the right of the computer. Her pretty, flowy script was scrawled over the lines, and I gently traced the letters.

Goddamn, I missed her. I hadn't been able to get a full breath since she'd been gone, the oppressive weight of depression sitting on my chest like a stone. My body physically hurt, like I was missing part of myself. I knew exactly what it was; Jules was the other half of my heart. I wouldn't feel whole, complete again until she was home.

I leaned back in the chair and stared at the ceiling. I was missing something. But what?

My phone rang, and I picked it up, more so just to give me something to do than because I actually wanted to speak with someone. "Donahue."

There was a brief hesitation at my gruff greeting, then a man's voice came over the line. "Hey, Sheriff. This is Ernie from the Gas 'N' Go."

I scrubbed one hand over my face. The Gas 'N' Go was situated only a few miles out of town near the Fox Hole, a strip club where several of the locals convened each night. There wasn't much crime in Pine Ridge, but it was unfortunately common for some of the younger kids to shoplift candy and other small shit.

"Hey, Ernie. What can I do for you?"

"I was at Rosie's earlier," the man began. "Word around town is you're looking for any strangers who may have been through recently."

"I am," I responded cautiously as I sat straight up in the chair. We'd questioned the owner, Lyle, but he hadn't seen anything. How the hell had we missed Ernie?

"Sorry I'm just now callin'. Had to visit my mama down in Kalispell in the nursing home there. She's got dementia bad, and…"

I made a frustrated gesture as I clenched my jaw to keep from screaming. Trying to hurry him up would do no good. It was like pushing rope; if I interrupted, the man would likely forget where he'd left off and have to start all over again.

"Well, anyway, two men stopped in for gas a couple mornings ago. Dressed all fancy-like, both of 'em in suits. Didn't think nothin' of it, just figured they was headed up to the ski resort. But now that I think on it..."

He trailed off and irritation surged inside me. I swore I was going to fucking strangle him if he didn't spit it out. "You see something?"

"Not sure," Ernie responded. "Only one came inside, bought a map and a pack of smokes. Never took his sunglasses off. You know them types? Didn't get a good look at the other guy out pumping gas. But it seemed a little off, if ya know what I mean."

"Did you see the plate when they drove away?"

"Didn't get a number, but pretty sure it had a picture of Abraham Lincoln on it."

That last bit of information brought me straight up in my chair, immediately alert. "You catch the make or model?"

"One of them expensive, big ol' Cadillac Escalades, looked like to me. All black, even the windows. They paid in cash, so I don't have any names for you."

"That's fine," I replied. "This is great. Thanks, Ernie."

I felt like a thousand pounds had been lifted from my shoulders as I hung up. Abraham Lincoln. The car was plated in Illinois. I had a lead—fucking finally.

A noise from the doorway drew my attention, and my gaze collided with a pair of bright blue eyes as Mia stumbled into the office.

"Oh." Her face fell as she drew up short. "I thought..."

Sadness creased her pretty features, tugging at my heartstrings. "Just me," I said softly.

Mia's gaze dropped to the floor, but not before I saw the glittering of tears hovering just above her lashes. Pushing from my chair, I rounded the desk and approached her.

Mia lifted her head as I rested one hand on her shoulder. "I'm worried about her."

I swallowed hard, resisting the urge to admit my fear of the same thing. It was literally as if she had disappeared into thin air, not even a trail of breadcrumbs to follow. "We'll find her."

My words lacked conviction, but I had to say them. I had to keep believing that she was out there somewhere, that I could bring her home to me.

Without warning, Mia threw her arms around my waist and buried her head against my chest. I let out a small grunt at the impact, then gently wrapped my arms around her shoulders in an awkward embrace. Sobs wracked her tiny body, and my strength leached away as her sympathy tore at my heart.

It never ceased to amaze me how many people loved Jules, despite the fact that she'd only been here for a few months. But she was sweet and lovable, and she had touched the lives of so many people, myself included. What would we ever do without her? I stood there feeling helpless, and I clutched Mia more tightly to me. Lowering my head, I closed my eyes against the now familiar burning sensation and fought to wrestle my emotions under control.

I had to find her—I *would*. We'd been through too much together, and I'd be damned if I let someone take her away from me.

SEVENTEEN

GIULIANA

I screamed as the back of my uncle's head exploded, and maroon droplets of blood splattered every surface. Suddenly, every man in the room was at attention, guns drawn and pointed toward Matteo. My body numb with shock, I watched helplessly. Though I stared at my uncle's lifeless body slumped backwards in his seat, head dropped back limply, I couldn't quite comprehend that it was real.

My eyes darted between Uncle Massimo and Matteo, who looked wholly unfazed. Calmly, he took his seat, then set the pistol on the table and pushed it away a few inches before lacing his fingers together in front of him. He stared across the table at Fox, whose expression was faintly bemused.

Why was everyone being so calm? I wanted to yell, to scream, to sprint for the door and leave this nightmare behind. Part of me was glad that my uncle was gone, but my mind couldn't quite reconcile it. After the years of hell he put me through, I'd come to think of him as indestructible. I glanced around the room. The familiar faces of men who had worked for my uncle registered shock and surprise. They seemed frozen in place, unsure how to react, and I sympathized with them.

Matteo's voice drew my attention back to him. "Now that the unpleasant part of the evening has been taken care of, we may speak."

I'd never been privy to the details of the work of my father and Uncle Massimo, but now it hit me like a ton of bricks. I knew men had died—probably a lot of them—but this was the first murder I'd personally witnessed, the only dead body I'd ever seen outside of a funeral, and it was jarring. My stomach heaved, and I made a gagging noise as I tore my gaze away from the gruesome sight. I slapped one hand over my mouth as if that could contain the bile creeping up my throat. My whole body shook as I pressed my palm to my mouth, terrified that the meager contents of my stomach would expel themselves all over the floor.

To Fox's credit, he didn't even blink. I wondered how often something like this had happened, and it sent a shudder through me. Fox lifted one eyebrow before directing his next words to Matteo. "She should not be present for this."

"She stays." Matteo's voice was hard and impassable.

I couldn't believe he was talking about me like a fucking dog. I directed a glare his way, but Matteo ignored me completely, his focus lasered on his future ally—or adversary. It could go either way tonight.

With a slight inclination of his head, Fox accepted Matteo's declaration. Matteo inhaled deeply before speaking. "I'd like to propose a new offer in lieu of the one Massimo suggested."

Fox arched one eyebrow, but Matteo continued, undaunted. "I think we can both agree that the Russians need to be stopped. They've pushed the boundaries for years, and it is time to bring their reign to an end. They've started a war, but I plan to finish it. To do so, I will need help. I would like your support."

Fox tipped his head. "I'm inclined to agree with you about the Bratva. Nikolai is reckless. I've heard rumblings about a plan to overthrow him."

"I have heard the same, and I would like to join forces. We will supply you with whatever you need."

Though I'd never been present for one of these meetings before, I wasn't stupid. It was what every criminal wanted—guns. I knew my family had access to weapons the likes of which I couldn't even begin to conceive.

My gaze jumped to Fox as he gestured toward me. "And the girl?"

"Off the table."

Fox pondered that for a moment. He was a strong negotiator, and he would make an excellent ally for my cousin. The thought was terrifying. "I want the west side, everything from the bridge over."

Matteo seemed to think it over. Over the years, dozens of different crime groups had sprouted up around Chicago, but the Bratva and *la cosa nostra* had gradually pushed them out, one by one. There were a few exceptions to this, and Fox was a living testimony to his will. There were a dozen different rumors about how the man had risen so quickly to power in just a few years, and I couldn't begin to contemplate it.

Finally, Matteo answered. "West side is yours, but I want 15% of the profits."

Fox shook his head. "Five."

Matteo's eyes narrowed slightly. "Ten, and that's my final offer."

Fox waited a beat before stretching out his hand. Matteo slipped his palm into it, and they shook. A handshake in our world was the measure of a man, the rock upon which all foundations were built. A simple handshake meant that the men would be forced to uphold their end of the bargain or face the consequences. I forced myself not to look at my uncle, but I couldn't help the relief that had settled over me. He was gone. Truly gone. Matteo had saved me, just as he promised he would.

Excitement and anticipation bubbled up inside me, and my body fairly vibrated with it. The men concluded their business, and Matteo extended one hand to help me up. His hand slipped around my bicep and gently tugged me to my feet, then anchored me against his side. Through it all, he never said a word. I took my cue from him and stayed silent as well. I didn't want Fox to change his mind before we were well away from here.

Fox and his men preceded us out of the restaurant, and silence hung heavily in the air as we followed. Matteo remained quiet as we made our way outside to the cars. Johnny held the door, and my cousin helped me in first, then slid in behind me. The door closed with a soft thunk, and a few moments later, Johnny started the car and pulled away from the curb.

A soft yellow glow strobed the interior of the car as street lamps whizzed past in a blur. Elation filled me as we exited onto the highway and headed away from the city. Now I could finally return to my real life. I could visit my friends and family without Uncle Massimo's censure. And Eric. I would no longer have to lie to him about who I was. As soon as I got out of here, I was going to tell him everything. I prayed that he would still want me. A mafia princess and an ex-cop didn't mix, but if a love could ever overcome anything... it was ours.

EIGHTEEN

ERIC

Doyle's name lit up my screen, and I eagerly took the call. "What do you have for me?"

"I've got a couple girls here who might fit the profile."

I exhaled in relief, my heart threatening to beat right out of my chest. "Thank God."

Doyle's next words doused my excitement. "Don't get ahead of yourself just yet. I limited my results to a hundred-mile radius of Chicago and checked every possible variation of the name. The search came back with seventy-two results."

"Jesus." I swiped a hand down my face. "So, what now?"

"I filtered them by age since you seem to be fairly certain of her birthdate. There are seventeen women with that name between the ages of eighteen and twenty-five."

That was doable, at least. I let him continue.

"I didn't want to restrict any physical features, because hair and eye color can easily be changed. I'll need you to look at the photos of each girl—specifically the facial structure—to be sure we've got the right one."

"No problem."

"First batch is on its way to you now."

I clicked open the email he'd sent and found five images attached. I opened the first photo and scanned it. The girl was pretty, with blonde hair and blue eyes, but she wasn't my Jules. I did the same for the other four images. "Not her."

"Okay. Next group."

I shook my head as I examined all five of those. "Not in these."

The last batch had six photos, none of which were Jules. I let out a growl and crossed my arms over my chest as I slumped back in my seat. "Damn. I thought for sure she would be there."

"There's one more."

Attention captured, I sat forward a bit, already reaching for the mouse. "Send it over."

"There are no verified photos that I can find," Doyle remarked cautiously. "She's practically a ghost aside from her birth certificate. There was nothing else in the system—no driver's license, no student ID, nothing."

What the hell ever. I didn't give a goddamn as long as it would lead me to Jules. "And?"

The exasperation in my tone was evident, and a long pause on his end ratcheted up my anxiety tenfold. Finally, he blew out a harsh breath. "Before I send this over to you, I need to ask you a question."

His hesitancy immediately set me on edge, and I answered warily. "What's that?"

"How well do you know this girl?"

The question sent tendrils of anger and heat snaking through my body in equal measure. I was fucking sick and tired of people questioning my relationship with her. I knew her better than anyone. I knew her hopes and dreams for the future. I knew every inch of her body like the flesh that covered my own and the blood that raced through my veins. I swallowed down the retort that jumped to the tip of my tongue. He had every right to ask since I'd reached out to him to find her true name. I answered as honestly as possible. "As well as anyone could, given her past."

There was another slight pause, then— "Did she ever tell you anything, allude to what may have happened?"

"No," I admitted. I wished I'd pushed harder, convinced her to trust me. "She said…" I choked on the words and started over. "She said she was engaged, but she didn't give me a name. Didn't say anything about him."

The thought of her with another man still made my gut burn with jealousy.

"Nothing else?"

I dropped my head into the palm of my hand and closed my eyes. "I have a feeling she's from the Chicago area, but that was only based on a conversation we had months ago. She was always reserved, even with me."

Doyle made a little sound. "You grew up there, right?"

"Til just a few years ago."

"I remember you."

I jerked back at his words. "From when?"

"Our teams worked together on the Capaldi crime case. I was at the warehouse that night. I didn't remember your name at first, but after Frankie told me about you…"

I knew exactly where he was going with that. It would be hard to forget the SWAT member who'd damn near had his head severed off by a crime boss. Unbidden, my hand moved to my throat.

"Capaldi was killed, but his brother took over operations."

"Yeah," I breathed. "I heard that."

Doyle spoke haltingly. "We researched the family for several months before we decided to move in. The bureau had Ignacio on their watch list for years, but he was a slippery fuck—always managed to evade any snare we set for him. I knew there was a brother—Massimo—but he wasn't there that night, for whatever reason.

"There wasn't much information on the other family members, so I didn't make the connection immediately. I went back through birth records, just to make sure I hadn't missed anything. Capaldi and his wife never had a son; their only child was a daughter who was sixteen at the time." He paused, letting that bit of information hang in the air for a moment. "Which would put her right around twenty now."

My heart stopped, and breath suspended in my lungs at the implication. *No. It couldn't be.* "How certain?" I forced the words from my lips.

Doyle sighed. "Damn near positive."

"Okay." I couldn't think of one single other thing to say at that moment.

His words sounded far away when he spoke. "Information is on its way over to you."

I managed a thanks and hung up. It didn't feel real. It couldn't be real. How could she do this? In startling clarity, I saw the events of the last few days line up. She'd begun to pull away after I told her about the mission and what had happened at the warehouse. I thought she was overcome with sympathy and pity for me. Instead, she'd been thinking of her father, a man who had tried to kill me and died at the hands of my partner instead.

I felt sick. I'd made love to her. Asked her to marry me. And she was the only child of the man who had tried to take my life. Where did her loyalties lie? Maybe she had left on her own, gone back to her fiancé—back to her family. I didn't want to believe it, but I couldn't refuse the evidence waving like a red flag in front of my face. It was entirely possible that she'd set this whole thing up. She wouldn't have driven her Cavalier; she was too smart for that. I could have it reported as stolen and have her found within hours.

By leaving everything behind and having someone come to collect her, she could effectively disappear from my life like she'd never been there at all. I hated her in that moment. Worse, I hated myself more. Because deep down, I was still in love with her.

NINETEEN

GIULIANA

Though I wanted to ask a thousand questions, I bit my lip and bided my time. Matteo had been silent the whole way home. He stared out the window, lost in thought, and I sneaked peeks at him every few seconds. I couldn't begin to imagine what he was feeling right now. He'd killed his own father… for me.

When we were younger, Matteo and I had spoken of what we wanted to do when we grew up. Even then it had been bittersweet and tinged with longing, knowing that it would never come to pass. We would never be free of the bonds of *la famiglia*. Whether he wanted it or not, Matteo was now head of the Capaldi family.

Headlights swept over the gates with the family crest on them, and they swung inward, allowing us entrance. I turned my gaze on the perfectly manicured lawn of my uncle's home. It was a veritable fortress, with eight-foot walls surrounding the five-acre plot of land on the outskirts of town. Soldiers armed with rifles patrolled inside and out, ensuring no breach of security. It looked harsh and cold, yet its familiarity tugged at my heart.

I wished things had turned out differently. I hated my uncle, but I never would have wished death on him. I closed my eyes against the memory of his blood staining the wall and ceiling, forcing down the bile that rose once more in my throat.

Matteo had taken the position of capo by force, and I was sure some of the soldiers were shaken and confused. I'd seen it written in their faces at the restaurant. We'd left immediately after the conclusion of the meeting with Fox, so I had no idea what they'd done with the body. Massimo had been head of the family and therefore deserved a proper burial. Though I had no desire to attend the funeral, I knew I didn't have a choice. I was bound by familial duty to attend. Once it was over, I could finally close this chapter of my life and move on.

The car slowed to a stop in front of the huge, carved wooden doors of my uncle's home, and the motion snapped Matteo from his trance. Johnny climbed from the driver seat, and I met his gaze as he held my door open. "Thank you."

Matteo nodded to him, then took my elbow and guided me up the stone steps. Inside the house, he escorted me to my room, then sat on the edge of my bed. Stonily still, he stared at the thick carpet beneath his feet. For several long moments, we remained quiet until I could no longer bear it.

"I can't begin to thank you," I said softly.

Matteo met my eyes, and the emotion in the dark depths rendered me speechless. It spoke of sheer torment, an anguish I'd never seen before. He turned slightly toward me and grasped both of my hands in his. "He should've listened. I couldn't let him give you away." He gave his head a little shake. "I couldn't stand it."

I squeezed his hands, and tears sprang to my eyes. "None

of this was your fault. You did what you had to do. You saved me, and I owe you my life."

His dark gaze slid over my face. "I would do anything for you, *principessa*. He deserved it after everything he did."

A niggling memory appeared in the back of my mind. "Matteo... Did he have anything to do with Daddy's death?"

His eyes closed for a moment, and he drew in a deep breath. "He wasn't supposed to die."

My heart thumped to an abrupt stop at the truth I'd been waiting to hear. Somehow, deep down, I knew my uncle was responsible. "What happened?"

"Massimo wanted your father out of the way. He thought he was getting complacent in his dealings with the Russians, and Massimo suggested an attack. Your father refused. Massimo wanted control of the entire city. If he could get your father out of the way, he thought he could push the Bratva out by force.

"He tipped off the Feds about an incoming shipment at the warehouse. I think your father knew something was happening, because they argued about a week beforehand, and things became very tense."

I remembered that, too. I recalled them sequestered in a corner at Richie's one night, my father's face angry and dark. Now I knew the rest of the story as well. Was that the reason Daddy did what he'd done? The Feds would have arrested him had they captured him. Had he chosen death instead? I had a feeling I'd never know for sure, and my heart dropped to my toes.

"I'm sorry," Matteo said quietly. "I knew what he meant to you."

I gave him a weak smile, though I still felt slightly sickened by what had taken place. "What about Mama? Does she know?"

Matteo's gaze shifted away. "I don't know."

There was something about his discomfort that piqued my curiosity. "Matteo… Where is my mother?"

He cleared his throat before speaking. "Last I heard, she was on Molina."

Our family owned a small chain of islands in the Caribbean, and the name of the largest one where my father's villa was located jumped out at me. I stared at him. "Is she there for safety reasons?"

He gave a slight shake of his head. "No, *principessa*."

I couldn't believe it. Any normal mother would have torn the world apart to find her child if they disappeared. Mine apparently went on vacation. The last sliver of hope I'd held onto for reconciliation hardened and dropped away from my heart. Anger and disappointment rendered me mute for another long minute.

"Can I ask you something?" Matteo tipped his head slightly to one side, giving me the confidence to continue. "How did he find me?"

"Sheer luck." His chest rose, then fell. "We traced you to Champaign until the signal on your phone stopped moving. Massimo got a hold of the video from the mall parking lot and figured out what kind of vehicle you were in. One of Massimo's contacts was able to get footage from a toll booth on I-39. He had every available man on the hunt, searching through hours of video footage until they finally saw you pass through.

"We knew you'd gone west. After that, it was anyone's guess. The trail went cold, and we'd almost given up. Then one day Patrick's wife was looking around online, making reservations for a ski trip. She came across this new resort in Montana, and Pat brought a picture to my attention. Standing there in the middle of a construction zone…" His voice softened. "I'd know your face anywhere."

I closed my eyes against the tears burning behind my lids. That damn picture. Mia had taken it during the initial phase of renovation and asked if it was okay to use when she showcased the development of the spa online. Though I'd debated it, I hadn't seen the harm in allowing her to post it. After all, it'd been taken from the side so most of my features were obscured. There was no mention of my name, and I'd been careful to cover my tracks after I'd fled Chicago. Apparently, I hadn't been careful enough.

I blinked my eyes open again and found Matteo's gaze on me, fierce and determined. "I was so upset when you ran away—but I understand why you did it."

I nodded, emotion still clogging my throat. "I'm sorry I left you to deal with him alone. But the thought of ending up with Nikolai, or worse…"

"I should have tried harder." He reached out and raked his fingers gently through the long strands of my hair and arranged them over my shoulders. It felt strange to have him touch me so intimately, but he seemed lost in thought as he curled one lock around his finger, and I forced myself to remain still. After a long moment, he continued. "I didn't have the resources in place to help you when Massimo arranged your marriage to Nikolai. I had only just met Fox, and I needed a strong ally to take him down."

Grateful tears clogged my throat, and I swallowed them down. "I just… you have no idea what this means to me. To finally be free. Uncle was terrible, to both of us. Now I feel like I can finally breathe again; I can finally move on."

"Now *we* can move on," he corrected with a small smile.

My brows drew together. He had to know I didn't plan to stay. "Matteo, I—"

His thumb swept over my bottom lip, halting my words. "I'm so glad you're back, Giuliana. God, I feel like I've waited so long for this. Just you and me, *principessa*. The way it was meant to be."

My stomach clenched with dread as a new light entered his eyes. He leaned forward as if to kiss me, and I jerked backward. Bringing one hand up between us, I placed it on his chest. "Matteo, what are you doing?"

He placed one large hand over mine, holding it against his heart. "You belong here with me. With Fox's alliance, and our union, we will be unstoppable."

I shook my head. "I can't stay here."

A furrow appeared between his brows, and he took both of my hands in his own larger, stronger ones. "Of course you can." He said it like there was no other choice. "With you back in your rightful place, we'll be stronger than ever."

"No." I met his dark gaze. "I'm not staying."

"You are." He squeezed my hands so tightly that I could feel the bones compress.

I let out a soft cry. "Matteo, stop! You're hurting me!"

His grip eased a fraction, but he didn't release my hands. "This is your home, Giuliana. You were bred for this role. You were meant to be queen of this city."

"I don't want this life, I never have." I shook my head. "You know how awful it is; I don't want my children to grow up this way. I want better for them."

His dark eyes bore into me. "Our children will have better."

A niggling of trepidation lifted the hairs on the back of my neck. He meant our respective children, right? Because there was no way he could be implying what I thought he was. We grew up together; we were family. For a multitude of reasons, there could never be anything between us.

I finally managed to pull my hands away and gave my head a little shake, speaking softly as I tried to make my point. "You've been like a brother to me, and I appreciate it more than I can say. You've done so much for me—but I don't belong here."

One huge hand cupped the back of my neck, and the possessive move took my breath away as his expression changed, became deeper and darker. "This is your place, Giuliana. You're staying."

Anger rose up, swift and hot. I ripped myself from his grasp and stumbled to my feet. "I'm not!"

He stood, towering over me, a fierce glare twisting his expression. "This is not up for discussion. This is your home. You're not leaving."

"I did it once," I snapped. "I'll do it again."

His eyes flashed, and he moved before I could blink. Sweeping me upward, the motion stole my breath as his shoulder slammed into my midsection, and I was flung upward.

Hanging upside down, I pounded my fists on his back. "Put me down! Let me go!"

Long, hard fingers curled into the back of my thigh, the pain immediate and acute, and I let out a little squeal as I kicked against the sensation. "Matteo, stop! Please!"

I watched upside down as he stormed through the house. My dress rode high on my hips, and I knew my ass was exposed to everyone we passed. Shame and humiliation coursed through me, immediately followed by anger. "Don't do this!"

My heart clenched in fear as we approached uncle Massimo's office—Matteo's office now. Oh, God. "Not the closet, Matteo, please!"

His hand slipped between my thighs, and I sucked in a breath at the intrusion. He pinched the sensitive flesh hard, eliciting a stifled scream. His footsteps thundered across the hardwood, and he dumped me unceremoniously inside the closet, then slammed the door.

Fury propelled me to my feet. I'd been in the same closet only a few hours ago, and now we had come full circle once more. I expected something like this from my uncle, but Matteo? He had always been my protector, my defender. How could he do this to me?

"Let me out!" I beat on the door, but only silence met my angry demands. "Don't do this!"

"I will never forgive you!" I screamed. I knew he waited just on the other side, listening to my pleas but refusing to help. I pounded both fists against the door as hard as I could. "You're no better than him! I hate you both!"

At that, the door was flung open, and my momentum carried me forward, right out the door where I landed in a heap at Matteo's feet.

The wood floor was cool against my cheek as Matteo swept my knees out from under me and grabbed both of my hands in his. His bruising grip wrapped around both of my tender wrists, and he stretched my arms high over my head. He settled himself on my hips, pressing me into the hard floor, and I heard the harsh rip of tape being torn from a roll.

"Matteo, don't do this!" I begged.

I began to fight in earnest as he wound the tape around my wrists. My shoulders and back ached from the struggle, and he was too heavy for me to throw off. Suddenly his weight was gone, and I breathed a sigh of relief. I opened my mouth to try to reason with him again, but a harsh crack on my exposed bottom stopped the words in my throat.

I cried out as a second hard blow came, this time on the other cheek, and I knew I'd bear his handprints. Rage and injustice bubbled up inside me. "Stop it! Matteo, please!"

"I've worked too hard to let you ruin this." Several more slaps rang out, echoing in the office as he paddled my ass and upper thighs, hard and unrelenting. "I won't tolerate your disobedience, Giuliana. It's time for you to learn your place."

Tears sprang to my eyes, but I bit my lip and forced them back as he threw as much force behind each stinging swat as possible. I clenched my ass cheeks in anticipation of the hard blows, but my muscles ached, and I couldn't endure much more. I closed my eyes and tried to block out the pain thrumming through my lower body.

Suddenly, it stopped.

"Get the car." Matteo's voice spoke from above me, presumably to one of his men. I heard footsteps move silently away from the office, and the last bit of hope I'd harbored fled. Someone had been there the whole time. And they hadn't tried to help.

Matteo fisted one hand my hair and leaned down to speak close to my ear. "You said you owed me your life when I saved you from Massimo. Now you belong to me."

TWENTY

ERIC

The anger I felt toward her was almost blinding in its intensity, and I'd had to pull over twice on the way here. I sat there alone on the secluded stretch of road raging at her, beating my fists against the steering wheel. I still wasn't quite sure how I'd ended up at the cabin; the drive was a blur of memories as I drove past the snow-covered pines. My body still shook under the force of my fury, and I tried several times to get the key into the slot before finally managing to get it unlocked.

I still hadn't begun to process Doyle's news. How was it possible that the woman I loved so deeply could betray me so badly? I prided myself on being able to read people, but with Jules… I'd never even seen it coming.

I pushed open the door to the cabin and stepped inside, then closed up behind me. I didn't bother to lock the door. I didn't plan to stay—just long enough to gather my things and head back home. I couldn't be here, surrounded by the memory of her. Everywhere I looked, I saw her. From the dishes stacked neatly by the sink to her tall leather boots sitting in the tray beside the door, she'd left literally everything behind when she walked away from me.

I let out a mirthless laugh. All of her mannerisms made sense now. I'd known instinctively that she'd come from money—it wasn't like a few articles of clothing mattered one bit to a woman like her. She was a mafia princess with the world at her fingertips; I could never give her the things she was accustomed to. Maybe she'd decided to go back to the life of luxury her fiancé could provide instead.

I couldn't believe she'd just thrown me over like that. She'd never given any indication that material shit mattered to her. With the exception of the couple of days prior to her disappearance, she'd seemed happier than ever. But I couldn't deny what was right in front of me. If she truly wanted nothing to do with me, then I would have to accept it. But, goddamn it, I wanted to know why—and who. It was almost sickening, the need to discover the man she'd left me for.

I pushed off the door and stomped upstairs to search our bedroom first. I studiously avoided the bed where she had lain next to me night after night, our loving filled with promise for the future. Steeling my heart, I methodically began to search her things. I started with the closet first, sifting through each article of clothing. I checked inside each pair of shoes, inside the pockets of her clothes, and inside her spare purse. I came up empty in each place, and I propped my hands on my hips.

It didn't help that I had no clue what I was looking for. I was praying for a cell phone, but I had a feeling I'd be shit out of luck on that score. Jules had claimed not to have one when she'd first arrived, and I believed her. She'd barely had enough clothes to wear, let alone any conveniences. Knowing Jules, if she had phone numbers or contact information written down, it would be on a piece of paper somewhere. I hadn't found anything when I'd searched her office at

Briarleigh, but maybe that was too obvious. Too many people had access to her things there, though I knew she kept the door locked. Wouldn't want someone stumbling across personal information, I thought with a sneer.

I looked behind the baseboard and in every nook and cranny I could find. I moved to the bathroom, rooting through each drawer and checking her meager cosmetics case, then I shook out each towel to make sure nothing was hidden within the folds. I checked the seam between the vanity and the wall, even inside the tank of the toilet. Still nothing. I moved to the bed next and ripped off the sheets. I checked inside the pillowcases, under the mattress, inside each drawer of the dresser. My ire grew as my search continued to yield no results.

Stomping back downstairs, I ripped apart the living room. I searched between pages of books, inside the zippered cushions of the couch, checked for loose stones along the fireplace. A hazy rage took over, and I moved toward the kitchen, where I searched the pantry and every cabinet, even inside the refrigerator and freezer.

Beyond frustrated, I let out an inhuman roar. "Goddamn it!"

Fury raced along my veins, and I lashed out. The coffee mug Jules had used several mornings ago sat beside the sink, and I palmed it, feeling its familiar weight in my hand. I could still see the faint outline of her lip print along the edge of the mug, and my heart constricted in my chest. Drawing my arm back, I slung it across the room and watched it shatter against the stone fireplace.

I scrubbed my hands over my face and felt the burning sensation at the backs of my eyes. How could she do this to me? I felt lost in my emotions, as if they were a rolling tide threatening to pull me under. I still couldn't believe she'd left. If she wasn't happy, why the hell hadn't she just told me?

That was the thing, though. She hadn't seemed unhappy

—not at all. In fact, she was almost a completely different person from the woman who'd shown up three months ago. The Jules who'd shown up just before Christmas was afraid of her own shadow. She'd kept one eye over her shoulder every second of the day, and her anxiety had been evident in the way she'd picked at her nails. It was a nervous habit, one she'd shed over the past several months. It was also something, I realized with dawning clarity, that had resumed full-force right before she'd disappeared.

What the hell did that mean? I stared sightlessly out the window as I replayed those last few days. She'd withdrawn after she'd learned of my tumultuous past with her father. Was that it? I dismissed the thought almost immediately. The following night, she'd made love to me almost frantically—as if she would never get to do it again.

I swallowed down the bile that rose in my throat. Maybe she'd needed me once more before she went back to *him*.

My eyes fell to the fireplace and slowly, like flame licking at kindling, a memory curled upward from the recesses of my mind. I'd made love to her just a few nights ago in that very spot. And I'd come inside her. My baby could be growing inside her right this very second.

Hell fucking no.

She was out of her goddamn mind if she thought I was just going to let her go. I would drag her ass back here just to prove a point if I had to. That new realization drove me to put one foot in front of the other as I continued my search of the downstairs. I stepped into the office, though she rarely spent time in here. I sank down into the leather seat. Leaning my elbows on the desk, I dropped my head into my hands. What the fuck had happened? Doyle's conversation played through my mind on loop, and I needed to know for myself.

As I reached for the power button on the tower, I realized it was already on. I jiggled the mouse to wake up the monitor and was rewarded a few moments later when the home screen popped up. I clicked over to the internet browser and typed in Capaldi's name. Dozens of photos of Giuliana's late father, Ignacio, popped up, but none of my girl.

I snorted bitterly. She wasn't my girl anymore. The more I reminded myself of that, the easier it would be to get over her. I hoped.

My gut tightened as the article about the raid at the warehouse popped up, and I read through it. The reporters had left out a lot of information, but that was no surprise. I was sure someone had paid them to look the other way— probably the Feds in this case.

My hand moved to the scar at the base of my throat, and I swallowed hard. Although Capaldi had tried to take my life that day, I couldn't help but wish that things were different. The knowledge of the truth behind his death had driven a wedge between Jules and me, and I wasn't sure we would ever be able to overcome it.

I kept coming back to the same question. What was she about to tell me that morning, and why? Part of my brain had blocked out the first part of her request, focusing only on the knowledge that she'd been set to marry someone else. Now it came back in its entirety.

"I think I need help. Before I came here, I… I was supposed to be married."

She'd said she needed help—but why? No one had seen anything, heard anything out of the ordinary. Everything had been fine until I'd told her about that damn raid. It was the catalyst that had thrown everything into motion, and I didn't know what else I was supposed to think. She'd run because going back to her family was better than staying with the man who'd been involved in her father's death… right?

I clicked up to the navigation bar, and began to type when the computer's search engine auto-populated the name of an email platform. I pressed enter, and my heart began to race in my chest as Jules's email account appeared on the screen. I opened it up and started at the top, clicking down through each new email.

One from an unknown sender caught my eye, and I hesitated for a moment before clicking on the video file. The subject line was grayed out, so I assumed Jules had opened it previously. Still, I didn't want to risk crashing the computer if it was a spam file, so I pulled out my phone and dialed the number at the top of my contacts list.

Jason answered after the third ring. "Doyle."

"I need your help with something," I began as my eyes skimmed the rest of the email, looking for a source. "Is there any way to find out if a video file is spam or if it's legit?"

"Want me to take a look?" Doyle asked.

Following his instructions, I found the IP address, and he connected to the computer remotely. I held my breath as the file loaded and began to play. I didn't recognize the young man and woman on their knees, but a sick sense of dread filled my gut. On their knees, they begged and pleaded for their lives.

"Fuck," Doyle said on the other end.

I cringed, my stomach revolting as we watched the brutal execution play out in silence.

Jason took a deep breath before he spoke. "Let me see what I can find for you."

He closed out the file and disconnected the phone call, and I sat there in silence. Somehow, I knew this was what Jules was about to tell me. I wasn't sure how or why; it was just a gut feeling. If she had been about to tell me of this video, I assumed she knew who was responsible.

I kept replaying our conversation from that morning through my mind. Why would she be so intent on finally opening up if she'd planned to disappear? Had some misplaced sense of guilt prompted her to warn me? And who the fuck was the guy who'd shot me? The fiancé? He could've —probably should've—killed me. But he didn't. Why the hell not? The pieces of the puzzle didn't fit, and it frustrated the hell out of me.

A sudden chill raced down my spine as the anger and hurt clouding my mind began to lift.

"I was supposed to be married…"

Was her fiancé responsible for this? She'd shown up months ago, bruises marring her face. I'd originally surmised that she was running from a boyfriend—or a fiancé. If he'd mistreated her, I seriously doubted that she'd have gone with him voluntarily. If he'd finally found her…

My eyes flicked back to the computer screen, and fear seized me. I needed to find out who the hell he was—before Jules met the same fate.

TWENTY-ONE

GIULIANA

Wrists bound, duct tape over my mouth, I glared at Matteo as he hauled me to my feet. Behind the thin gray barrier I swore a blue streak, but all that came out was a muffled cry. My curses were immediately cut off as Matteo wrapped one huge hand around my neck, his lean, strong fingers pressing into my pressure point. I let out a sharp shriek as pain radiated down my spine, and he forced my gaze to his.

"Do not push me, Giuliana. I promise you'll regret it."

With one last withering glare, he shoved me out the door. I threw a beseeching look at Johnny, but he avoided me completely, his expression cold as he directed his words to Matteo.

"Would you like an escort, sir?"

Matteo waved him off. "No. Stay here."

I threw an angry glare in Johnny's direction, but he was already moving away, presumably headed back to his normal post. What the hell was wrong with these men? Why would no one help me?

I stumbled in my heels as Matteo forced me through the

mansion and out the front door. A car idled quietly out front, and my cousin opened the back door, then practically shoved me inside. I fell to my stomach on the buttery leather, and Matteo shoved me out of the way. My ass slid off the seat, and I landed on the floor with a jarring thump. I yelled at him from behind the tape, but he ignored me as he spoke to the driver. "Go."

The car accelerated, throwing me off balance again, and I fought to catch myself. Before I could move, darkness descended over my face. I screamed out, and a pair of strong arms hauled me upward. Matteo settled me on the seat next to him, one hand on my bound wrists.

"It's just a hood. You'll be fine."

Condescension dripped from his tone, and I turned a glare on him as if he could see my mulish expression. The glow of street lamps permeated the fabric as we flew down the street. Where the hell were we going? I shifted uncomfortably, my bottom and legs aching from his brutal spanking. I'd never felt so demeaned in my entire life, and I wanted to throttle him the second my hands were free.

Matteo remained silent, and the minutes bled away until finally the car slowed to a stop. "Stay here."

I knew from the tone of his voice that he wasn't talking to me; where the hell was I going to go anyway? Bound and gagged, a hood over my face, I wouldn't make it ten feet on my own. Didn't mean I wouldn't try the first chance I got. The second he let down his guard, I was getting the hell away from these crazy assholes.

Cold air invaded the car as the door swung open, and goosebumps broke over my skin as the wintry chill washed over me. Suddenly I was being dragged across the seat again as Matteo pulled me from the car. He set me on my feet for a moment then, without warning, his shoulder pressed into my midsection and he tossed me over his shoulder once more. I curbed the instinct to fight back. I couldn't see a damn thing and with my luck, he'd drop me straight on my head. Then I'd really be shit out of luck.

I bit back my curses and focused instead on the sounds around me, trying to figure out where we were. I didn't hear anyone follow us, but all of Matteo's soldiers were adept at blending silently into the background. For a brief time, we stepped inside a building, and several people's voices filled the air. Unfortunately, the duct tape over my mouth prevented me from calling out for help.

I felt the tell-tale dip as Matteo started down a set of steps. The bouncing motion as he walked turned my stomach, and he set me on my feet when I made a gagging sound. He grabbed my hand and tugged me along, causing me to stumble. My cry was hampered by the tape over my mouth, and Matteo let out an exasperated sound before looping one arm around my waist and urging me forward.

It felt like we walked forever, only a sliver of light visible through the face covering, as if everything else was pitch dark. I followed along as Matteo led me through the dank air and down a second set of steep stairs, wondering where the hell we could possibly be going. The air was cool, and I shivered involuntarily before I could stop myself. My body wanted to lean instinctively toward Matteo, to try to absorb his heat, but I refused to give in. Pushing the cold from my mind, I leaned slightly away from him.

My shoulder bumped against the rough wall, and the duct tape pulled against the skin of my wrists as Matteo tugged me along. I stumbled as I stepped off the final step, and the ground rushed up to meet me. My chin hit the hard floor, sending a shower of stars sparkling in the darkness before my eyes. Instead of helping me to my feet, Matteo let out a small sound of disgust, and I heard him move away, the soles of his expensive leather shoes scuffing against the hard floor.

Shifting my weight, I finally managed to pull my knees under me in a kneeling position. The air was cold and damp, and the floor was hard and rough under my knees. Concrete, maybe? Where were we?

The footsteps returned, and suddenly the hood covering my face was ripped away. I blinked as the room around me came into focus. The room was small, maybe only twenty feet deep by twenty feet wide, and it would only take a few steps for a person to cross from one side to the other. Soft light spilled from two old-fashioned oil lanterns attached to the walls, one on each side of the small room, and my brow creased in confusion. The walls, the floor, the ceiling— everything was made of thick, wide stone. It looked… old.

A hook dangled from the ceiling, threaded through a metal circle and attached to the wall to my left, like a primitive pulley system. Horror clashed with understanding as Matteo loosened the rope to lower the hook. I scrambled to my feet and made a mad dash for the door, but his hard body slammed into mine, pressing me against the hard wood just as I reached it.

His hot breath washed over my cheek as he pinned me in place. "I warned you not to fuck with me. I told you you'd regret it."

A sharp cry tore from my mouth as he fisted one hand in my hair. Tear spring to my eyes, but I refused to give in that easily. I threw an elbow into Matteo's midsection with as much force as possible considering my hands were still bound in front of me. A tiny kernel of satisfaction bloomed as he let out a harsh grunt, but it was overshadowed seconds later as he grasped the long strands of my hair and yanked hard. My back arched under the strain, and pain exploded across my scalp as he dragged me backward. The agony was almost paralyzing, and Matteo had me strung up before I could fight back.

Arms suspended high above me, Matteo tugged on the rope until I was standing fully upright, my heels barely able to touch the floor. He secured the rope in place, then took three steps to stand directly in front of me. He glared down at me, and I notched my chin up in challenge. With a quick jerk, he lifted a corner of the tape over my mouth and ripped it off.

Damn, that hurt! Tears clouded my eyes and I let out a sharp cry as pain burned across my skin. I rolled my lips together to try to ease the fire there, but it didn't diminish. Infuriated, I glared at my cousin.

"If you think this will get me to change my mind, you're wrong." Though my words were full of false bravado, I couldn't quite keep my voice from shaking. Fear vibrated through me, and I swallowed hard, forcing it down.

A confident smirk lifted one corner of his mouth. "We both know that's not true."

I mimicked his smirk. "Really? I escaped once. What makes you think I won't do it again?"

He dropped back a step, hands propped on his hips, and the smile slipped from his lips. Then he did the last thing I expected. He laughed. Cold and completely devoid of mirth, the sound sent a chill down my spine. My heart raced, and my stomach clenched as his deep chuckle bounced off the stone walls, filling my ears and sending goosebumps over my flesh. I pressed my lips into a firm line and stared at him until, finally, his laughter trailed off.

Dark eyes met mine, cutting through me like a knife. "Oh, Giuliana. Still so naïve."

I recoiled as he closed the distance once more and took my chin between his thumb and forefinger. "You think you will escape me?" I didn't deign to answer, and he gave his head a little shake. "Do you have any idea where you are?" His voice was deceptively soft, smooth as silk, and I recognized the calm before the storm.

In hell. I wisely kept the retort to myself and stared at him like it didn't matter in the least. I tried like hell to keep my expression neutral and not show my curiosity—because I did want to know where we were. How far were we from people, from any place I could seek help?

Matteo tipped his head slightly to one side as he studied me, seeming to anticipate my reaction to whatever he was about to impart. "Did you know there are hundreds of tunnels beneath the city?"

Oh, God. My shoulders tightened. I'd lived in Chicago my whole life; of course I'd heard of them. Had I ever been down there? Hell no. It was too creepy to contemplate.

"Is that where we are? In one of the tunnels?" The thought of being locked away underground, where no one could hear me, sent chills down my spine.

"You, *principessa*, should be more well-versed in our family's history."

Anger curled through me. "Maybe I would if my family actually shared information with me."

It was the same with all the women in *la famiglia*. We were involved on a strictly need-to-know basis—and more often than not, we didn't need to know. I knew a lot of the other women preferred it that way; they didn't want to know what kind of monster their husband or father or brother was.

Matteo turned finally and smirked as he crossed his arms over his chest. "Then I shall enlighten you. This"—he spread his arms upward in a Y shape—"is Saint Paul's Church."

My mouth opened, then snapped closed again. I'd been to Saint Paul's hundreds of times over the course of my life. I'd been baptized here, attended mass, dozens of weddings, and more funerals than I cared to admit. Never in all those years had I ever seen anything like this. "How did you know about this place?"

A condescending smile curled his lips. "Oh, I've used this room several times over the years."

I looked around the room again, and suddenly… I knew exactly what this room had been used for. I swallowed hard. "Why did you bring me here?"

"Privacy," he said simply. "Can't have anyone interrupting."

"Matteo…" I recoiled as he pushed off the table and strode toward me.

"You hated that closet, didn't you?"

I glared up at him. What the hell kind of question was that? He knew I did. I didn't bother to respond, and his head tipped slightly to one side after several tense seconds of silence. "Is it the dark?"

He waited a bit, then shook his head. "No, not the dark. Is it the confined space?"

Again, I refused to answer. I wouldn't give him any more ammunition to use against me. I watched as Matteo moved in a wide arc around me, and I turned my head, eyes fixed on him until he moved out of my peripheral vision. Hands bound above me, I was helpless as Matteo stepped up behind me, pressing himself against my back. I arched, trying to hold myself away from him, but the limited range of motion in the restraints made it difficult. Or was it the stale air? I tried to focus beyond the dull pain radiating through my shoulders. What was he asking about?

One large hand slid over my shoulder, brushing my collarbone, then wrapped around my throat. "Must be difficult to breathe in such a small space," he observed, tightening his hold.

My breathing turned shallow and rapid, and Matteo let out a soft chuckle. "That's it, isn't it? What do you think it would be like to be left for dead, buried alive? Wondering when your oxygen would run out. If anyone would ever find you, or if you would die all alone in the dark, trapped in that tiny space."

My lungs hitched, and my heart thundered in my chest. Blood thrummed through my veins, and I could hear the rushing of it in my ears as black dots danced in front of my eyes. I tried to jerk away, my instinct for survival overriding my fear.

Matteo moved in front of me again and cocked one eyebrow as he studied me. "Massimo was much too lenient with you. You see," he continued, "he didn't take the opportunity to get to know you. Not like I know you."

A shiver of foreboding slid down my spine as his eyes darkened.

"He put you in the closet because you hated it, but he didn't really understand why you hated it so much."

I hated that he could read me so easily. I glared up at him. "What if you're wrong?" I challenged.

Matteo laughed. "I'm not wrong. You hate the idea of being completely helpless, being at someone else's mercy."

I swallowed hard, but refused to answer him. He was right; we both knew it.

"How do you feel now?" He lifted his hand, trailing his fingers lightly down my right arm as he circled me again. "Strung up like a marionette, dancing only when I pull the strings?"

As if to prove his point, he tugged lightly on the rope where it wrapped around the cleat mounted on the wall. The quick jerk tugged on my wrists, lifting me to the balls of my feet. I cried out as pain shot through the joints of my shoulders. He released me, and I fell back to my heels with a panting breath.

"Fear is the greatest motivator," he remarked as he moved toward one flickering lantern. The golden glow danced over his face as he lifted the glass globe and leaned close, then blew out the flame. The room immediately dimmed, and my heart lurched in my chest.

Oh, God. "Please don't!" I begged. I could deal with a lot of things, but the stark darkness of a torture chamber buried deep beneath the earth had the power to break me.

Matteo met my gaze as he crossed to the second lamp. The

leaping flames reflected in the dark depths of his eyes, making him look like the epitome of the devil. "Will you obey me if I let you go?"

I could have told him yes, but we both knew it would be a lie.

"That's what I thought." He took a deep breath then exhaled, and the smell of smoke lingered on the air as the light was extinguished.

"Matteo!" Desperation laced my voice as he swung the door open. I couldn't see a damn thing, and my heart raced as I began to hyperventilate. "Oh, God... Please don't! Don't leave me!"

"Sorry, *principessa*." A slight hesitation. "This is for your own good."

The door slammed behind him, and the key in the lock sounded deafening in the small room. I tugged on my bonds, my breath coming in rapid pants in the dark. "Matteo!"

A soft scraping noise met my ears, making me jump. Unable to see, I envisioned spiders crawling along the walls, rats scurrying along the stone floor. "Matteo! Don't leave me here! Don't do this!"

I screamed until my throat was raw, but no one came. I was all alone in the dark, left here to die alone.

TWENTY-TWO

ERIC

"Sheriff?" Hawkins called from the front office.

I moved to my doorway. "Yeah?" He hitched one thumb over his shoulder. "Got a guy on the phone who wants to talk to you."

I waved my hand in the air dismissively. "Get a call-back and I'll touch base with him later."

I was too busy to deal with any bullshit right now. I had just entered my request for vacation, effective immediately, and I had a ton of loose ends to tie up before then. I planned to head to Chicago tomorrow and meet up with some of my old teammates, do some digging of my own. I'd put in a call to Doyle to pull everything he could on Massimo Capaldi and his family in the meantime. He'd put me in touch with a contact from the Chicago field office, and we had a meeting arranged for the following day.

I was going to find whoever was responsible for taking Jules away. Then I was going to make damn sure justice was served, one way or another.

"I tried," Hawkins apologized with a grimace. "But he says he has something you might want to hear."

My heart leapt in my chest, but my mind told me to proceed with caution. Any time there was a case like this, false tips poured in like rain. We had to investigate every single one, and more often than not, it was a waste of time and resources. Still, I would at least hear the guy out before I left.

"Send him over," I snapped. The transfer rolled through just as I reached my desk, and I swiped up the phone. "Donahue."

My response was gruff and curt, and the chuckle that came from the other end sent prickles of ice down my spine. "You sound frustrated, Sheriff."

Immediately on guard, I tamped down my anger. "Who is this?"

The man made a little sound in the back of his throat. "I believe we have a mutual… acquaintance," he responded.

I ground my molars together. "Is that so?"

"You must've made quite an impression on her, Sheriff," the man taunted. "She's awfully distraught."

I balled my hand into a fist and placed it on the desk. I wanted to reach through the phone and wrap my hands around his neck and choke the life out of him. Somehow, I managed to form words through the anger choking my throat. "Then maybe you should let her go."

Another chuckle came from his end. "I don't think so," that smooth cultured voice spoke again. "If you want her, you'll have to come take her."

"Tell me where." There was no hesitation this time, only my resolve to find Jules and bring her home to me.

"There's an old warehouse down by the river," he said. "I'm sure you remember it."

Trepidation stole up my spine as I remembered the last time I was inside that Godforsaken abandoned building situated next to the Calumet River. *Motherfucker*. He was leading me right back to the spot where I'd almost lost my life three years ago. If that wasn't a fucking omen, I didn't know what was. But there wasn't a damn thing I wouldn't do for Jules, and if facing my demons meant keeping her safe and bringing her home, I would do it if it killed me. Maybe literally.

"When?"

"Tomorrow evening, eight o'clock. Don't be late."

With that, the man hung up, and I stared at the phone for a long moment. "Goddamn it!"

I banged my fist against the wood of the desk as I slammed the receiver down. I was going to murder the bastard. I'd been chasing the wrong lead all along. Though he hadn't identified himself, it had to be none other than Massimo Capaldi himself. By ordering me to meet at the warehouse, he'd practically handed me his identity.

Hawkins hovered in the doorway. "Sheriff?"

"She's in Chicago," I ground out. "I've gotta go."

I was already halfway out of the station when I spun on my heel. Fuck. What the hell was I thinking? I met Hawkins's gaze, and he gave his head a little shake. "Go. I'll take care of everything."

I tipped my chin and was out the door seconds later, already climbing into the cruiser. The cold air battered at me, but I didn't notice as I shoved the key into the ignition and peeled out of the parking lot. I dug my phone from my back pocket as I drove and hit a number on speed dial. Jack picked up on the second ring.

"Donahue. What's up?"

"Need a favor," I said without preamble. "Can you find me the first flight to Chicago?"

There was a moment's pause, then— "Did you find her?"

"Yeah," I breathed. "Fucker called me out, told me to meet

him at a warehouse on the outskirts of town tomorrow night."

"Good. Let's go," Jack responded.

"No fucking way," I cut in. "You're not going."

"Fuck you," Jack said blithely. "Are you going to stop me?"

"Don't be stupid." I growled. "You've got a kid on the way, for Christ's sake."

"Yeah, well, around here, we take care of our own." Keys tapped in the background, and Jack's voice came back over the line. "First flight out is in about five hours. Should give us time to get to the airport and get through security."

"Book it," I groused. "But you're not coming with me."

Jack entered my information into the airline system as I drove toward home, my heart pounding in my throat.

"All right," Jack said finally. "You're on American 1273 into O'Hare. Flight leaves at 8:05."

"Thanks, man. I really appreciate it."

"Thank me later," Jack said. "I'll be at your place in 30."

The line went dead, and I growled my frustration as I tossed my phone onto the dash. Fucker couldn't listen to save his life. Still, I couldn't help the gratitude that welled up inside me. I slid to a stop in front of the cabin, then practically ran inside. Hastily, I grabbed clothes and shoved them into a duffel bag. I didn't bother with toiletries. I wasn't going to dick around with trying to get them through security, and I could buy everything I needed once I got there, if the hotel didn't provide it. Right now, I felt the overwhelming need to get on the road and get going.

I waited impatiently, hovering by the front door, and my ears perked up as I heard a car turn into the gravel drive. Duffel in hand, I locked the door and slammed it behind me, and I was already waiting in the driveway by the time the Tahoe came to a stop. Surprise rendered me speechless when I saw Mia behind the wheel of the giant SUV.

Yanking open the door, I tossed my duffel in and climbed into the backseat and shot a look at Jack. "No fucking way. She's not coming with us."

"I'm just driving," Mia said helpfully as she turned around and headed back down the main road. "Not that it would stop me from going if I really wanted to."

I rolled my eyes. It was probably true, but I refused to let a pregnant woman walk into danger. I had no idea what had transpired over the past several years with the Capaldi family, and I wasn't sure how strong they were, or what kind of resources they had. Showing up in Chicago was a gamble in itself. Jack and I could be taken out the second we stepped off the plane.

I rubbed my forehead. "You guys really shouldn't be involved in this."

"And you should really learn to stop arguing and just say thank you when someone wants to help," Jack commented from the front seat.

I couldn't help the worry that spread through me. "Listen. It's not that I don't appreciate what you're trying to do, but—"

"You're not walking in there alone." Jack's voice was flat and implacable.

"He's right," Mia piped up. "You walk in there alone, and he'll kill you. We'll lose both of you forever. That's not something either of us wants to live with."

I met her gaze in the rearview mirror and swallowed hard. "Thank you."

"Look at that," Jack drawled, his voice thick with sarcasm. "He does have manners."

A tiny smile cracked my mouth. "Only when it comes to Jules."

Because she was my whole world, and I'd burn it down to save her.

I'm coming for you, baby.

TWENTY-THREE

GIULIANA

Everything hurt. My shoulders ached from the weight of my body pulling downward, and the cuffs cut into my wrists, grinding against the delicate bones. I hung there limply, completely helpless, nearly frozen with cold. Fear had been my constant companion, as was the darkness. I had no idea how long I'd been down here. Hours, at least. Maybe even a full day. Every cell of my body radiated with pain, from the tips of my toes to the top of my head. The blood had drained from my arms, leaving behind a prickly sensation like they'd fallen asleep long ago.

My stomach growled, hunger having finally caught up to me. I didn't remember the last time I ate anything of substance. I'd barely managed to force down a couple pieces of dry toast after the doctor had examined me when I arrived at my uncle's house, but I hadn't had anything after that. After Uncle told me Eric was dead, I hadn't been able to drum up any appetite at all.

As it always did, Eric's image floated to the forefront of my mind. God, I missed him so much. The crazy thing was…

I swore sometimes that I could feel him, as if he were still alive. My heart wanted to believe it, but my mind knew better. *La cosa nostra* didn't let people just walk away. Especially not someone like Eric. He'd been everything to me —my savior, my friend, my lover. Would I ever get over him?

The grief came then, almost crippling in its intensity. This was all my fault. I knew better than to get involved with someone like him, but loving him had never been a choice. I knew from the moment we met that he was different—and my selfishness had cost him his life.

I still couldn't fathom it, didn't want to believe it. Eric was so strong and vital that the idea of never seeing him again was unthinkable. The bridge of my nose burned, but my eyes remained dry. I'd exhausted the last of my tears hours ago, and my body was too weak and dehydrated to form more. My chest hurt, and my heart constricted, like the life was literally draining out of me. Without Eric, what did I have? I could go back to Pine Ridge, back to my job and the friends I'd made there, but it wouldn't be the same. I had nothing left.

On the heels of despair came anger, hot and fierce. I hated Massimo, and I hated Matteo for what he'd done to me. For years I believed him, trusted him, and he betrayed me in the worst way possible. He was even worse than his father.

A soft scuffling sound broke the silence, and my ears perked up, hope causing my heart to skip a beat. Had Matteo come back for me? Fear mingled with hope in my chest. Escaping wouldn't be easy, but all I needed was a chance. I would force myself to withstand whatever torture he had planned next, then I would figure out a way to get out of here. A soft creak filtered over the still, dank air, and I could practically envision the heavy wooden door swinging open. There was no light to speak of, and the thought sent another shiver down my spine. I didn't want to consider how far underground we were. If what Matteo had said was true, no one would ever find me down here. My resolve to break free strengthened.

There was a soft clink of metal that I assumed was the lock sliding into place. More shuffling assaulted my ears, my body hyperaware of every movement, the sounds seeming to echo in the small room. Suddenly, a flame flared to life in the oil lantern on the wall, and the soft light illuminated Matteo's face.

Pushing down my fear and discomfort, I lifted my chin and met his gaze head on. He paused at the sight of me, something akin to surprise lighting his eyes before it slipped away, and a smirk took its place. "How are you faring, *principessa*?"

I refused to show any weakness, and for several long moments, we remained locked in a silent battle of wills. Despite the exhaustion of my body, I forced the slight tremor in my muscles to still. *Stay strong, no matter what.* I knew men like Matteo; I'd grown up with them. They lived for fear— thrived on it. They wanted their enemies to squirm and beg, but I refused to give him the satisfaction.

Finally, he broke the silence. "I see your attitude hasn't changed."

Striding toward the wall, he deftly uncoiled the length of rope from around the cleat. I cried out in agony as the bindings around my wrists loosened, and pain shot down my arms. I collapsed to the ground, tucking my arms in close to me. Head bowed, I watched as Matteo came closer, the polished black shoes coming to a stop a foot away. "Have you learned your lesson?"

I swallowed hard, forcing the pain away, then I lifted my head and glared at him. "Never."

His jaw clenched, and he let out a tsking sound before turning abruptly on his heel and striding toward the workbench. I watched him warily and took the brief reprieve to massage some feeling back into my arms. Reaching beneath the workbench, he retrieved a sack and carried it over to me.

"What is that?"

Without bothering to answer, he upended the bag in front of me, and the contents spilled out. Snowy white grains made a small mound on the floor, and I lifted my gaze to his. "Rice?"

He arched one eyebrow. "Do you know anything about corporal punishment?"

I sucked in a breath, my mind automatically conjuring images of cat o' nine tails, whips, and canes.

"You should've paid more attention to your history lessons." A malicious smirk lifted the corner of his mouth as he used his foot to spread the grains so there was a thin layer covering the uneven stone. "In fact, it's still popular in some cultures."

Bile rose up, stinging the back of my throat. "Why rice?"

"Because the grains are small and hard." He took a step closer and cupped my chin in one large hand. "The smaller the surface area, the more pain will be inflicted."

My entire body went rigid, and my mouth parted but nothing came out. What the hell did he plan to do with that?

As if reading my thoughts, he released me and pointed at the small heap of rice before me. "Kneel."

"Matteo, please. I..." I stiffened as he moved around behind me and slid his hands under my armpits. "No, please, no more!"

I tucked my elbows in close to my side in an attempt to block him, but he was too strong. I fought his hold and crashed to the floor as I struggled to get away. A scream ripped from my throat as he grabbed my wrist and tugged me upward. The tears I thought I'd cried blurred my vision as pain tore through me as he yanked my arms upward.

"Your choice," he said coldly. "Arms above your head or behind your back."

Slowly, I pushed to my knees and crossed my wrists at the small of my back. He wrapped a strip of duct tape around my wrists, then pointed toward the pool of granules in front of me. "Kneel."

On my knees, I shuffled closer, and I grimaced as the sharp grains cut into my skin. "Matteo…"

His hand fisted in my hair, the motion both keeping me upright and propelling me forward. I moved my other knee forward and sank my teeth into my lower lip to keep from crying out. The skin stretched tightly over my kneecaps, and each tiny granule felt like a needle stabbing straight into the bone. The grains of rice dug into my skin as they shifted beneath me, and I winced.

When he was satisfied I was in place, Matteo began a slow circuit around me. I stared straight ahead, avoiding his gaze completely. With a harsh exhale, he stomped over to the workbench, and I watched in my peripheral vision as he grabbed the metal folding chair. My body recoiled, my toes curling and my fists clenching tightly as he slammed it to the floor in front of me and slouched into the seat.

In this position, my eyes were at chest level. I took in the clean shirt, the newly pressed suit. He'd changed. That meant he'd at least had time to go home, and I suspected I'd been here far longer than the couple of hours it would have taken him to do so.

Reluctantly, I moved my gaze upward until it collided with his. He stared at me for a moment, his head cocked slightly to one side. "You won't win."

The words were deceptively soft, borderline regretful. It triggered something inside me, and I tried to appeal to him once more. "You don't want to hurt me, I know you don't." His expression darkened, and his mouth parted as if to speak, but I cut him off. "For as long as I can remember, you've been there for me. When Uncle locked me in the closet, you tried to help. You always wanted me to be safe. What happened? Why are you doing this?"

A flicker of hurt appeared in his eyes. "I have always wanted what was best for you."

"Do you really think this is best for me? You're hurting me, Matteo. Please let me go," I pleaded.

His brows were furrowed slightly, as if my question confused him. "Don't you realize how much it hurts me to do this?" He shook his head. "This is your birthright. This is where you belong."

"I don't want this. I don't want any of this!"

"You're a Capaldi," he shot back. "This is your legacy. This is how it's meant to be."

"No." I shook my head. "My last name doesn't dictate my future, and it doesn't have to determine yours either."

Matteo let out a mirthless laugh. "That's where you're wrong, *principessa*. My name has everything to do with it."

Despair settled over me. What if he refused to see reason? I knew that, for the men, *la famiglia* took precedence over everything. Once you were part of *la Cosa Nostra*, you were in it for life. But I was a woman. I was absolutely powerless. With my father gone, I had literally no say in anything that happened—not that I'd held much sway to begin with. No one would care now whether I lived or died.

"I don't understand," I cried out. "If I wanted to turn you in, I would have tried already. All I want is to be free. Please let me go," I begged.

He shook his head sadly. "I can't do that."

Anger took hold, and I snapped at him before rational thought kicked in. "Why the hell not? You're torturing me to what—prove that you can control me? That's not very manly of you."

Before I could blink, Matteo lunged toward me. Breath suspended in my chest as his fingers bit into my biceps, and he thrust his face barely an inch from mine. "Don't you dare fucking speak to me that way. Not if you want to live to see another day."

My inner flight mechanism kicked in, and I mentally retreated. I dropped my chin, my gaze glued to his chest as it rose and fell rapidly. After a long minute, he slowly released me and settled back into the folding chair. Silence descended over us once more, and I finally summoned the courage to look at him again.

"Why are you doing this?" I asked. "You killed your father for me, and—"

Matteo let out a mirthless laugh. "He was never my father."

My brows drew together. I knew they'd had a tumultuous relationship, but for Matteo to so blatantly deny Massimo was inconceivable. I tried again. "I know you didn't get along—"

Matteo cut me off with a wave of his hand. "You don't understand. He's not my father; we're not blood."

I blinked up at him, my mind frozen. Not blood? "What are you talking about?"

We'd been raised side by side for two decades. Surely I would have known something this important.

Matteo let out a gusty sigh. "I don't know who my real father is. It was no secret that my mother's marriage to Massimo was unhappy. He drove her into another man's arms about a year after they'd married, and she ended up pregnant.

"I think deep down I always knew." His voice was sad, resigned. "I always felt... different. Like I didn't belong."

Oh, God. It explained so much. I'd never understood why Massimo treated him so abominably, but now it made perfect sense. They weren't flesh and blood, and Massimo resented the fact that Matteo was a bastard. Massimo had to claim him publicly, but he punished my cousin for his mother's sins.

"I'm so sorry," I whispered. "I never dreamed..."

Matteo slumped down in the chair, elbows resting on his

knees, looking uncomfortable for the first time since he brought me down here. "My mother was always the most important person in my life."

I wasn't surprised by his admission. Considering the way Massimo had treated him, I was sure he relied heavily on his mother to protect him.

"Of course she was," I soothed. "She was your mother. She loved you."

His lips curled into a sneer. "Not enough."

To this day, I had no idea what had happened to Aunt Helena. "Did Uncle Massimo...?"

I couldn't finish the thought. Rumors had swirled for years, but no one dared speak directly of her. It was as if, with her death, her name had been wiped from everyone's vocabulary.

"He didn't kill her," Matteo said. "Though that would've been preferable to the truth."

My jaw dropped as I regarded him. "How can you say that?"

"It's true," he snapped. "What kind of mother leaves her son?"

I shook my head, confused. I knew he was hurting, but... "Your mother passed away," I said softly. "She—"

Matteo leaned forward, so close that our noses almost touched, and wrapped one hand around the back of my head. "Do you want to know what really happened?"

Did I? I wasn't sure. Haltingly, I nodded. Dark eyes bore into me for a moment before Matteo spoke. "Massimo was right when he called her a coward. She couldn't take it anymore, and she killed herself."

My eyes widened. Surely he was mistaken. Whatever Massimo told him must be wrong. "Matteo, she wouldn't do that to you. She wouldn't—"

I winced as he squeezed tighter. "She did. She left me with

that monster. She knew how awful he was, yet she didn't spare a thought for what it would be like for me."

"Matteo." Aunt Helena had loved him so much. She was more a mother to me than my own, and I believed with all my heart that she would have given her life for him. "Do you really believe that? After all the lies Massimo has told you over the years, after everything he's done to you—do you really believe he would tell you the truth of your mother's death?"

Indecision flashed in his eyes, then promptly disappeared. "No, *principessa*, it is the truth. Do you remember her funeral?"

I thought back to that awful day nearly a dozen years ago. I remembered standing beside her closed casket, thinking it odd even at the time that she wasn't in the family plot. My brows moved together as snippets gradually came back to me.

Matteo watched my facial expressions, then finally released me and stood. "They wouldn't even say mass for her."

I bit my lip. Of course they hadn't. According to the Catholic Church, suicide was one of the greatest sins you could commit. Most believed that if you took your own life, you were doomed to an afterlife in Hell. I didn't know what to say. It was awful no matter what had happened. I wanted to offer encouragement, but I couldn't find the words. Would his mother be proud of him kidnapping me and holding me hostage below the church that had cast her away? I seriously doubted it, but I kept my mouth shut.

Matteo strode to the workbench and leaned against it, his arms spread wide as his hands rested on the roughhewn table. "I loved her more than anything, and she turned her back on me. Maybe I'm not worthy of love," he murmured dejectedly after a long pause.

"Of course you are," I said softly. "I'm sure she would take it back if she could."

He didn't bother to acknowledge me, and I wondered if he was lost in thought. "I'm sorry," I said. "For all of it. I'm sorry your mom left you, and I'm sorry you were subjected to Massimo's abuse for so many years. If I'd known..."

Nothing would've changed. Had I stood up for Matteo, Massimo probably would've killed him on principle. We could've figured out something else. I winced again as the grains of rice shifted beneath me, and I couldn't hold back my cry of pain this time.

Matteo turned, watched me for a moment, then picked something up and strode toward me. Moving behind me, he lifted me to my feet and brushed away the granules that had stuck to my skin. With a blade he drew from somewhere, he cut loose the duct tape binding my wrists. I rolled my shoulders in relief, and brought them in front of me as I massaged the store flesh.

"You're the only good thing in my life," Matteo said quietly. "You were always there for me. Until you ran away. Why did you have to leave me, too?"

I turned toward him and met his gaze. "I understand you're upset. But please let me go. I had nothing to do with this."

The sadness from a moment ago had leached away, giving his tone a harder edge. "Yet you are willing to walk away from me, from your family?"

Annoyance flared once more. "They are no more my family than they are yours," I said. "Family doesn't treat each other the way they treated me, or you, or even your mother."

"I deserve this. *We* deserve this," he stressed. "Don't you see? We can make them pay for every wrong that was ever inflicted."

That's not what I wanted. They could kill each other for all I cared, but I wanted no part of it. "My life is no longer here.

You don't have to do this," I said. "Just walk away. You're not blood anyway."

I didn't have time to react as his hands snatched up my wrists and yanked me close. "I've thought of nothing but this for the last dozen years. I waited and bided my time, and now we can finally be together. You're mine, Giuliana."

"Please don't," I pleaded, and he yanked me close when I tried to pull away. "You don't know what you're saying."

"We're not blood; there's nothing stopping us now."

Panic made me blurt out the truth. "I don't love you!"

As soon as the words left my mouth, I knew I'd made a mistake. Matteo's head tipped slightly to one side, his eyes cold and blank as he studied me. "But you love him. Your cop."

I couldn't bring myself to lie to him, so I appealed to his emotions. "Please, Matteo, please try to understand."

He glared at me for a long moment, his long fingers still wrapped around my wrists, holding me in place. "This is your birthright, your duty," he spat at me. "You've turned your back on your family. Where is the honor in that?"

"What would you know about honor?" I shot back. "Do you really think this will change my mind? I will never love you the way you want."

He transferred my wrists to one hand as he reached up to snatch the leather band. I twisted and writhed against his hold, but he held fast. I kicked backward, and he released me with a grunt as my foot connected with his knee. I jabbed at him with my elbow and finally managed to break free. My gratification was short-lived as one strong arm came around my waist and spun me so I was locked in his embrace, my back firmly against his chest. His free hand moved to my neck and pressed lightly against the vagus nerve there—just hard enough to send a spike of pain through my body. My knees went weak and I cried out as I slumped against him, black spots bursting before my eyes. He took advantage of my momentary impairment and locked the cuff around my wrists, then yanked them over my head and secured the rope in place.

Stepping in front of me, he took my chin in his hand. "Good thing I don't need your love, *principessa*. Just your obedience."

I blinked rapidly to clear my vision, and Matteo thrust me away before striding toward the workbench. His hand danced over the implements cluttering the tabletop before he made his selection. He approached slowly, the long cane swinging like a pendulum at his side.

"What are you doing?" Fear caused my voice to shake as I watched him warily.

"Ready to surrender yet?"

I shook my head. "N-no."

His gaze narrowed, darkening with anger. "Do you dare defy me?"

I swallowed hard, unable to rip my stare away from the narrow rod hanging loosely from his fingers. Steeling my voice, I spoke with as much conviction as I could muster. "You'll have to kill me first."

He bent and pulled an object from a sheath attached to his ankle, and my heart stuttered as the blade of the knife shimmered in the dancing light.

My eyes widened. "Matteo..." I twisted, pulling against the restraints as he circled me, my false bravado fleeing. "Please," I begged. "Please don't!"

He stepped forward, his face a mask of concentration as he pressed the tip of the knife into the fabric of my dress. Tears spilled over as he drew it downward, the black material parting in its wake, baring my breasts to him. I turned my face away, unable to bear the humiliation as the dress fell from my body and pooled around my feet.

My chest rose and fell on silent sobs, and I forced them under control. I would weather this; I would endure whatever he planned. Then I would run. I just needed to play along for now until he thought I was too cowed, too weak. Matteo was too confident; he thought he was breaking my spirit. He was wrong. As soon as he turned his back, I would escape. And I would make him pay.

Blinking away the tears, I retreated deep into myself and turned off my emotions. I had to stay strong no matter what. Somehow I resisted the urge to flinch as Matteo held the cane up.

"Ten lashes."

I let out a sharp cry as the cane connected with my back, and I arched under the pain.

"Count."

I shook my head, and the cane landed in the exact same spot. "One!"

"Not so hard, now was it?"

Before I could answer, the narrow rod slapped against my skin again, a mere inch below the last. I bit back a cry, refusing to show weakness. He had to know how badly it hurt; I wouldn't reinforce his control with cries of mercy.

The cane hit the same spot again. "Count!"

"Two." The single word left my mouth on a resigned breath, and I gritted my teeth against the humiliation welling up inside me. I counted each strike as it landed against my skin until I was sure my back looked like a ladder of red welts.

Matteo touched one finger to the small of my back, just above my ass. I swayed forward as if to get away, but he kept his touch firm. Slowly, it trailed upward over the ridges of raised flesh until he reached the base of my neck. His hand slid over my collarbone as he circled my throat.

"Take heed, *principessa*." He leaned forward, so close that his breath stirred the strands of hair near my ear. "I will break you. And when I do, there will be nothing left."

TWENTY-FOUR

ERIC

People swarmed into the aisle, eager to disembark, and I grabbed my duffel from the overhead bin. Jack and I exited the plane in silence, then went our separate ways. I headed straight for the rental agency to get a car for the next couple of days while Jack ducked into the bathroom, exactly as we'd discussed during the flight.

As soon as I stepped outside, I felt eyes on me, and I surreptitiously scanned my surroundings as I entered the rental office. There were several people in front of me, and I took my place in line. The hairs on the back of my neck bristled, and the tingling feeling along my spine intensified. From the corner of my eye, I watched the cars entering and exiting the arrivals lane. Passengers greeted their drivers with hugs and kisses, loaded suitcases into the trunks, then pulled away from the curb. Except one car.

A black Escalade remained in the same spot just outside the glass double doors of the baggage claim area, and people swarmed around it on their way to the parking lot. I could feel the man's eyes on me from here, and I shifted my stance slightly so I could see him better. Jack entered the office moments later, a dark look on his face. I could tell from the set of his shoulders that he had either seen or felt the man's presence as well. I shifted my attention from Jack and turned back toward the counter, my foot tapping an impatient rhythm on the thin industrial carpet.

The line moved along, and fifteen minutes later I filled out the paperwork for a small sedan. Palming the keys, I made my way to the parking lot, feeling the man's eyes on me the entire way. As soon as I pulled into the flow of traffic, the man steered into the lane behind me. I supposed I should be thankful he hadn't put a bullet in my head the second I stepped out the doors. Whatever Capaldi was planning, he would require it face-to-face. He was the type of man who liked to see his prey dangling from a hook, writhing and begging before he put them out of their misery.

I merged onto the freeway, then headed toward the outskirts of town. At this time of night, traffic had slowed a bit, making it easier to navigate. The warehouse was several miles outside of town, past the projects. I exited into a relatively popular tourist area and pulled into the first hotel I saw. I parked the rental under the covered walkway in front of the lobby, then made my way inside.

In my peripheral vision I watched as the black car turned into the drive and back into a parking spot diagonal from the entrance. I had decided against making reservations ahead of time. Without knowing exactly where I was staying, it would make it infinitely more difficult for anyone to bug my room before I got in there. I wasn't able to bring any detection devices, and though the agents we were meeting would be able to, it would be obvious to anyone watching outside what we were doing. I was going to have to wing this part of it and hope for the best.

The concierge greeted me with a smile, and I told her that I would need a room for two nights. Hopefully. Tomorrow night really depended on what went down at the warehouse and whether I walked away or not.

"Preferably on the back side away from the main drag," I told the woman.

With a nod, she clicked away at the keyboard. "We have rooms available on the ground floor as well as the third floor. Which would you prefer?"

"Third floor, please." That would deter anyone from having a direct line of sight into the room.

With a smile, the young woman handed me the programmed keycard for my room, and I made my way back outside. Climbing back into the car, I started it up then pulled all the way around to the back of the building. Hopefully, the man in the Escalade would follow me and wouldn't see Jack when he arrived. If the man recognized Jack from the airport and put two and two together, it could throw everything off.

I gathered my things and crossed to the single door at the back entrance. I slid my keycard inside to unlock it and stepped inside just as the black car pulled around the corner. The hotel was only five stories tall, and though the other man didn't know exactly which room I was staying in, it would be easy enough to detect new movement in the rooms above. I stepped into the elevator and punched the button for the third floor. It was just high enough off the ground to conceal most of my movement and, with luck, discourage putting a bullet through the window. I didn't think that would happen, but it was better to err on the side of caution.

The elevator doors slid open, and I glanced at the numbered doors to get my bearings before making my way down the hall to my room. I stepped inside and flipped on the light, then made my way deeper into the room to drop my duffel on the small table in the corner. As I did so, I flicked a quick glance out the window without turning my head. In the shadows, away from the glow of the street lamp, I could just barely discern the bulky shape of the Escalade parked almost directly across from my room.

I grabbed the remote off the dresser and flipped on the TV, then shut off the overhead light. I moved to the bed and settled in to wait. Twenty minutes later, a knock came on my door. I flipped on the bathroom light and turned on the faucet before I checked the peephole and opened the door. Hopefully the noise of the running water would conceal our conversation if someone happened to plant any devices, either inside or out, and the light from the bathroom would overpower the shaft of light coming in from the hallway.

An agent slid inside the narrow opening, as I cracked the door, and he studied me. I jerked a thumb over my shoulder. "Black Escalade directly across from the window. Only one man that I could see."

He nodded, and I traded places with him, slipping silently out the door of the hotel room. Now the agent would make himself comfortable on the bed I had just vacated. He was similar enough to my height and build that three stories up, the man in the car wouldn't notice a difference.

I swiveled my head left and right as I stepped into the hallway, and a man hovering near the elevators tipped his chin at me. In silence we stepped into the car and rode up to the fourth floor where we exited and I followed him down the hall to Jack's room. After a brief knock, the door was thrown open, revealing Jack and a half dozen men I didn't recognize.

The man who had led me to Jack's room turned to me as soon as the door closed and held out a hand. "SSA Martinez."

I gave him a single hard shake. "Donahue." The Supervisory Special Agent looked familiar. "Have you been working the Capaldi case for a while?"

He dipped his chin. "I was at the warehouse a few years ago when shit went down."

My jaw set in a tight line. Now I remembered. He'd looked younger then, and he seemed to have aged decades over the past three years. He knew better than anyone—better than most anyway—how important it was that we not fuck this up. They'd slipped off the hook one too many times; I promised myself it wouldn't happen again.

Martinez led me further into the room and made introductions to the other agents assembled around the living room of Jack's suite. SSA Martinez leveled a stare at me. "We've got one man undercover inside the house."

"How long has he been in there?"

"Nearly four years."

My eyes widened. "Christ." That was a hell of a long time to be undercover. "Why so long?"

Martinez lifted one shoulder. "We needed to cultivate loyalty. Trust. He entered the organization just before the operation at the warehouse. Pulling him afterward would have looked too suspicious, so he stayed in place. He's been close to the new capo and working on gaining his confidence."

The new capo? Ignacio's brother, Massimo, had taken over when he was killed. Had Massimo passed now, too?

"What do we know so far?" I asked.

"There's been a definite shift the last couple days," Martinez replied. "Seems there was some kind of dissent in the family, and an argument broke out over the girl. There was a meeting the other night at Richie's," Martinez said, mentioning the family-owned restaurant downtown, "and shit apparently went sideways. Matteo Capaldi shot Massimo at point-blank range and has assumed the head of the family."

I blinked at Martinez. "He shot his own father?"

"Looks that way," the man replied.

"Jesus." The man wasn't fucking around. He was a loose cannon, and I hated the thought of Jules being anywhere close to him. I glanced out the window in the direction of the warehouse and ran one hand through my hair. So it was Matteo I'd spoken with. What the hell did he want from me, other than a human sacrifice? Was it to prove a point to Jules for running away? It was possible, but somehow I thought it went deeper than that.

What the hell had happened to prompt him to kill his own father? If what Martinez said was true, they'd fought over Jules. I knew from the information we'd received that the elder Capaldi had planned to marry her off to the leader of another local syndicate in an effort to settle affairs between the two groups. Had Matteo killed Massimo in an effort to protect her?

"There's another problem," Martinez said, his dark stare never leaving mine. "Our guy says he hasn't seen her in more than twenty-four hours."

My spine stiffened. "What the fuck are you talking about?"

"They had a disagreement last night and he apparently dragged her out of the house. My guy tried to go along, but Matteo took only the driver. Nobody knows where they went."

"Son of a bitch." Fiery rage swept through my veins, and a red haze filled my vision as my body trembled under the force of my fury. He wasn't going to walk away from this; I vowed it on my life. Whatever happened tomorrow night, I would never let him hurt anyone ever again.

Over the next hour, we discussed our plans for the following evening. After we were done, the agents filtered out the door and made their way back to their respective rooms. Jack propped his hands on his hips and stared at me. It was after one in the morning, but I still found myself wound like a spring. I couldn't relax, wouldn't be able to until I saw Jules for myself.

Jack drew in a breath. "Are you ready for this?"

I felt like I was standing at the end of a loaded barrel playing Russian roulette. Was anyone ready to walk into a situation knowing that it might cost them their life? I thought once more of Jules. Sweet, innocent, naïve Jules, she was the reason my heart continued to beat, and I would gladly sacrifice myself for her. I nodded. "I'm ready to end it once and for all."

"Okay." His face was set in a resolute expression. "I've got your back no matter what happens."

"Thanks, man." If there was anyone I could count on, it was Jack. Former Army Ranger, he was one of the smartest, most relentless men I knew. He wouldn't go down without a fight, and he'd do his damnedest to make sure we all walked out of there alive.

I turned away and swallowed hard. I didn't even want to contemplate all the things that could go wrong. Ever since I'd gotten that phone call, a thousand scenarios had played through my mind—all of them brutal and gory. Except this time there was an added component—Jules. I prayed she wouldn't be there tomorrow to witness whatever went down. Because I knew without a doubt that it would end in bloodshed, and a lot of it. I would never forgive myself if anything happened to her.

I faced Jack once more. "See you tomorrow."

I exited Jack's room and made my way back down to my own. The agent inside slipped out just as quietly as he'd arrived, and I made my way to the bed. Not bothering to undress, I collapsed backward on the scratchy comforter and flung one arm over my face. The TV blared in the background, but the dismal thoughts raging in my mind drowned them out.

Just the thought of going back into that warehouse again sent my heart rate into a rapid tempo. I knew exactly why

Matteo had chosen it. He wanted the advantage of my discomfort. Well, I wasn't going to give it to him. I was going to shut that shit down, lock it away somewhere dark and deep where it could never be found. The only thing that mattered was Jules, and if I didn't have her, I wasn't sure I even wanted to walk out of there alive.

TWENTY-FIVE

GIULIANA

The heavy clank of the lock disengaging reached my ears, but I didn't lift my head. My thoughts were muddled, clouded by pain and exhaustion. I hadn't slept at all, and I wondered vaguely how long it'd been since I'd eaten anything. There was no light, no sense of time to speak of. It could have been hours or days. I was betting on the latter. It felt like weeks since I'd been stripped from Eric and immersed in this hellish nightmare.

"Ciao, bella." Matteo's tone was mocking and insincere as he shut and locked the door behind him.

I closed my eyes and listened to the soles of his shoes scuff softly against the worn stone floor as he moved around the small room. "I had the most wonderful vintage from Nonna Scali's vineyard. Perhaps we shall go and visit when this is all over. What do you think?"

Over my dead body. I kept my eyes closed, my head bowed as he spoke, not bothering to respond.

The smell of something savory wafted on the air, and my stomach grumbled.

"Hungry, *principessa*?"

Saliva pooled in my mouth, and I forced myself to swallow. I refused to show how much it affected me.

He reached for the folding chair again, then flipped it around so it faced me. He swaggered around it and took a seat barely a foot from me. Suspended once more from the ceiling, I stared straight down at the container of food settled on his lap. I drew in a deep breath and immediately averted my gaze as the scent of garlic and savory herbs filled my nostrils.

"You must be hungry. It's been several days. How much longer will you continue to pine for your lover?"

Forever. I gave my head a little shake even as my stomach clenched and let out another audible growl.

"You know what you have to do."

He opened the carton and forked up a bite of lasagna, the stringy cheese stretching and tempting me with its lure. He held it up, inches from my face. "Tell me."

I swallowed hard and closed my eyes. Hunger pains twisted my stomach into knots, and tears crept into my eyes, burning the bridge of my nose. I hated him for what he was doing. I would never give in; I would never give myself to him.

"Why must you make this harder than it needs to be?"

I remained stubbornly silent, and he barked out my name so loudly that I jumped.

"Giuliana! Tell me. Tell me you're mine."

Pushing down the pain, I blinked my eyes open and met his dark gaze. "You know I can't do that."

"Can't or won't?"

He tipped his head and lowered the fork back to the container. Despite my best efforts to control it, my gaze dropped longingly toward the pasta and my stomach clenched on another rumble.

"You know you want to. It would be so easy," Matteo

cajoled. "Give yourself to me, and you can have whatever your heart desires."

I met his gaze. "Even freedom?"

His eyes hardened. "Except that."

"Then I refuse."

His chest rose on an inhale. "It appears we are at an impasse."

He stood and carried the container to the workbench. Without turning to me, he spoke. "Do you think I enjoy this, Giuliana? Do you think I want to hurt you?"

There was a fine line between love and obsession, and he'd crossed it long ago. Though he claimed he was doing this for my own good, I knew he got off on the power he wielded over me.

"I think you crave control."

He paused for a moment, then let out a little laugh. "You are not wrong about that, *principessa*."

There was no longer any doubt in my mind that I would die down here. Matteo would never let me go unless I submitted to him, and I would rather die than ever give myself to him.

"I have one request."

He didn't even bother to look at me as he shuffled articles around on the workbench. "And what is that?"

"I want my ring."

Face carefully blank, Matteo turned to me. "What?"

"My ring." My words were raspy, and I licked my parched lips. "I want my ring."

Eric might be gone, but I wanted that one last piece of him.

Matteo's head tipped to one side. "Why?"

I met his gaze head on. "I want to wear it when I'm buried so he'll always be with me."

At my words, his jaw clenched, and his eyes went hard and dark. He strode toward me, his steps long and determined. He bent slightly at the waist, bringing his face level with mine. "Even now you think of him?"

"Always," I replied, my gaze unwavering. "He is the only man in my heart."

Fury stained his cheeks red, and his hand went around my throat. "How dare you say that to me? After everything I've done for you?"

I jerked backward, and his hand fell away. "Everything you've done? Like this?" My eyes flew around the dank, dark room. "Holding me captive and torturing me? You think that will make me love you?"

I glared up at him. "That's not love, Matteo. That's manipulation."

His eyes narrowed as he straightened. "Do not test me, Giuliana."

"Or what?" I challenged.

His left eye twitched, a clear indication of his anger. "I'll show you just how bad it can be. I will break you, push you until there's nothing left."

A defeated sigh lifted my chest before filtering through my lips.

Matteo drew in a sharp breath and stood ramrod straight, his hands balled into fists at his side. His chest heaved on ragged breaths, and his muscles trembled as he fought to control himself. "I planned to have mercy on him. Now you force my hand."

What? My gaze jerked toward him. "What are you talking about?"

His mocking stare met mine as he moved to the work table. He picked up a whip and slid the narrow leather strip across his palm. "Did I not tell you? Your sheriff is coming for a visit."

Eric was alive? *He was alive!* Hope and joy bloomed, only to be doused a mere second later. "Perhaps I shall bring him here so you can watch."

The whip was a thin black blur cutting through the air, and I screamed as it connected with my flesh. Fire burned along my side, but I was hampered by my bonds as I tried to twist away. I gritted my teeth against the pain and summoned every bit of anger boiling inside me. "I hope he kills you."

"I wouldn't count on that."

A shriek ripped from my throat as the lash connected with my skin again, in the exact same place. Sweat beaded at the back of my neck, and I felt fluid run down my hip. *Blood.* "I will never submit to you."

He chuckled and moved in a wide arc around me. "We shall see."

The next lash was harder than the two previous, and I bit back an oath as I grimaced at the pain exploding over my nerve endings.

"Dissociate. You must retreat."

Johnny's words resounded in my mind. I closed my eyes and tried to bring the beach into focus. It was my safe place, the thing I'd concentrated on while I spent hours locked away in the closet. Another slice of the whip ripped me from my reverie, dragging me back to the cavern deep underground.

"Had enough, *principessa*?"

"Fuck you."

"Language," he admonished. "Another foul habit you picked up from your sheriff."

With a flick of his wrist, the leather cut through the air and snapped across the flesh of my bottom. "I'm going to kill him slowly. Brutally. Make him wish he'd never met you."

I gritted my teeth against another lash.

"You're not the man I thought you were," I panted. My back and sides were on fire, and spots danced before my eyes. "And you're not half the man Eric is."

The whip connected with my back, hard enough to make me stumble. I lost my balance and began to tumble, stopped only by the bonds suspending me from the ceiling. The leather cuff constricted around my wrists, but it was no match for the weight of my body as it pulled me down. I let out an unholy scream of pain as a loud pop filled the air and my shoulder joint slipped out of its socket.

The whip fell several more times, and I lost count, unable to conjure even a single muffled cry. My mind had begun to shut down; my body would be next. I hung there limply, my mind clouded by agony, the only noise in the room the sound of Matteo's heavy breathing.

My gaze was blurry, unfocused as Matteo moved into view. Black creeped into the edges of my vision, and I blinked rapidly. Suddenly, the binds tethering me to the ceiling loosened and I crashed to the ground. I hissed in a breath as the grains of rice on the floor pricked the open wounds on my sides and back, sending sparks of searing pain throughout my body.

My left arm refused to cooperate, and I looked at it where it lay limply on the ground next to me. My breath came faster and faster, and the pain threatened to pull me under. I felt more than saw Matteo's palm slide beneath my chin, and I met his dark gaze as he lifted my face to his. "If I can't have you, no one will."

***

The stone was cold beneath my cheek, and I barely stirred when the now familiar creak of the door met my ears. The lantern flared to life, illuminating the room in its soft glow. Around me, I heard scraping sounds and a heavy thud, as if something heavy had been dropped on the floor. From my vantage point I could see Matteo's dark shadow moving as he crossed the room.

Familiar eyes met mine as he squatted down. "Had enough?"

I closed my eyes and tried to shut him out. I had no idea

how long he was gone last time. My arm was numb, and the rest of my body felt heavy with fatigue. I'd tried to conserve what little energy I had left and slept restlessly. The floor was hard, but I'd hardly noticed. Without food and sleep, my body was slowly shutting down. I was running out of options. Only the knowledge that Eric was still alive kept me going. Somehow, I needed to get out of here so I could find him.

Matteo lightly slapped my cheek. "I asked you a question."

It took a minute for his face to come into focus as I blinked up at him. I didn't say anything; I couldn't. Formulating words was beyond me at this point. My tongue felt thick and dry from lack of water, and my head spun deliriously.

He blew out a harsh breath and pushed to his feet. I allowed my eyes to slide closed again, and seconds later I felt his hands slide under my armpits. I gritted my teeth as he shifted me into a sitting position and propped me against the cool wall. Every inch of my flesh, still sore from his last punishment, screamed as it came into contact with the rough surface.

A spark of pain shot down my arm, and I cried out. Gently, I maneuvered it into my lap and cradled it to keep it from being jostled further. It still hurt, though Matteo had wrenched it back into place before he'd left last time. The agony, on top of my body already being broken and sore, was unbearable, and I'd passed out on the cold floor. My muscles were stiff, but my nerve endings felt like they were on fire. I wasn't sure how much more I could take.

My gaze skated over the lower half of my body, marred with streaks of blood. No wonder I was so sore. I hadn't been able to see the extent of the damage before, but now I examined the wounds on my legs, some of which still seeped fluid. The whip had cut deeply in some place, and rivulets of dried blood clung to my skin. My back had borne the brunt of his wrath, and I could only imagine what it looked like.

Matteo was moving around again, and I lifted my head to track his movements. Something off to the side caught my attention, and the noise from earlier clicked in my brain. About three feet long by two feet wide, the box was crudely constructed of pine, and my breath caught in my throat when I realized just what I was looking at.

A coffin.

Matteo turned and met my gaze, then dropped his eyes meaningfully toward the box. "You thought the closet was bad, hmm?"

He nudged the metal folding chair aside with his foot, then bent and lifted the lid, allowing it to rest against the stone wall so it would stay open. "I will give you two choices." He made sure I was looking at him before he spoke again. "End this now. Tell me you'll stay and we'll rule this city the way it was always meant to be. Or"—he tipped his chin toward the coffin—"we do it the hard way."

I licked my cracked lips and stared at the pinewood box. I couldn't get in that damn box. I just couldn't.

"What's it going to be?" he asked. "Me or the box?"

With no small amount of effort, I struggled to my feet. Heavy pants left my lungs as I staggered forward a step. Victory gleamed in his eyes, and I could see the corners of his mouth already curling up in pleasure.

I swallowed hard, trying to wet my dry mouth. After two tries, I finally managed to choke out the words. "You win."

The smirk became a full-fledged smile, and he cupped my face in his hands. "I knew you would see it my way."

He turned toward the workbench, still talking as he did so. Biting my tongue against the anticipation of pain, I reached out and grabbed the metal folding chair. The slight squeak of its legs alerted Matteo, and he glanced over his shoulder at me just as I swung upward. He let out a roar of pain as it connected with the side of his face, but I didn't pay attention.

My vision wavered as I bolted toward the door, my muscles protesting with every jolting stride. Grasping the old-fashioned iron handle, I yanked as hard as I could and nearly toppled backward when the door flew open. It banged against the wall with a thud, and I darted through the opening as fast as my feet could carry me. The stone steps were rough and uneven, and my foot slipped as it landed on the edge of one tread. I pitched forward, and my chin glanced off the stairs, sending a shower of stars exploding in front of my eyes. Before I could get my feet under me again, I felt myself being yanked back.

I tried to scream, but it came out a muted growl as I writhed and scratched and kicked at Matteo as his arms closed around me. I threw my head backward, and a sense of satisfaction bloomed as my skull connected with his nose.

"Stupid bitch!"

I stumbled forward as he released me and barely managed to catch myself on the workbench. Panting hard from the effort, I dredged up the tiny reserve of strength remaining and forced myself to move. I pushed off the workbench and spun to face Matteo, whose hands had flown up to cover his face, leaving himself completely open to my kick. My foot landed hard in his groin, and he let out an anguished howl as he dropped to one knee.

Part of me wanted to inflict as much pain as possible, just as he'd done to me. But what little energy I had left was slowly leaching away. I could barely stand, let alone fight my cousin who outweighed me by nearly eighty pounds. All I cared about now was getting away from Matteo—and back to Eric.

I'd taken two steps when his hand shot out and wrapped around my ankle. The motion caused me to stumble midstep, and I cried out, my arms flailing wildly. I kicked at him, trying to shake him off, but he only pulled harder. I leaned the opposite way, trying to break free of his hold. Suddenly, his fingers slipped free and for a moment I hovered in midair. Off balance and unable to correct myself, I reached for the workbench. As I fell through the air, my fingers grasped the edge—then slid off. My head connected with the corner of the wooden coffin as I plummeted downward, and everything went dark.

TWENTY-SIX

ERIC

The huge metal building loomed in front of me, looking just as daunting in the moonlight as it did in my dreams. To anyone else, it was just an old warehouse, rusted and rundown. To me, it was the epitome of malevolence and loss.

The industrial gray siding was unassuming, hiding the evil that lurked inside. The things that had happened three years ago couldn't hold a candle to the shit that would go down here tonight. Maybe it was instinct that made the hairs on the back of my neck lift in warning. Maybe it was because I had an emotional tie to the situation. Either way, the next hour would determine my future—if I would have one.

I wasn't stupid. My chances of getting out of here were 50/50, at best. I wasn't armed, and I had no way to protect myself other than my own two hands. Yeah, I could inflict some damage that way. But in a room full of men armed to the teeth with guns and knives, I'd be lucky to take one man out before I caught a bullet.

My heart rate increased, and I took a deep, steadying breath as I slowed to a stop about twenty yards from the entrance. I counted four of Capaldi's soldiers as they stood guard around the outside of the building, and two approached the car as I put it in park and shut off the ignition. I kept my hands on the wheel, not making any sudden movement; I didn't need to give them any reason to get trigger happy and kill me before I'd even made it inside.

One moved to the passenger side, the muzzle of the rifle leveled at me through the window. I kept him in my peripheral vision, focusing on the one who'd approached the driver door. I studied him, my eyes canvassing every inch. He didn't carry a rifle like the others, but I was sure he had at least one weapon concealed on his person.

He grabbed the handle and wrenched the door open. "Put your hands behind your head and step out of the vehicle—now."

His phrasing struck a chord, and my ears perked up as I followed his orders. It was almost identical to the command we used during traffic stops. Was the man ex-law enforcement? I couldn't discount the possibility. He was big and broad, with a hardened edge to him. I knew Capaldi's tentacles of power stretched deep into the political system. He owned half the politicians, though most of the residents didn't have a clue.

Fingers laced together at the base of my neck, I maneuvered through the narrow opening. The man closed the car door then grabbed me and spun me around. I let out a grunt as he slammed me against the hood of the little rental car. He kicked the inside of my ankles until my legs were spread wide, then frisked me.

He wasn't going to find anything; I hadn't even bothered to bring any weapons with me. It was a pain in the ass to get them on the plane, and I knew they would've just been confiscated the second I stepped onto Capaldi's property.

Satisfied that I wasn't hiding anything, the man grabbed me by the back of the shirt and hauled me up, then marched me toward the industrial metal door on the side of the building. I kept my chin up, my expression firmly in place as we entered the last place I ever wanted to see again. The interior was dim, lit only by a handful of dingy, ancient fluorescent bulbs that dangled precariously overhead.

The warehouse was a wide open space, undivided by walls or offices. Any machinery that had once run here had long since been removed, and the man shoved me forward, through the maze of discarded pallets and crates. I forced my face into an expressionless mask as I fought to bring my heart rate under control.

Two folding chairs had been set up in the center of the room, and a man occupied one. His posture was insouciant, borderline defiant, and I immediately recognized Giuliana's cousin Matteo. He smirked at me as the guard led me closer then slammed me down into the seat. "Nice of you to join us, Sheriff."

The guard who'd led me inside moved away and took up position to Matteo's left. Two other men took his place, stationed on either side of me, but I ignored them completely. Instead, I made a show of looking around. "Hasn't changed much since the last time I was here."

My glance around the place revealed several things. There were several soldiers posted around the warehouse. I'd counted at least a dozen, though more were probably hidden in the shadows. There was no evidence of illegal contraband, which told me they'd probably ceased using this warehouse as a sort of base after the last raid. And most importantly—Jules wasn't here. I thanked every deity known to man for that. At least she'd be out the way when all hell broke loose.

I turned my attention back to Capaldi. "Haven't done much with the place. But I guess the war with the Russians has been taking up too much of your time and money."

Matteo's eyes narrowed on me. "Yes, well, I expect that to change soon," he replied.

I snorted. "Not likely."

"Hmm…" Matteo hummed a noncommittal sound, and I affected a bored expression.

"Want to tell me why the hell you dragged me all the way out here?"

I kept my expression cold and distant, and Matteo stared at me for nearly a minute. Finally, I broke the silence and tipped my chin at him, alluding to his attempt at intimidation. "Does that work for you?"

A tiny smile quirked his mouth. "I admire your confidence, Sheriff. Makes this all the more fun."

"If you say so." My gaze landed on the bruising around his nose and eyes. I indicated the wound with a quick jerk of my head. "Looks like you were on the receiving end of some blunt force trauma."

His lips thinned. "Courtesy of Giuliana."

I bit back a smile as vicious pride filled me. *That's my girl.*

"No matter." He waved a hand dismissively. "She learned her lesson."

My gut clenched at his words, and foreboding filled me as Matteo reached inside the pocket of his immaculate black suit and withdrew a little box. It was a small square, only a few inches wide, but the sight of it filled me with dread. There was only one reason for him to present something like that— just large enough for an appendage.

Smirk still in place, he lifted his chin and tossed the box to me. "A gift from your precious fiancée."

I caught the box deftly, and my fingers turned to stone as I tried to open it. The air felt as if it had been sucked out of the room, and I forced myself to drag in even breaths as I lifted the lid away.

Tiny smudges of brown marred the paper inside, and bile rose in the back of my throat. Blood? Jesus, I prayed that wasn't the case, but I wouldn't put it past him. Capaldi had killed his own father; what would stop him from hurting Jules to strike out at me?

I moved aside the tissue and barely held back a sigh of relief. No finger, no ear; no body parts to speak of. *Thank God.*

I lifted her engagement ring from the bottom of the box and held it up, then arched a brow at Matteo.

"She won't be needing that anymore," he replied to my unspoken question.

That still wasn't an answer. I needed to know if she was alive and well somewhere. He already knew I'd hop on the plane at the drop of a hat for her, which explained his lack of surprise when I asked, "She's okay?"

"Depends on your definition." He paused and arched a brow. I ground my molars together and clenched my hands into fists where they rested on my thighs. I wanted to knock that smug look right off his face, then rip him limb from limb.

"If you're asking if she's alive, then the answer is yes. For now."

The diamond cut into the skin of my palm, reminding me that it was still there, and I forced myself to relax. If Capaldi was telling the truth—and he had no reason to lie since I was already here—then I had to trust that she was still alive.

I gave a little half nod and slid the ring into my pocket, leaving my hands free. "I thought we were here to make a trade..." I let the words hang in the air for a second.

"I beg to differ," he responded when I didn't continue. "We never discussed a trade, per se. What are you suggesting?"

Fucker was being deliberately obtuse. "Where the hell is she?"

"She's been... detained," Capaldi replied, a trace of a smirk tipping up the corners of his mouth.

I inhaled deeply. I had zero illusions of what could happen tonight, but I wasn't going to go down without a fight. "Let her go."

One dark eyebrow rose toward his hairline. "And what do I get out of it?"

I gritted my teeth. "We'll walk out of here and pretend none of this ever happened. You'll never see either of us again."

Capaldi's lips twisted into a petulant moue. "I don't think so. You see"—he leaned forward and rested his elbows on his knees, pinning me with his intense dark stare —"she belongs here. This is her home. Giuliana belongs with me."

Crazy fuck. "Have you even considered what she might want?"

He let out a little laugh. "Does that matter?"

"Yes," I snapped. "It's the only thing that matters. You're her cousin; you should care about her."

Matteo's smile disappeared in an instant. "She means everything to me."

I blinked. For some reason, I hadn't expected that. Maybe he truly did care about her; I tried to appeal to him one more time. "I want her happy. And we both know she's happy with me."

"So it would seem." His eyes narrowed with hatred. "A life for a life. Isn't that why you're here?"

I hoped to hell I got to walk out of here, but I'd gladly give myself up for her if she would be safe. I spread my arms wide. "Then take me."

"How very noble." He sat back in his chair and eyed me. "I despise you."

I snapped my mouth shut and lifted a brow. Was that supposed to surprise me?

He gave his head a little shake. "This is her place. She could have anything she wants—money, clothes, jewels. Yet she would rather go back to that Podunk little town with nothing. Except you."

His lip curled, and satisfaction unfurled in my chest. It

died away just as quickly as he continued. "You're the only one she wants, the one she cries for."

It gutted me to think that I hadn't been here when she needed me most. "Just let her go."

"I said I'd let her live," he corrected as I opened my mouth to argue with him, but he spoke over me. "Though it might be a bit late for that."

Anger surged, hot and fierce, forcing me forward in my chair. "What the fuck does that mean?"

Matteo lifted his left hand, and in a silent communication, signaled the man to his left. The soldier lifted his pistol and trained it on my forehead.

"I'll fucking kill you if you hurt her!" As soon as the words ripped from my throat, a loud commotion erupted behind me. I didn't bother to look; I knew that sound all too well. The Feds had breached the entrance and were cutting through the soldiers, one by one.

I locked eyes with the man who had his gun pointed at me. All of a sudden, his arm swung to the side, and he popped off two quick rounds, dropping the soldier to my left. I was already out of my chair as the undercover agent turned his pistol on Capaldi, my hand wrapped around the forearm of the man beside me. I jerked his arm upward as his finger squeezed the trigger, and splinters of wood rained down from the wooden beam above us.

Pushing down with my thumb, I put pressure on the bones of his wrist until his grip loosened and he let out a grunt of pain. Using his body as a shield, bullets whizzing through the air all around me. I took control of the gun and shot two more guards before putting a bullet in his temple.

His body hit the floor with a thud, and I whirled toward Capaldi. He was still firing rapidly at the undercover agent, but the fight was over. He'd taken several rounds to the torso, and dark maroon stains bloomed over his pristine white shirt. The agent popped off another round and Matteo jerked backward under the impact. He stumbled and fell over the chair he'd vacated just moments ago, then remained sprawled on his back, deathly still.

Taking a quick glance around, I saw that the Feds had the soldiers rounded up and were busy cuffing those who were still alive. Stomping over to where Matteo lay on the ground, I kept my pistol trained on him. His Beretta lay next to him, and I kicked it out of reach. His eyes opened to narrow slits before closing again.

He was rapidly losing blood, but the fucker wasn't dead yet. I dropped to one knee next to him. "Where is she?"

His voice was thin and thready when he spoke. "You'll never find her. No one will."

I used the muzzle of my pistol to press down on one of the open wounds. The man let out a ragged groan of pain but made no attempt to fight back or speak.

"Tell me where she is, and you might get to live." The man's lips moved, and I lifted my gun away from the wound. "What was that?"

"In hell," he choked out as blood spilled from the corner of his mouth.

My molars clenched together. This was clearly a wasted effort. He would rather die than tell me where she was. I stood and pointed the pistol at his forehead. "See you there."

The man's body jerked as the bullet hit its mark, leaving a small hole in his forehead. The back side wouldn't be so pretty.

Agent Martinez materialized beside me, his face an angry red. "Goddamn it, Donahue. What the fuck was that?"

I stared back impassively, then turned my pistol around and extended it toward him. "I did what I had to do."

He made an agitated gesture before propping his hands on his hips. "You get anything, at least?"

I shoved the weapon into my waistband and shook my head. "Nothing."

He blew out a harsh breath and dropped to one knee. Yanking a pair of nitrile gloves from his coat, he slipped them on. Capaldi's suit jacket had fallen open, and Martinez ran a hand over the inner pockets, first one side, then the other. He extracted a wallet, phone and…

"What the hell is that?" I gestured with my chin toward the object, and Martinez held up what appeared to be an old-fashioned key.

"Skeleton key." He slid it into a clear plastic bag, then handed it to me.

I turned it over in my hands, inspecting it. "What the hell is this for?"

"Not sure." He finished searching the body, then pushed to his feet. "But we're damn sure gonna find out."

He passed the evidence bags to one of the techs, then turned to address his agents. "As soon as the suspects have been transported, search the property." He turned back to me and clamped one hand on my shoulder. "We'll find her, Sheriff. We've got warrants to seize his assets and search his home and business. If we have to, we'll tear this city apart."

TWENTY-SEVEN

GIULIANA

He's alive.

It was the first thing that came to mind as soon as I pushed through the layers of fog cloaking my mind and came fully awake. I blinked into the darkness and replayed his words in my head.

"I'm going to kill him slowly. Brutally. Make him wish he'd never met you."

Matteo had slipped; he'd threatened to kill Eric—which meant he was still alive. My heart leaped with hope and, despite everything, a smile came to my face. I'd thought he was gone, but he was out there somewhere. I knew he'd be looking for me. I needed to get to him before Matteo did.

I lay on my side, my legs drawn up so that my thighs rested against my stomach, and my left arm had fallen asleep. Thank God for small favors. It was back in place, but it still ached like a bitch. I tried to stretch my legs out but the movement was hindered as my feet collided with something hard.

What the hell? Gritting my teeth through the pain, I forced

my left arm to move and tried to sit up. Agony speared through me as my head smacked against something hard, and I collapsed to my back. I rubbed at my forehead, trying to get my bearings. It was jet black in here, like it was perpetually night, so I couldn't see a damn thing.

I tentatively stretched out my arm and my fingers brushed something smooth just inches from my face. My brows drew together as I lifted my other hand and pressed both palms flat against the cool surface. It felt almost like… wood? My mind spun furiously, trying to make the connection, and it finally hit me.

I was in the box.

My heart lurched in my chest, and I sucked in a breath as I slapped my palms against the lid. It didn't budge. Putting as much force behind the movement as possible, I pushed upward, but it refused to give. My rapid breaths filled my ears, coming much too quickly.

Spurred by the need to get out, I frantically searched the seam where the lid met the sides of the box, searching for any kind of latch or hook. Nothing. My heart rate increased with every second that passed, and disbelief quickly gave way to panic. In the limited space, I kicked against the lid. The sound reverberated in my ears, but the wood refused to give.

For a moment, I paused and focused on the sounds outside the box—or, rather, lack thereof. It was almost deathly silent and still. Had Matteo left me again? I had no idea whether I was still in the room under the church or if he'd transported me somewhere different. Why else put me in a box if he didn't plan to move me… or bury me.

Oh, God. The thought alone made me sick, and I had to force down the urge to retch. He was going to kill Eric if I couldn't get out of here. Anger welled up. I was so close! Furious with myself, with Matteo, I pounded my fist on the lid of the coffin.

I beat on the wood with everything I had. I kicked and

punched at the lid until my knuckles were sore. Scream after scream ripped from my throat as I clawed at the wood of the too-small box. I knew I was using up valuable oxygen, but I couldn't stop. I felt crazed, out of control. If I didn't get out of here, I would die. Eric would die.

Suddenly my throat felt too tight, the air too thick. My head felt fuzzy and I could practically feel the room spinning around me.

No.

No, no, no, no, no.

I had to get out of here so I could help Eric. I had to...

My hands fell limply to rest on my stomach, and I closed my eyes, my breathing hard and labored. Depleted of nutrients and past the point of fatigue, my body could only take so much strain. My head rolled to the side as exhaustion claimed me once more, and I gave up the fight to stay conscious.

TWENTY-EIGHT

ERIC

I raked my hands through my hair as I stumbled out the front door of the restaurant. Where the hell could she be? The agents had searched Capaldi's home as well as several other holdings the family owned locally, but their efforts had yielded nothing. Though we'd questioned several of the staff members, no one had seen her for two days. The thought made me physically ill. I didn't want to contemplate what that might mean.

I lifted my head, and my eyes collided with an ancient church across the street. Unbidden, my feet carried me in that direction. I paused in front of the huge carved wooden doors, and I placed one hand flat on the wood. It'd been years since I stepped foot inside a church, and it felt foreign, unfamiliar. With a deep breath, I tested the door. Unlocked. I braced myself, then pushed my way inside. This late at night, it was dimly lit, not a soul in sight. I made my way up the aisle between the empty pews that looked eerily vacant. I knew the stained glass windows set high along each wall depicted

Christ's crucifixion, though the darkness outside obscured the images.

I stopped just before the altar and stared up at the cross. I had no idea what I was looking for here. Hope, maybe? Guidance? I had nowhere else to go, no trail to follow. Maybe it was time to seek a higher power, because I was at a dead end. I'd exhausted all of my options, put everything I had into it, but it hadn't been enough.

I sank into a pew and linked my hands together where they rested over the back of the pew in front of me. I closed my eyes and bowed my head the way I'd seen others do. I had no idea how to pray. How did you speak to someone you weren't sure even existed? I'd seen enough evil over the past two decades to believe God was a figment of someone's overactive imagination. Surely no deity would ever allow such horrible things to happen.

A soft noise brought my head up, and I stared at the stooped little priest in the corner. He hadn't registered my presence or, if he had, he'd chosen to ignore me. He lit a candle and I saw his lips move in prayer. He made the sign of the cross, then shuffled my way.

I watched warily as he took a seat beside me, and for several long moments we remained silent. Finally he turned to me. "What brings you here?"

I lifted one shoulder. "I'm not really sure."

He nodded slightly. "Anything I can help with?"

Tears burned the backs of my eyes, and I quickly blinked them away as I sat back against the hard wood. "I don't think so, Father. I'm not sure anyone can."

I felt eyes on me, and I craned my neck as I glanced around the large open space, trying to find the source of my discomfort. Except for the priest, the church was empty. A blast of cool air hit my skin then was gone as quickly as it had come. Beside me, the priest rubbed his hands briskly over his arms. I eyed him. "Did you feel that too?"

He tipped his chin. "The spirits have been active."

I didn't know what to say to that. I didn't believe in ghosts, but I was certain that, given his profession, he was required to believe in otherworldly elements.

"Do you…?" I wasn't sure how to finish the sentence.

The old priest seemed to know what I was asking, because he spoke up. "They speak to me sometimes."

I tried not to judge, but being here was creeping me the fuck out. I was just about to excuse myself when his next words stopped me cold. "She's a mournful one."

I turned a bewildered gaze on him. "What?"

He nodded his head toward the candle he'd lit when he first entered the room. "She's sad. Tormented."

She? "How do you know?" My question was barely a whisper.

The priest seemed to think it over. "It's just something that I feel. It's almost tangible, her sorrow."

I dug in my pocket for Jules's ring and turned it over in my hands, staring at the diamond like it would impart some much-needed secret. It'd been days since anyone had seen her. Where was she? Was she still alive? Capaldi's words had been confusing at best. He'd spoken in present tense but like he assumed her demise was imminent. I couldn't fucking imagine never seeing her again.

I closed my eyes against the moisture gathering there and fisted my hand around the ring. Dropping my head backward, I sent up a silent prayer. We'd searched damn near every place Capaldi had access to, yet we'd found no trace of her. What if we were truly too late?

My eyes popped open. No. I wouldn't even let myself think it. Martinez and his men were researching every angle. We would find her; we just had to. It was so damn hard to believe that, though. I knew how many cases went unsolved, how many victims were never found. Faith wasn't a luxury I could afford, but it was the only thing I had left.

I turned my gaze back to the crucifix suspended over the altar. "How long have you done this?"

"Nearly fifty years," the priest replied. "I was born and raised here in Chicago."

"Same here." I drew a deep breath. I loved this city, but I hated it for so many reasons at the same time. "I'll bet you've seen some things."

"Indeed," he agreed. "More good than bad, thankfully."

I nodded, and we lapsed into silence for a long minute. Suddenly, the candles in the corner flickered, sputtering out almost completely before reigniting. Icy fingers clawed at my spine, and my blood ran cold. What the fuck was happening? This wasn't real. Spirits didn't exist… Did they?

"Did you see that?"

He nodded slowly, then glanced around before rubbing his hands together again. "Sometimes I feel like they're really calling for help." He let out a soft chuckle. "I actually walked the tunnel yesterday to make sure I wasn't hearing things."

My head snapped toward him. "Tunnel?"

"The original part of this church was built back in the late 1600s, before Chicago was officially appointed a city, and they made several additions over the centuries," he replied conversationally. "In fact, the restaurant across the street is where the old rectory used to be, but it burned down nearly a hundred years ago now. As the city grew outward, the catacombs under the church were established for the residents to bury and honor their dead. Everything back then was connected by underground tunnels, but they've been forgotten over the years."

I knew there were tunnels running under the city, mostly recreational or transport, but this was the first time I'd heard anything about catacombs under the church. If the restaurant somehow connected to an underground tunnel, was it possible…?

"How do you access the catacombs?" I asked.

The priest grasped the pew in front of him and slowly rose his feet. "Come with me." He led the way deeper into the church to another sturdy oak door. He pulled it open and flipped on a single bulb. "The stairs here lead to the basement. Once down there, the tunnels break off in several directions. The rooms have been locked for decades," he remarked, "as we have no use for them. We also can't have people disturbing the dead."

"Would you mind if I took a look around? I promise I won't damage anything," I said when he paused.

He studied me for a moment then finally relented. "I'll be right here."

I used the flashlight from my phone to illuminate the steps in front of me as I made my way down to the bottom. As he said, the landing broke off and tunnels veered in several directions. I slowly turned in a circle, eyeing the long, dark tunnels and debating which way to go. Suddenly, the craziness of the situation hit me.

What the hell was I doing?

Jesus. Was I so desperate for answers that I was willing to look for the most ridiculous and sensational solution? I turned and placed my foot on the step to return to the church. As soon as my shoe made contact with the hard stone, the bright light flickered. I froze in place, positive whatever I'd just seen was a malfunction. Though the phone wasn't new, I'd never had issues with it before. I jiggled the device, but this time the beam of light remained steady and strong. Shaking my head, I took another step. The light flickered once more, and my heart jumped into my throat.

What the fuck was happening here?

I took a step backward as the light flashed off then quickly on again. I held it up, the hairs on the back of my neck standing straight up as I swept my arm in a wide arc. The white light danced as it flickered over the old stone walls of one tunnel, then the next. Suddenly, the light went out completely.

A heartbeat later, it came back full force, seeming to lead me down the tunnel to my right. The light seemed brighter, stronger, and I tentatively took a step in that direction.

I walked several dozen feet until I came to a sealed room. Dropping my gaze to the floor, I noticed the dust and dirt had recently been disturbed. My heart beat frantically in my chest as I grasped the smooth iron handle and shoved the swollen door open. Just beyond a small landing lay a set of stone steps that seemed to descend straight into Hell itself. I stood there motionless, staring into the yawning mouth of darkness, wondering with dread what lay at the bottom.

TWENTY-NINE

GIULIANA

A shiver rocked my body, and my legs instinctively curled tighter into my body. Not like they could get much closer. The box limited my movement in every direction, and agony ripped through me every time I tried to move.

I swore I could feel the air thin as I tried to drag in a deep breath. I was slowly running out of oxygen. How much time did I have left? Tears crept from the corners of my eyes as I pressed my hands to the lid only inches from my face. I couldn't even get enough leverage to push up on it or kick upward. I ran my fingers over the seams, searching for any weakness in its construction.

I'd been in and out of consciousness, fighting to stay awake and alert. Here in the dark, time had no meaning. Did Matteo plan to come back for me at all? Or did he plan to let me die down here, all alone? I was growing weaker and weaker, staying awake for shorter periods of time. A shudder rolled through me and a sob tore from my throat. No one could help me now. I was locked away somewhere underground where my body would never be found.

I prayed that death would come quickly. The last set of lashes were the hardest I'd endured yet, and my skin was flayed open in several places. Those wouldn't kill me, though. What I dreaded most was dragging in one breath after another, slowly using up all of the oxygen inside my small tomb until it was gone. I already felt lightheaded. It wouldn't be long now.

I cried for myself, for Eric, for the life we would never have. It was stupid to use up my reserve of oxygen, but I couldn't help the great, gasping breaths that heaved in and out of my lungs. I hated Matteo and everything he stood for. I closed my eyes and employed the strategy Johnny had instilled in me years ago.

The darkness of the box dissolved away, and my breathing regulated, my tears slowing as the beach came into focus. Here in my own little world, I knew every blade of grass, every grain of sand. I felt the sun on my face, the wind in my hair. The cool water tickled my toes as the tide lapped gently at my feet. But there was a second presence that hadn't existed before.

"Daddy!" Tears burned the bridge of my nose as his familiar arms enveloped me, pulling me close. "I missed you so much."

He stroked one hand over my hair. "I've missed you, too, *tesoro*."

I leaned away and met his green eyes, so much like my own. If Daddy was here… "Is this Heaven?"

He smiled gently. "It seems that way, doesn't it?"

Dread settled like lead in my gut. I'd tried so hard to be strong, to keep going, but it hadn't been enough. Eric was somewhere out there, and I couldn't even warn him that Matteo was coming for him. I couldn't do anything at all, because now I would never see him again.

Burrowing my head against Daddy's shoulder, I vented my frustration, my grief. Through it all, he held me close.

"He took everything from me." He squeezed my shoulders tighter as my voice broke. "I loved him so much, and…"

I trailed off, and my father gently stroked my back. "Everything will be all right. You'll see."

I shook my head against his chest. How could he say that? I'd been betrayed by my own cousin; we'd both been betrayed by people we'd cared about. I pulled back to look at him. "Massimo sold you out."

An acute look of sorrow entered his eyes. "I know."

"How could he? He took you from me, and then Matteo —" Choking back a sob, I glanced up at him. "I lost everything. I loved him so much, and now I'll never see him again."

"Of course you will, *tesoro*." A large palm slipped beneath my chin and lifted my gaze to his. "Your cop is a good man. He loves you very much; I can tell. You will be happy together."

My father spoke in present tense though we both knew better, and a sad smile lifted my mouth. "I'm so glad we're together again."

"I have missed you, *piccolina*." He gave a little shake of his head. "But this? This is only temporary."

"Why?" Panic flared around my heart. "What are you talking about? Why can't I stay with you?"

He leaned forward and pressed a kiss to my forehead before meeting my gaze again. "You're not ready yet."

"But—"

Daddy shook his head and placed a heavy hand on my shoulder. "I will always be here, in your heart."

"No!" Tears welled up, blurring my vision. I couldn't bear to lose him again, not when I'd just found him. "Daddy—"

"Jules."

My ears perked up at the sound of my name as it carried toward me on the slight breeze. My brows drew together, and

I whipped my head left and right as it came again, closer this time.

"Jules."

I shielded my eyes from the glare of the sun as a lone figure strolled along the shore. Each step that closed the distance between us brought the man more into focus.

Eric.

My breath caught, and I took a step toward him before I remembered. I spun back toward my father, tears in my eyes. "Daddy..."

He lifted one hand and cupped my cheek. "Go."

Pushing myself up on my toes, I kissed his cheek. Tears swam in my eyes as I stared up at him. "I love you."

"Ti amo."

With one last watery smile, I ripped myself out of his arms and sprinted across the sand toward Eric.

"Come back to me, Jules." He stopped and spread his arms wide, a smile on his face as I launched myself toward him.

I'm coming, Eric.

THIRTY

ERIC

I followed the other officers down the dank, narrow stone steps and paused as Martinez pulled the skeleton key from the bag and inserted it into the lock. The click of the lock disengaging seemed to echo in the narrow space, and I held my breath as the door swung open.

Inside the room it was completely dark. I don't know what I was expecting. Even the warehouse had been dimly lit. Here, though, there was nothing, no indication of life whatsoever. The air seemed thick and stale, and the tiny kernel of hope I'd harbored began to dissipate.

Beams from the mens' flashlights bobbed and weaved as they swept the room. Golden light washed over the wall as one of them lit an ancient looking lantern suspended in a holder on the wall. I froze just inside the doorway as I quickly scanned my surroundings. A roughhewn workbench stood against the wall to my right, various implements scattered over its surface. But that wasn't what made my heart stop.

In the middle of the room sat a pinewood box. It was the

only thing of substance in the room—and it could only be here for one reason.

The room went deathly silent, so quiet I swore I could hear the beating of my heart echoing off the stone walls as the men tossed uneasy glances at one other.

I looked at SSA Martinez. "What the fuck is that?"

"Donahue, maybe—"

I shook my head, one hard, fast shake, and the agent's lips pressed into a firm line. He shot a quick look at Jack, who stood next to me. I didn't look at him; I couldn't take my eyes off that Godforsaken box. What the hell was inside? Deep down I knew, and my gut clenched into a tight knot.

In my peripheral vision, I watched Jack give a terse nod.

As if realizing I wasn't going anywhere, Martinez moved to the far end of the box and accepted the crowbar one of his men extended to him. Two agents stood at the ready, pistols trained on the box, prepared for the worst. Martinez slid the narrow end under the lid and levered upward. The nails screeched loudly as they pulled free of the wood, and I cringed at the sound. Martinez set aside the crowbar and swore softly as he lifted the lid.

My heart clenched and my hands curled into fists as pale skin was revealed an inch at a time. I wavered on my feet, suddenly lightheaded, and I locked my knees to keep from falling. Even from here I could see the dark brown stains on the inside of the lid. *Claw marks.* My body turned numb, dense as cement, and the light in the room grew intensely bright before fading once more.

I quickly blinked and fought for control as my heart thudded against my ribcage. Everything bottled up inside me felt like it would shatter at any second, and I drew a deep breath, forcing oxygen into my lungs. I had to stay strong.

The two agents holstered their weapons as Martinez dropped to one knee and dipped a hand inside the box. He placed his fingers on Jules's neck, then looked up at me. I stood frozen, not daring to breathe until he gave me a slight nod. Then my feet were moving of their own volition, and I found myself in front of the box.

I hit my knees, tears of fury burning my eyes. Jules lay inside, curled into the fetal position, one arm tucked protectively over her head. Her skin was riddled with cuts and bruises, stained various shades of red and brown from the blood that had encrusted her skin along with the new wounds that still seeped liquid.

A steel band constricted around my chest as I stared down at her. I felt helpless, so furious that I wanted to rip something apart with my hands. I regretted that Matteo was already dead, because he deserved so much worse for what he'd done to Jules.

"Jules?" I spoke softly. "It's me, baby—Eric."

I didn't dare move her arm; I had no idea what she'd been through, and I didn't want to risk her trying to fight back. Instead, I gently pressed two fingers to her throat so I could feel her pulse myself. It was there—barely.

My gaze swept over her, and I blinked the moisture from my eyes as I took in the full extent of the damage done to her body. Lacerations and welts riddled her body, from her lower calves to the top of her shoulders. Dressed only in her underwear, there hadn't even been a fabric buffer between her delicate flesh and whatever implement of torture Capaldi had used. I swallowed hard, wondering if he'd inflicted damage where I couldn't see. Had she been raped and left for dead? Christ, I couldn't fathom the thought.

Using my large frame, I turned slightly to block the others' view of her, though I knew they'd moved away to give us space. I'd heard Martinez call for the medic, so I only had a few more moments with her before they would come take her away.

"I don't know if you can hear me, sweetheart"—I gently touched her hand where it rested over her head—"but it's over now. He won't hurt you anymore."

I stroked one finger over the back of her hand, taking in the ragged, blood-stained nails. The sight made me physically ill. There wasn't a single inch of her that wasn't battered and bruised, and it fucking broke me that I couldn't even hold her to comfort her. I was furious with myself for not looking harder, finding her sooner. How could I have ever believed, even for a single second, that she would leave me? Had my hesitation done this to her? While I'd been cursing her for her betrayal, she'd been tortured at Capaldi's hands. What if even those few hours could have made a difference? God, I couldn't bear to think of it.

"We're going to take you to the hospital, honey, and get you all fixed up." I slid my fingers around hers. "Squeeze my hand if you can hear me."

For several heartbeats I just waited.

Nothing.

Panic welled up, and I ruthlessly pushed it down. I wouldn't lose her now; I refused to let her give up. Not when we were so close. "Come on, baby. Squeeze my hand. Let me know you're still in there."

Nine heartbeats. Ten.

My breathing increased. "Come on, Jules. Fight for me, baby! Squeeze my hand!"

Jack laid a hand on my shoulder. "Donahue—"

I shrugged him off. "No, I—"

Then it happened. So light I almost missed it, her fingers curled around mine.

"Jules!" A relieved breath rushed from my lungs, and I gave her a gentle squeeze back. "Hang in there, sweetheart. I'm here now."

She'd withdrawn completely, and she was in shock—but she was in there. A shudder rolled through my body. God.

How close had I come to losing her? I didn't even want to contemplate it.

"Sheriff?"

One of Martinez's men stood off to the side, crowbar in hand. He lifted it toward me. "We'll need to disassemble the box so we can transport her."

I nodded but didn't move. They could work around me; I refused to leave her side. As the man went to work loosening the nails that held the walls together, I spoke quietly to Jules, walking her through each step of what was happening and offering what little comfort I could.

Three sides fell away, leaving only the one I was currently leaned over, holding Jules. "Almost done, sweetheart. We'll get you out of here soon. I'm going to have to let go of you now."

I started to pull away but was stopped by the feel of her fingers around mine. My breath caught, and I squeezed back. "Jules?"

Her fingers constricted around mine, and the arm covering her face twitched. I swept tiny circles over the back of her hand with my thumb. "Just lie still, sweetheart. I won't go anywhere."

A tiny whimper left her throat as her arm moved again. It slipped lower, and she tucked it against her chest. Seeing her move, seeing her fight, filled me with hope. I leaned further over the edge of the box and brushed one hand over her hair.

"Wake up for me, baby. Let me see you."

Her long dark lashes fluttered for a long moment, then fell closed again. Her chest rose on a deep inhale, then, as if it took all the strength in the world, she blinked. Once. Twice. Her eyes were glassy and unfocused, and several heart beats passed as I waited for her to meet my gaze. The sight of her gorgeous green eyes was the most beautiful thing I'd ever seen.

Relief and joy and a feeling I'd never experienced before

billowed up inside me. I bit my tongue against the urge to pull her into my arms and bury my head against her throat. Instead, I bowed my head and kissed our hands where they were still joined. I swallowed hard and forced a smile to my lips as I lightly brushed her cheek.

"I'm right here, sweetheart. I'm never leaving you again."

THIRTY-ONE

GIULIANA

A jolt of pain shot through my body, and I jerked awake. This was the first night that I'd slept on my back since I arrived at the hospital, and the sensation felt like a thousand needles pressing against my skin. The nurses made me turn constantly so as to not put pressure on the wounds any more than necessary. As fatigue melted away, I became aware of something else. Someone was in the room.

Curling my fingers into the fabric of the thin blanket, I slowly turned my head toward the darkened corner of the room. A man sat in the standard issue chair, elbows resting on his widespread knees, his head bowed as he stared at his clasped hands. Despite him being hunched over, there was no mistaking his familiar form. As if he felt my gaze on him, his head jerked up, and his dark chocolate eyes met mine.

For a long moment, we remained frozen, suspended in time. He had been my jailer for nearly the entire time I lived with my uncle, yet here he sat, assessing me with that unsettling gaze. A chill swept up my spine. Was he here to kill me? Was he here to carry out my cousin's final order and tie up all the loose ends?

I recoiled as he pushed from the chair, and he held his hands up in a placating motion. "I'm sorry. I don't want to scare you, I just wanted to make sure you were okay. I'll leave."

His hands dropped to his sides as he took a step toward the door. I didn't know what to think. Why was he here? Johnny had never hurt me. In fact, he was the one who'd introduced me to the idea of dissociation to weather my uncle's abuse. But I couldn't believe he was standing in front of me here today. From the snippets of conversation I'd caught over the past few days, I was under the impression that all of my uncle's men had been arrested—at least the ones who'd been present in the warehouse. I was sure several of them had gotten away, but Johnny most certainly would've been present.

"Did you get out?"

He paused for a long moment then shook his head in the negative. It wasn't unheard of for some of the soldiers to be granted immunity or to make bail once they'd been incarcerated. "Not exactly."

I lifted a brow, and Johnny heaved a sigh as turned to face me. With one hand, I surreptitiously pulled on the cord for the remote to call the nurse. I wanted to have it close by in case anything happened. Unfortunately, he didn't miss the slight movement, and his eyes flicked over my shoulder before they met mine again. "Are you in pain?"

I gave my head a little shake. "I'll be fine."

It was his turn to cock a brow at me. "You *are* fine, or you'll *be* fine?"

I stared up at him, my expression impassive, but I didn't bother to respond. "I'm sure the meds have worn off by now," he replied as he tipped his head toward the remote. "You can call them if you want."

They'd actually weaned me off the morphine two days ago, per my request. I hated the way it made me feel sluggish and drowsy. After everything that had happened with Matteo, I wanted my senses at full height. I felt the overwhelming need to be aware of everything around me at all times.

My brow furrowed. "I don't understand. Why are you here?"

He lifted one shoulder as he shoved his hands in his pockets. "I told you. Just wanted to check on you."

"No." I gave my head a slow shake as I watched him. "That's not it. What's going on?"

A tiny smile lifted the corners of his mouth. "You're too perceptive. Anyone ever tell you that?"

Again, I didn't bother to respond to his question. I'd spent every day of nearly the last three years studying my uncle's posture and facial expressions, watching for any nuance that would indicate the slightest change in his hair trigger temper.

Johnny's smile slipped away. "I'm sorry, I shouldn't have…" His words trailed off, and I watched several emotions flicker over his face as he seemed to carry on some kind of internal debate for speaking again. "I infiltrated the organization nearly four years ago under the direction of the FBI."

I sucked in a sharp breath as he flicked open his jacket, revealing a shiny badge clipped inside the lining. "Are you crazy?" My eyes widened, and hysteria caused my voice to raise several octaves. "They'll kill you! You have to—"

He dropped his jacket back into place and took two steps toward the bed. "It's fine."

"It's not fine!" I shot back as I struggled to sit up. "If anyone finds out—"

He shook his head. "All of your uncle's associates have been taken into custody. Even if they do get out and try to come for me, they won't find me."

"What are you going to do?"

Another little smile curved his mouth. "Disappear. Technically, I don't exist anyway, and…" He trailed off and gestured toward the long scar along his cheek before shoving them back into his pockets. "Too identifiable for field work now."

Guilt sliced through me once more, and I choked out the whispered words. "I'm sorry. I had no idea—"

He held up one hand to stop me. "I'd do it all over again."

My brows drew together as I thought back to that morning. "Did you see me?"

He nodded slowly. "I kept talking with Lila, praying you'd have time to get away."

"Thank you."

He shrugged as if it meant nothing, but he shifted uncomfortably. "It killed me to have to bring you back."

"So, it was one of Uncle's men I saw in the parking lot that morning, wasn't it?"

"It was." He nodded regretfully.

"But the plates…. How—?"

He gave a quick shake of his head. "We switched them with another car that was parked at the resort. We had eyes on you for a couple days before moving in."

"Of course." Bitterness seeped into my tone, and my head spun as memories washed over me. Four years. He'd watched my uncle abuse me for years, yet he'd done nothing. He must've seen the heartbreak on my face, because he sobered. "Believe me when I tell you I did everything possible to get you out of there."

Tears burned my eyes, and I fixed my gaze to the wall directly across from me, trying to ignore his presence.

"Every time we got close, every time we had something in place, your uncle would slip right off the hook." He sighed. "Then all this shit with the Russians went down, and things escalated from bad to worse."

I wanted to blame him, but I knew it wasn't his fault. He had done what he could at the time, though I still felt betrayed. "Was it you who kidnapped me?"

His head moved in a solemn nod. "I tried to convince your uncle it would only be a one-man job, and that I could take care of it. He wouldn't let me go by myself, so I brought one of the new young soldiers with me and told him I wanted to be the one to take care of Eric. Had it been anyone else…"

He trailed off, and I picked up his train of thought. Had Massimo sent anyone else, Eric would be dead, and I would've been someone's plaything until they tired of me and killed me, too. Anger surged, hot and fierce. "So… what? You brought me back here instead of letting me go? How was that helping me?"

Johnny dragged the chair next to the bed and sank down, dropping his head into his hands. He was silent for a long moment before meeting my eyes. "It wasn't supposed to go down like that. None of that was supposed to happen. We had a plan to get you out, but Massimo scheduled that dinner and threw everything off. And Matteo…" his voice softened. "Christ. I wish I could make him suffer for everything he put you through."

He looked genuinely distraught, and sympathy tugged at my heartstrings. "It's not your fault."

"It is." He scrubbed his hands over his face. "I would take back everything if I could."

Though I'd known the man for more than three years, I'd never seen this side of him before. His reaction seemed genuine, and I felt the need to console him. "Whatever you did, you did to survive. Just like me. Had you gone against my uncle's orders you would've been killed. That's on his hands, not yours."

His eyes went cold, his expression stony, at my words, and apprehension washed over me. I thought about the video I'd found just two days before my abduction. Lila and her boyfriend had begged for their lives before their execution. I knew one of the men was my uncle. The other I hadn't been able to identify at the time. But now…

"You did it, didn't you?"

His expression shuttered, and he swallowed hard but refused to speak. Tears burned over the bridge of my nose, and one slipped down my cheek as I turned my head toward the window, hiding my face from him. I closed my eyes and cried; for myself, for Lila and her boyfriend, for the man beside me who'd been forced to choose between his life and another's.

After several long moments, I finally managed to compose myself. I dabbed at my eyes with my knuckles and turned back to Johnny just as the door to the room opened with a quiet click. Eric froze, one foot in the room, his keen gaze missing nothing as it swept over first me, with my red, swollen eyes, then Johnny sitting next to the bed. His brows lowered, and I could see the storm brewing in his eyes as he started toward us. He opened his mouth to speak, but I cut him off.

"Eric."

The sound of his name halted him in place, and he tore his gaze away from Johnny to look at me before returning to the other man. "What the hell happened here?"

"It's fine," I assured him.

Johnny hadn't moved, just sat there with his arms crossed over his chest, looking impassive as ever. Eric glared at him before turning his attention back to me. "Are you sure? If you don't want him here…"

I shook my head. "He came by to check on me, that's all."

Eric's lips settled into a thin line as he regarded the other man. Seeming to accept my response, he lifted his chin and reluctantly extended one hand. "Thanks for your help."

They shared one firm shake before dropping their hands

away and lapsing back into silence once more. After a tense moment, Johnny turned to me. "I should get going anyway."

"Thank you," I said softly. He'd given me the closure I needed, no matter how much it hurt. "Will I see you again?"

He stood and gave an almost imperceptible shake of his head. "No, ma'am."

My mouth lifted in a brittle smile as I watched him make his way toward the door. He paused with his hand on the doorknob before glancing back at us. "Good luck. You deserve it."

With that, he was gone.

Eric stood frozen as he watched the door shut behind Johnny, then he turned back to me, concern furrowing the space between his brows. "You sure you're okay?"

"I'll be fine." Part of me wanted so badly to tell him everything, but I couldn't bring myself to say the words. Instead, I forced a smile to my face. "I'm just tired."

Eric nodded, but the expression in his eyes told me he didn't believe me. I swallowed hard, watching Eric as he watched me. Except for the police report, we hadn't discussed what had happened over the past couple of weeks. He didn't pry, and I didn't offer up more than necessary. Eric had been attentive without smothering me, and for that I was grateful.

All I wanted was to put the past behind me and move on. The only problem was, I had no idea if we could ever go back to the way we'd been.

THIRTY-TWO

ERIC

My eyes popped open, and I swept out a hand, automatically searching for Jules. The sheets were cold, and I propped myself on an elbow as I scrubbed the last vestiges of sleep from my eyes.

I hadn't meant to fall asleep. I wanted only to give her a little bit of space, but the sheer exhaustion of the past couple of weeks had apparently caught up to me. I glanced at the clock on the nightstand, its digital red numbers glowing in the darkness. I'd only been out for about two hours, but it was too long without having her next to me.

Throwing aside the covers, I slipped from the bed. A pair of jeans lay discarded on the chair in the corner, and I hastily stepped into them. The lights were all off downstairs, but moonlight streamed in through the floor-to-ceiling windows that spanned the back wall of the cabin. My heart clenched, and I paused on the landing at the top of the stairs as my gaze landed on Jules. Knees drawn up to her chest, she was huddled in a small ball on the floor, staring sightlessly out the window. She didn't acknowledge my presence as I quietly descended the stairs and moved closer. She remained silent, and I took a seat next to her, resting my forearms on my knees.

For several long minutes, we sat there together, just staring out the window. I turned my gaze to her, studying the pretty profile of her face. Long dark curls had tumbled forward, and I swept them back over her shoulder. She flinched at my touch, and her chin dropped to her chest. I snatched my hand away and replaced it in my lap, my fingers curling into a tight fist. The sound of my heart hitting the floor was deafening to my own ears, and I wondered if she could hear it shatter in the silence.

I swallowed hard and pretended like her rejection hadn't just gutted me. I'd seen the evidence of the abuse all over her tiny body, and it sent rage curling through me once more, hot and volatile. I had no idea what she'd endured during her time with him, and I had no idea how to make it right. She'd been different since the night we'd found her, wary and closed off. Something inside her head had changed, and I had to face the fact that whatever I did might not be enough. She might very well walk away from me. After everything we'd been through, I might still lose her. The thought terrified me, but I had to do what was best for Jules.

"Can't sleep?" I finally ventured. She gave her head a little shake but didn't speak. I'd seen cases like this before, and the internal damage was often so much worse than the wounds inflicted on the outside.

"Do you want me to get your medicine? I—"

Another shake of her head cut me off. "It's not that."

Hope caused my breath to suspend in my lungs. There was an interminable silence before she spoke again. "How did you know?"

I tipped my head to one side. "How did I know how to find you?" I clarified.

Her eyes stared straight forward, but her head moved in a

jerky nod. I drew in a deep breath. "Right after you moved in with me, we had a discussion about the Tavern. Remember that?" She didn't bother to respond to my rhetorical question, so I continued. "I grew up in Chicago, and I had this gut feeling that you had too. I still have friends there, and I asked a contact with the bureau to find any information on you that he could. That's how I found out about your dad."

My voice cracked a little bit as memories washed over me, but I pushed them down. "I knew that's where you had to be."

A tear slipped down her cheek. "Why did you come after me?"

"Because I love you," I said baldly. "There isn't a single thing that I wouldn't do for you. I'd have burned the world down to bring you home if I had to."

More tears squeezed from her eyes, and she dropped her forehead to rest on her knees. I scooted behind her and swung my right leg around her, then eased her into the vee of my legs. She turned slightly, and I wrapped my arms around her as she curled into my chest. I gently rubbed her back while she cried, each sob cutting through me like a knife. She turned her head into my neck, and I stroked one hand over the silky locks of her hair until she finally quieted.

"I feel dirty. Broken."

The pain in her voice caused my heart to constrict, and I clenched my jaw so tight my molars ground together. God, I wanted to kill Capaldi all over again for what he'd done to her. She moved as if to shift away, and I tightened my hold on her. I couldn't help wanting her close to me, and though I wanted her to feel comfortable and safe, neither could I find it in me to give her the space she was begging for.

"You are stronger than anyone I know. Half the men and women I went to the Academy with couldn't have done what you did. You trusted him, and he..." I broke off, emotion choking my voice. "You didn't deserve any of that. You're not broken, baby. You're the strongest, most amazing person I know."

I cuddled her closer and pressed my cheek to the top of her head. For nearly a moment, neither of us spoke. "I'll understand if you don't want to tell me what happened."

The marks on her body told a story of their own anyway, and I could put the pieces together well enough. She sniffled but remained quiet, and I drew in a deep breath.

"Just know that if you ever need anything"—my voice faltered as tears burned the backs of my eyes—"you can always talk to me. Wherever you are, whatever you do, I'll always be here for you."

Another sob tore from her throat, and I pressed my lips to the top of my head as I clenched my eyes closed and steeled my heart. Though I wasn't nearly ready to let her go, this felt like goodbye. I would never tether her to me against her wishes. I would respect whatever she chose to do, no matter how badly it hurt. She'd already been through so much; letting her go, allowing her to be free, was the least I could do. I just had to hope and pray that one day she would find her way back to me, because my heart would remain with her forever.

Time slipped away as we sat huddled on the cold floor, wrapped in each other's arms. Ten minutes, an hour—I wasn't sure how much time had passed. I couldn't let her go. If this was the last time I ever got to feel her in my arms, I was going to commit every second to memory.

THIRTY-THREE

GIULIANA

Guilt crashed over me like a wave. Here in the circle of Eric's arms, I felt safe, protected, and I didn't deserve one bit of it. I'd lied to him about my past, about who I was. How could he say he still loved me after all that? My thoughts brought on a fresh bout of tears. Through it all, Eric held me close, lending silent comfort.

"I don't understand you," I finally choked out.

Beneath my cheek, the muscles of his chest tensed. "What do you mean?"

Reluctantly, I peeled myself away from him and dabbed the tears suspended on my cheeks with the pads of my fingers. "Why are you being so nice to me?"

His left arm dropped to rest on his knee, still propped up on one side of me, but his other hand remained at the small of my back, his touch light but sure. Eric answered my question with one of his own. "How long have you known?"

I assumed he was talking about our entangled past. "I didn't put the pieces together until you told me about the incident in the warehouse."

I should have told him that night. Instead, I'd withheld the truth and put both of our lives in jeopardy.

"That was just a couple days before you were abducted," he clarified. I stiffened at the word, but I couldn't dispute the truth of it. It sounded so dire, so distorted, but that was exactly what Matteo had done. With no regard to myself or anyone else, he had taken me away and done the unthinkable.

"What about the video?" he asked softly.

I flinched and closed my eyes against the memory of it. I wasn't sure I would ever get those images, the sound of Lila's screams, out of my head. Eric's hand slipped up my spine to cup the back of my neck. I blinked my eyes open, and my gaze collided with his.

"The day before the accident," I admitted softly.

Still staring deeply into my eyes, Eric nodded. "Is that what you were going to tell me that morning?"

I nodded and licked my lips nervously. "I... I knew I needed to tell you, I just wasn't sure how."

He was silent for several long moments as he studied me. "I can understand that—but that's my point. You were going to tell me."

I nodded faintly at his statement, and his fingers tightened ever so slightly around the base of my neck. "You asked me why I'm doing this, how I can just put it behind me."

His hazel eyes bored into mine. "Forgiveness," he said simply. "I love you, and I will always forgive you. But you need to forgive yourself."

Tears sprang to my eyes, and I threw my arms around his waist as he hauled me against his broad chest. I held on for dear life as sobs welled up in my throat then finally ripped free, emotion pouring from me like a tidal wave. It was cathartic, like a cleansing, and after several long minutes, I felt as if I'd exorcized the fear and anger and guilt from my heart.

I slipped my fingers up his chest and rested them on the scar at the base of his throat. "Every time I see this…" I choked out as a shudder rolled over me. "I can't help but think—"

"This was not your fault." Eric grasped my fingers and pressed them to the faint pink line. "None of this was your fault."

"But my father—"

Eric gave a hard shake of his head. "You're not him. And I don't care who your father was. All that matters now is you and me." He lifted my hand to his mouth and kissed my fingers before releasing me. "In some twisted up way, it brought us together."

I blinked rapidly. "But if he hadn't—"

"Then what?" he asked as he slipped one hand over my cheek and into my hair. "We lived in Chicago our whole lives and never crossed paths. If shit hadn't gone down that day, I would probably still be working with my team, and your dad would still be in charge of the family. You could be married off to some mafioso, or in college somewhere halfway across the world."

I knew he was right, but it didn't diminish my guilt. "I just wish…"

He seemed to read my mind, because he picked up my train of thought. "I wish things had turned out differently too. I would sell my soul to take back all the hurt you've endured."

His words filled me with lightness. Selfless to a fault, his first thought had been of me instead of himself. Though I knew things between us wouldn't always be easy, and we would still have to work to overcome our past, I clutched onto the tiny kernel of hope in my heart. "Do you think it will ever go away?"

He shook his head. "No, and I don't want it to. I fell in love with you because of who you are. I want all of you, forever."

Shedding the last of my reserve, I swayed toward him. His hand tightened in my hair, and he yanked me forward, sealing his mouth over mine. The kiss was urgent and frantic, primitive and animalistic. Our teeth clashed, and our tongues tangled in an exotic dance as old as time. Wrapping his free arm around my waist, Eric fell backward, pulling me down to the floor with him. I sank my fingers into his hair, shaggy now with recent growth. I'd never seen it this long before, and I twined my fingers in the light brown strands.

He let out a little growl as I turned, and his hands slipped down to cup my bottom, long fingers kneading the flesh. I winced, sucking in a sharp breath, and he immediately released me, ripping his mouth from mine. "Fuck. I'm sorry, baby. I'm so sorry." He pushed up on his elbows, but I shoved him back down.

"No."

He cocked an eyebrow as he lay back and watched me. I stripped my shirt over my head and felt his hard arousal swell beneath my hips where I straddled him.

"I need your hands on me—all over me."

Reaching behind my back, I flicked the clasp of my bra and drew it down my arms. I bared myself to him completely, and he eagerly took up the reins. Tentatively, gently, he placed his hands on the indent of my waist then ran them upward. I let out a little hiss as his thumbs swept along the underside of my breasts, then up and over the hard peaks of my nipples.

He rolled us to the side, taking extra care as he gently lay me back on the rug.

"Good?"

I nodded, and he brushed his lips over mine. I opened for him as he swept his tongue inside, his familiar taste like a balm to my soul. God, I'd missed him so much. I let out a little whimper as he pulled away.

"Right here, baby. Just feel." He kissed down the cord of

my throat, one hand cupping my breast and teasing the stiff point. I shifted my hips as he knelt between my legs, his knees brushing the inside of my thighs and forcing them farther apart. His long fingers coasted over every inch of me, his mouth trailing soft kisses in their wake.

"Whose hands are all over your body?"

"Yours," I breathed.

"Who's the only man who will ever touch you?"

"You." My fingers curled into the thick pile of the rug beneath me as his mouth moved lower. His tongue dipped into my belly button, causing me to jump before he continued his descent.

"That's right," he said before kissing the space just above my clit. "Me and only me, until I take my last breath."

His tongue sliding through my drenched slit took my breath away, and I arched at the heady sensation. Spreading my legs wide and opening me to his intense perusal, he delved back inside, a man on a mission. He stroked and licked and sucked on the tiny nub, each ministration pushing me closer to the edge. A wave of ecstasy crashed over me, and I rode it as it lifted me up, close enough to touch the stars. Then it gradually lowered me back to reality, into the safety of Eric's arms.

Right there in the light of the moon, he chased away the demons and darkness crowding my mind. He filled my heart with love and joy, leaving no room for anything else.

THIRTY-FOUR

ERIC

Time ceased to exist as I made love to her. Her body turned to putty in my hands, the tension draining from her muscles as her chest rose and fell with each breath. She looked so beautiful—so open, so free.

Taking one hip in my hand, I gently rolled her to her belly on top of the soft rug. Her muscles tensed as her back was exposed to me in the silvery light. Stark lines crisscrossed her body, from the top of her shoulders to the backs of her calves, and though I had seen them before, the sight still made my heart stutter in my chest. Her hands curled into fists, and she ducked her head as if to hide from me.

I skated my hands up her sides, then placed them on either side of her and leveraged my body directly over her. Her back arched slightly, her bottom lifting toward me, practically urging me to sink inside her. My dick swelled against my zipper as her ass pressed against me, and she gave her hips a little wiggle. It was tempting as fuck, but there was something I needed to do first.

Her body went rigid as stone when I kissed the first scar.

My tongue and lips followed each dark line as if I could erase the memory of betrayal and anger burnt into her skin, and replace it instead with love and tenderness.

Over the past week, the wounds had begun to heal, and in time, they'd be gone completely. But the scars inside would remain until she purged them from her memory. I planned to be by her side for the rest of her days, replacing every bad memory with ten good ones.

I kissed another mark right above her bottom, and she inhaled sharply. Keeping one hand firmly on her back, I used one hand to flick open the button fly then worked the waistband down my legs. I kicked free of the fabric and fisted my cock as she shifted restlessly.

"Eric..."

"I know, baby." Sliding my free hand under her belly, I lifted her hips until her pretty pussy was exposed to me in the moonlight. I let out a little hiss as I eased my shaft inside, and it was immediately enveloped by her wet heat. I wanted to bury myself deep inside her, stay there forever.

"Fuck, Jules..."

She pressed backward, and I sank in to the hilt. Our mingled gasps filled the air, and I clutched at her hips as I tried to clamp down on my control. The urge to move hard and fast was overwhelming. It'd been too damn long, and I needed to feel her.

I guided her to a sitting position, her back against my chest. Then I began to move. I nibbled along her neck and collarbone, the view as I stared down at her incredible. Her tits bobbed up and down with each shallow thrust, and I cupped them in my hands, feeling their familiar weight. Her nipples strained, tight and erect, and I brushed my thumbs over the sensitive peaks.

Her head dropped back to rest on my shoulder, and I bit down on the space where her neck met her shoulder. She let out a soft cry, and her pussy clenched around me. Fire burned low in my belly, and I knew it wouldn't be long. Slipping one hand down her stomach to the apex of her thighs, I dipped into the silky wet heat. Her swollen clit was distended from her earlier orgasm, and she moaned as I circled the bundle of nerves.

One hand on her breast, I tweaked and teased the tiny point until she writhed in my arms, hovering on the precipice once more. She came apart with a ragged groan, her body falling forward under the force of her orgasm. She let out a little whimper as I pulled out, her sensitive inner muscles clutching at me as I withdrew. My dick ached to be back inside her, and I bit back an oath as my gaze swept over her perfectly shaped ass, evidence of her arousal glistening on her thighs in the moonlight.

Her legs quivered, and I stroked one hand over her bottom, cupping the perfect globe. "So beautiful."

Her pretty green eyes watched me intently as I lay down next to her. "Come here, baby. I want you right here where I can see you."

She braced her hands on my chest as I lifted her over me, and I lined myself up with her opening. Then I thrust hard. Gripping her hips, I fucked her slow and steady, so deep she'd feel me forever. Her teeth dug into her bottom lip, her eyes closing as her face contorted into an expression of sheer ecstasy. Just watching her pretty face turned me on, made me so damn hard. A tingling shot up my spine, and I knew I was getting close.

"You're mine, Jules." I threaded one hand through her silken locks and pulled her down to me. "Only mine."

She made a sexy little sound as I rolled my hips, and I claimed her mouth, curling my tongue over hers. She ripped herself away, panting as she ground herself against me. "Come for me, baby… Need to feel you one more time."

As if my words spurred her on, I felt her walls clench around me, and she let out a keening cry. Her pussy clamped down on me, and I gritted my teeth, trying to stave off my orgasm. I started to lift her off me, but her knees gripped my thighs like a vise.

"Jules… Goddamn it, baby, I—"

She shoved herself down on me one more time, setting off my release, and I let out a ragged groan. "Fuuuuck!"

Hot cum spurted deep, filling her up, and I pumped up into her twice more before collapsing on my back, Jules slumped over me. My cock still seated firmly inside her, I could feel our mingled lovemaking, and the sensation was erotic as hell.

We lay there in a tangle of limbs on the cold floor, moonlight streaming in around us, bathing us in a silvery glow. I stroked a hand up and down her back, our chests heaving, the only sound our labored breaths.

"Sweetheart?"

"Hmmm?" Her rumbled response vibrated through my chest, and I fought a smile at the sleepy sound of her voice.

"I didn't pull out."

"I know." Her words were soft but sure.

Hope flared. Did that mean she planned to stay around?

"What if you get pregnant?"

She lifted her head and blinked those sensual emerald eyes at me. "You want kids, right?"

With her? Hell yeah, I did. "Only yours."

"And I want yours."

I framed her face in one hand and took her mouth in a single hard kiss. I'd meant what I said; She was mine, and I was never letting her go.

Jules lifted herself off me, then slipped down to cuddle against my side, and I sifted my fingers through her hair as I turned my attention to the night sky outside. Not a cloud in sight, thousands of bright stars shimmered against the inky backdrop. I dredged up a memory from what seemed like a lifetime ago, and I repeated the same words to her now as I had then. "Gonna be a cold night."

I felt her smile against my chest, and she tipped her head up to look at me. "I never did look into that. Still sounds a little fishy."

I let out a chuckle. "You don't need to look it up. You should just assume I'm always right."

She smacked my chest lightly, playfully, a smile curling her mouth. Suddenly, it slipped away and her eyes turned serious, her expression taking on a quality of remorse. "There's something I need to tell you."

She laid her left hand over my chest, and her gaze dropped to it for a moment. "I lost my ring. My uncle took it when I got to his house, and I couldn't find it." Tears clouded her eyes. "I'm sorry."

Delving both hands into her hair, I drew her further up my body and kissed her forehead. "Don't worry about that, baby. Besides…" I swiped out with my right hand, searching for my jeans. I felt a tiny bulge in the front pocket, and I fished it out. "You didn't lose it. I have it right here."

Her mouth formed a small O, and her eyes lit up. "You found it!" She practically snatched it from my fingers. "But how?"

No fucking way was I ever going to tell her that story. I lifted one shoulder and traced my fingers over the back of her hand as she slipped it on. "It was returned to me afterward."

Not a complete lie, but it was the best she was ever going to get from me.

"I was so worried it was gone forever," she lamented softly.

Once more, I wondered what had transpired at her uncle's house. "If it holds bad memories, if you want to replace it…"

I wasn't sure how I would swing it, but I was sure I had some kind of return policy.

Jules's chin jerked up. "No!" Her fingers curled into a little fist. "I want this one. It's perfect."

My stomach let out a little grumble, and Jules let out a tinkling laugh. "Did you work up an appetite?"

A smirk tipped up the corners of my mouth." Yeah, but I'm not sure if I'm hungry for food… or for you."

Jules kissed my chest. "How about food, then me?"

It sounded like the best thing I'd heard in a long time.

THIRTY-FIVE

GIULIANA

"You ready?"

No. "Yep!" My voice was high and thin, and too damn chipper, a fact that went unmissed as Eric studied me.

"You'll be fine, babe. Like ripping off a Band-Aid. Just gotta get it over with."

"Right." Sarcasm flowed from my tongue as I threw a glare his way. I really wasn't in the mood for his tough love today.

He set down his coffee mug and stepped toward me, curving his hands around my shoulders as he studied me. "It's because I love you that I'm doing this."

"Mhmm." I hummed a noncommittal sound as my gaze slid away. I couldn't look at him. Those hazel eyes read me too well, and I was terrified of what he'd see deep inside. Fear. Cowardice. *Shame.*

"Sweetheart."

I ignored him and stared fixedly at the wall.

"Look at me."

His tone brooked no argument, and I forced myself to do as he commanded.

"This woman in front of me"—he gently squeezed my biceps—"this isn't you. Don't think I haven't noticed. You've practically worn a hole in the floor from your restless pacing around the room. You're anxious and on edge. But mostly..." He waited until he was certain he had my full attention. "You're bored."

I opened my mouth to refute his statement, but his lifted brow had me closing it again almost immediately.

"You need a purpose. Something to occupy your time. Being cooped up, even when I'm here, isn't good for you. You need to go to work, get back into your routine."

Two weeks had passed since I'd been released from the hospital, and I hadn't stepped foot outside. It was stupid, I knew, but I couldn't help it. There was no longer a threat hanging over my head; Massimo and Matteo were both gone, and no one was after me. Still, I couldn't bring myself to leave the cabin. Every time I thought about it, my heart raced, and I felt on the verge of having a panic attack.

Eric had been encouraging me—pushing me, rather—for the past several days to go back to work. I knew I needed to get back into the swing of things, but I couldn't get out of my own head. Finally, this morning, he'd threatened to throw me over his shoulder and carry me out the door kicking and screaming if he had to.

"I just..." I took a deep breath and directed my gaze out the window so I wouldn't have to see the disappointment in his eyes. "I'm not sure I'm ready."

His hands slid down my arms and laced our fingers together before bringing them to his lips. "Sweetheart, you're the strongest person I know. I'll never say I understand exactly what you're feeling, but believe me when I say I can speak from experience. I've been in a situation similar to yours.

"Life as I knew it was over after that operation at the warehouse. I'd lost my partner, my best friend, and was damn near killed in the process. All I wanted to do was bury my head in the sand, turn off my heart and mind, and forget it ever happened. So I took the easy way out and ran; I left everything behind and moved out here. But you know what?"

He waited for me to meet his gaze again before continuing. "I missed it. I missed not working, not having a reason to get up every morning. You're the same way. You're letting dark memories hold you back from the future."

He placed one finger over my lips as they parted to speak. "It's hard as hell to keep moving, to keep putting one foot in front of the other. It's going to take time to feel safe again, I understand that. And I'll always be here for you. You need something, I'm just a phone call away. Jack and Mia are there, and they can't wait to see you.

"It's time to go back to work, baby. It's time to take control again instead of letting them win. Stay in your office all day if you have to, but you've gotta get out of this house."

I hiccupped a little sound, a combination between a laugh and a sob, and his huge hand lifted to cup my face. "Please, Jules. I'm not asking you to do this for me. I'm asking you to do it for *you*."

I closed my eyes against the stupid, irrational tears gathering there and nodded against his calloused palm. "I know. I'm just… I'm a mess."

He lifted my chin, directing my gaze to his. "If that's true, you're the most beautiful mess I've ever seen."

I smiled despite myself. "Gee, thanks."

His other hand slipped around to my lower back and pulled me close. "You know I love you."

I melted into his embrace. I could hear those words every day for the rest of my life and it still wouldn't be enough. "I know."

He dropped a kiss on my lips, then swatted my bottom. "Now, get that cute ass in gear."

"Yeah, yeah," I grumbled as I peeled myself out of his embrace. "I'm going."

I slipped my purse over my shoulder, then picked up my keys from where they lay on the table beside the door. I watched as Eric clipped the duty belt around his waist, then shrugged into his coat, all the while thinking about what he'd told me.

He was right. I needed to take control of my life again. Though I hadn't wanted to admit it initially, I'd been going crazy. Being stuck in the house was just as bad as the thought of going out in public, just in a different way.

I'd grown up spoiled and, if not lazy exactly, complacent. I never had to work, didn't even have to go to school. Everything had come to me. Clothes, tutors, money; I'd never had to work for any of it. But what I'd discovered when I got a job at Briarleigh was that I truly enjoyed working. I liked being independent, actually thrived on it. It was so different than anything I'd ever known, and now that I'd had a taste of freedom and independence, I wanted more of it.

"Eric?"

He didn't even look at me as he palmed his keys and took a step toward the door. "Yeah?"

I took a deep breath. "I want to do this myself."

That got his attention. "What?"

Hazel eyes bore into my own, both bolstering my courage and making me feel incredibly bashful. "I… I think you're right. I need to do this." I paused. "On my own."

"Okay." His head moved up and down in a slow nod. "You're sure?"

"I am."

He stared at me for another long moment, then closed the distance between us. "I'm proud of you."

That meant more than anything else he could have said.

Eric was the bravest, strongest man I knew; for him to admire me was almost more than I could bear. I certainly didn't deserve his admiration, but I would find a way to prove myself worthy.

He cupped my chin in his hand and brushed his lips across mine. "Good luck today. And remember—I'm just a phone call away."

I nodded, knowing exactly what he meant by that. He wouldn't come running to me at the drop of a hat. He would, however, be there to listen. If I was worried or scared he would make the time to listen to me, to offer encouragement. "Thank you."

With another soft kiss, he ushered me out the door. "See you after work."

I made my way down the mountain to Briarleigh, my heart threatening to beat out of my chest. It was so strange to be surrounded by so many people, yet it was welcome at the same time. I loved Eric, and I truly enjoyed spending time with him. But I needed this. I fit in here, and I knew I was good at what I did. I thrived on the feeling of satisfaction of a job well done.

The employee door was unlocked, and I made my way down the hall to my office. I paused just outside the thick oak door and took a deep breath before sliding the key into the lock and stepping inside. I quickly closed and locked the door behind me, then moved behind my desk.

My purse slid from my shoulder as I sank into the chair, and I dropped my head into my hands. Baby steps, I reminded myself. I'd made it here without encountering anyone; that was half the battle. Truth be told, I was more worried about that than anything else.

What would people say? They knew I'd been kidnapped; Eric had told me of his tearing the town apart after the accident and trying to find me. I couldn't stand to be on the receiving end of their curious or judgmental looks. I had a feeling Eric knew the same. It was probably the only reason he'd waited so long to force my hand. But gossip wouldn't die down until I took control and showed my face in public. I needed to put on a happy appearance and pretend that it didn't bother me.

In reality, it was the furthest thing from the truth. Eric had been my saving grace over the past two weeks. He was there each time I woke from a nightmare, sweaty and screaming, the feel of the whip still fresh on my skin. He never offered me pity. To see that would have broken me. Instead, he'd coached me through each episode, using the comfort of his touch to slowly erase the nightmare I'd endured.

For the past four nights, I hadn't dreamed at all, and it felt like I was finally starting to move on. Though I'd resisted at first, I was glad Eric had pushed me to do this.

Drawing in a deep breath, I booted up my computer and began to scroll through emails. I'd received hundreds over the past few days, and I carefully read through each one.

An hour later, a soft knock came on the door.

I warily made my way to the door, then unlocked it and opened it a crack.

Mia peeked her head in, a bright smile on her pretty face. "Hey."

I smiled back. At least, I tried. I knew it felt forced, but she didn't seem to mind as she slipped inside and I closed the door behind her. "I didn't want to jump you right away on your first day back."

"You're fine." I tensed, waiting for the inevitable questions. But Mia surprised me.

"The spa is almost finished. Want to go check it out?"

A pang of disappointment thudded in my chest. The addition had been my baby, and I'd missed the completion of it. I would never get that time back, never…

I shook off the thought. It was just a room. All that mattered was that I was here. Safe. I had Eric and all of my friends. We had another thousand moments just like this one ahead of us.

"I'd love to." I reached for the door, but Mia hesitated, looking more than a little uncertain. It immediately put me on guard, and I froze in place, one hand on the knob. "Are you okay?"

"Yeah." She gave a tiny smile, one that didn't reach her eyes. "Just…"

She opened her arms slightly, her expression pleading. I didn't realize how much I needed the hug until I found my feet carrying me forward of their own volition. Her arms locked around my waist, and I clutched her tightly. Her body shuddered, and the knowledge that she was crying brought tears to my own eyes. For several long minutes, we remained that way. She was my best friend, practically a sister to me. God, I'd missed her so much.

She gently peeled herself away and swiped at her cheeks with the backs of her hands. "I'm sorry, I—"

"No, really." I blinked the moisture from my eyes. "You have no idea how much I needed that."

"I missed you."

Her blue eyes were sincere, and I realized just how difficult my absence had been on her, too. Though I'd been home for two weeks, I'd refused offers to see anyone, including Mia. Now I regretted it deeply.

"I'm sorry," I said by way of apology.

"Don't be." She waved away my concern. "I understand. I just want you to know how important you are—to all of us," she added. "I knew you wouldn't have just left. I knew something was wrong; I could feel it."

I nodded but still couldn't bring myself to tell her everything. From the slightly curious look on her face, I suspected Jack hadn't told her what had happened. Though I'd wavered in and out of consciousness, I knew he'd been there when they found me beneath the church. Eric told me that Jack had flown home the following day, but part of me was glad he hadn't told Mia. I wanted to leave that behind. It was bad enough that I'd been kidnapped; I couldn't bear to have her look at me with pity and sympathy instead of her usual cheer.

Pasting on a bright smile, I tipped my head toward the door. "I can't wait to see what you've done with the spa."

Mia held the door for me and chattered excitedly as we made our way down the hall. "We kept to the original plans, and the tile finally came in last week. Everything came together really well. Now all we have to do is finalize the name and some last-minute details, and we'll be good to go."

We'd been debating on a name for the past month but hadn't come up with anything official. I almost hesitated to offer my opinion, because I didn't want to sway Mia. This was the Prescott's resort, and I wanted to make sure she was happy with it. "That's awesome. What are you thinking?"

She slid a look my way. "I kind of liked your idea."

"Which one?"

"Rêverie."

I couldn't help the tiny smile that formed on my lips. It had been my favorite as well. The last several months—for myself as well as Mia—had been a dream come true. She'd rekindled her love with Jack and found her place in her late father's company. I'd been lucky enough to get this job at Briarleigh, create this amazing spa, and fall in love with Eric. It seemed fitting somehow that the spa be named for all the dreams that had come to fruition.

"Well, it's up to you. It's your spa."

She hummed a noncommittal sound just as we reached the doorway. "You ready?"

Butterflies kicked up in my stomach, battering against my rib cage. I was both excited and nervous—but mostly excited. I couldn't wait to see it. "Yes!"

She unlocked the door and swung open one of the heavy,

carved oak doors. The lights were already on, and my heart clenched as I looked around the space. Gone was the plastic sheeting and drywall dust. In their place were gleaming dark wood cabinets and shiny marble tiles. I stepped inside and ran my hand over the gently textured wallpaper, marveling at how gorgeous it was. It literally brought tears to my eyes. The tiny samples we'd chosen from could never do the finished product justice.

I glanced back at Mia, who stood in the doorway grinning hugely. "Gorgeous, right?"

I turned in a slow circle, taking it all in. "It's… perfect."

We spent the next half hour walking around the space, investigating every tiny detail, delighting in the silliest of things like the soft-close drawers and doors on the cabinets.

As Mia moved to turn off the lights, she looked up at me. "Hey, I have a meeting in a few minutes I'd like you to sit in on."

"Are you sure?" My heart raced at the thought of being surrounded by people who would be scrutinizing every move I made.

"Of course. Remember I told you we met with the lawyers in Spokane?" I nodded, and she continued as we moved toward the front door. "We need to firm up a few details about the spa, so it'd be great if you had time. It'll just be the lawyer, Jack, Carter, and myself."

I hated feeling so weak and insecure. Swallowing down my discomfort, I straightened my shoulders and forced a smile to my face. "Sure. Why not?"

Mia led the way back toward the small conference room. I smiled at the men seated around the table as I stepped inside, then waited while Mia closed the door. She gestured for me to take the seat at the head of the table while she slid into the chair next to Jack. Carter was situated to my left, and a man I didn't recognize—the lawyer, I presumed—sat at the opposite end of the table facing me. He smiled benignly, and I returned it.

Carter turned to me. "Welcome back."

"Thanks." My cheeks burned, and I quickly turned my attention to Mia, who had begun to speak.

"Thanks for coming, Mr. Jeffries."

He dipped his head in a slight nod. "My pleasure."

Mia pointed in my direction. "Mr. Jeffries, this is Jules. Jules, Mr. Jeffries."

I smiled. "Nice to meet you."

"You as well."

"Alright." Mia clapped her hands softly. "Let's get to it. Carter?"

Glancing to my left, I watched as Carter withdrew what appeared to be some kind of agreement from a manilla envelope. He met my gaze. "Have we decided on an official name for the spa?"

I flicked a look toward Mia, who nodded encouragingly. Why she was leaving it up to me to tell him I had no idea, but I relayed the information regardless. "We like Rêverie."

"Perfect. No changes necessary, then."

I lifted a brow. If Mia had already chosen a name, why had she asked my opinion? I started to question her, but Carter's next words stopped me before I had the chance.

"We've invited you here because we'd like to discuss something with you."

Caught off guard, my eyes widened, and I leaned back slightly in my chair. "Um… sure?"

Carter peered at me. "Have you ever heard of a rent-to-own agreement?"

I bit my lip, ashamed of my inexperience, and darted a quick look around the table. Jack and Mia offered reassuring smiles, and I returned my gaze to Carter. He gave no indication of making fun at my expense, just stared at me, waiting for my response. Slowly, I shook my head. "No. I don't know what that is."

He gave a little perfunctory nod. "Let's say you were leasing a space. Like the spa, for instance. Basically, you would pay rent throughout the lease, and a percentage of the payment would be applied to the purchase price."

My brows drew together. "Okay... But what does that have to do with me?"

"Jack and Mia would like to sell you the spa on a sort of rent-to-own agreement."

They what? For a long moment I sat statue-still, too shocked to think. My mind became a blank void, and I struggled to formulate words. Finally, I managed to shake off my stupor. "I'm sorry, I don't understand."

"Typically a business would move into a particular space, then make payments over the duration. In this case, you would be buying the entire business."

Was he messing with me? A quick glance toward Jack and Mia told me that they were, in fact, very serious. I understood the logistics of what he was telling me, but I needed to hear the words. "You want me to buy the spa?"

"Only if you're interested. Look it over and see if it sounds agreeable to you." Carter slid the sheaf of papers toward me, but I remained frozen to my chair, completely stunned. "Mr. Jeffries is here to answer any questions you might have, and I've reviewed it myself. It's a great deal."

Still unable to believe it, I turned to Mia and Jack. "Why?"

"Because we believe in you," Mia said softly. "This was all your idea, and you deserve to be recognized for it."

I blinked. "You're losing money."

They had to be. I'd only glanced at the first page of the agreement, but I knew the number listed as the purchase price wasn't even close to the spa's true value.

"Consider it an investment. Mia and I have been discussing the possibility of expanding and constructing several more resorts," Jack said, his dark eyes on me. "We'd like you to consider putting a spa in each of those resorts."

A spa in each resort? I gaped at them, completely blown away. "I just…" I shook my head. "I'm sorry. I'm not good at this kind of thing."

"Actually, you are," Jack interjected. "You did a phenomenal job in the pro shop, and the spa wouldn't have turned out the way it did without your input. I think you're very well qualified. This is common practice," he added. "But instead of investing in a franchise of some billion-dollar company…. We'd rather invest in you."

His words brought tears to my eyes. I'd always thought of Jack as being intense and reserved, cold and hard, but that was the furthest thing from the truth. For the first time ever, I saw his true character, and I understood why Mia loved him so much.

Mia smiled gently. "It's your choice, of course. But we'd love to work with you."

"I… I don't…" I swallowed hard, hot tears burning across the bridge of my nose and clogging my throat. "I don't know what to say."

Carter grinned and tapped the document with his index finger. "Sign it, Jules. You deserve it."

My hand fluttered to my throat, and I shot a quick glance at the lawyer, who until now had silently watched on. "Is this for real?"

He, too, grinned at me. "Very. And it's a wonderful deal. I would advise you to take it as well."

I whipped my head back toward Mia and Jack, my gaze ping-ponging between them. "Are you sure about this?"

Jack smiled widely and dropped an arm around Mia's shoulders. "We're positive."

"But take your time if you need to," Mia quickly spoke up. "I don't want you to feel like we're pressuring you or forcing you into it."

If the price on the front page was accurate, then this was a total steal. Still… I bit my lip. "Would you mind if I spoke with Carter and Mr. Jeffries?"

"I'd expect nothing less," Jack said. "If you'd like to get your own lawyer just to make sure—"

I was already shaking my head. "No, no. I trust you. I just… It hasn't quite sunk in yet."

I wanted to make sure I understood what was required of me, and I needed someone to break it all down for me.

"Why don't we give you guys some privacy?" Mia gestured around the table. "We'll be back in, say… an hour."

She and Jack excused themselves, and the three of us delved into the contract. I read through it, asking the occasional question when I came to a section of legal jargon I didn't understand. Carter and Mr. Jeffries outlined everything from payments to liabilities to future additions. By the time Jack and Mia returned, I was feeling much more confident and almost overwhelmed with gratitude.

It was going to be a hell of a lot of work, running a business in addition to my work as the events coordinator, but I looked forward to it with an enthusiasm I hadn't felt in… maybe ever. Mia and I had talked about posting a job listing soon to hire a manager for the spa, and I couldn't wait to get the ball rolling.

We signed the necessary documents, and Mr. Jeffries left to return home and begin the proceedings. The men congratulated me once more, then excused themselves to get back to work. Mia turned to me, one hand resting on her tiny baby bump. "Thank God, they're gone. Now we can talk about the wedding!"

I let out a little laugh. "It's been killing you, hasn't it?"

"You have no idea." Mia rolled her eyes dramatically. "You know, I'll bet our amazing events coordinator will work magic."

She side-eyed me, and I grinned at her reference to my new title. "Well, I do have a couple ideas…"

THIRTY-SIX

ERIC

I drummed my fingers on the countertop and let out a little growl. Where the hell was she? I glanced at the clock again, though it'd been barely thirty seconds since I'd last checked.

I'd felt anxious all day, on edge, nervous for Jules. I bet I'd checked my phone a hundred times over the past seven hours, expecting a call, a text—hell, *anything*—but the screen remained infuriatingly blank. I was proud of her for tackling this all by herself, but damn… I'd be lying if I said I didn't want her to need me, to rely on me to shoulder all of her burdens.

Almost as soon as the thought crossed my mind, I shoved it away again. The last thing I ever wanted to do was hinder her or hold her back from something. What I'd told her earlier was the truth: she was so incredibly strong, and I loved that about her. She'd endured something terrible, but she'd picked herself up, lifted her chin, and carried on. I loved her independence, but a huge part of me wanted to hold her close, protect her, tell her that she could depend on me.

What the hell was wrong with me? I couldn't quite explain

the conflicting emotions that rioted in my heart, turning my stomach into a tight knot. Maybe that was love, though. I'd never felt this way about anyone before; I wanted to push Jules to be the best she could be yet, at the same time, I wanted to tell her not to worry, that I would take on everything life threw at her.

The familiar crunch of gravel from the driveway reached my ears, and I damn near jumped out of my skin. I pushed off the counter, already striding toward the front door when I stopped midstep. Christ. What was I doing? I forced myself to change directions, and I headed back to the kitchen where I leaned against one of the cupboards, arms crossed over my chest in the most relaxed pose I could muster.

One minute passed, then two.

I let out a low growl and was half a second from storming outside when the front door swung inward. Jules stepped inside, bringing with her a wintry swirl of snowflakes that melted as soon as they touched the wood floor.

I didn't spare them a glance as I watched her set her purse and keys on the table, then hang up her coat and toe out of her boots. She turned and met my gaze, and for a moment, we were both silent. She looked a little dazed as she started toward me, and I was already halfway across the room, reaching for her.

"Jules?"

Silently, she wrapped her arms around my waist and leaned her head on my chest.

Immediately on guard, I folded her in my arms. "What happened? What's wrong?"

She shook her head, and I felt her chest rise and fall on a deep inhale before she peeled herself slightly away and angled her head to look up at me. "Everything is… perfect."

I studied her for a long moment, unsure whether to believe her or not. Finally, I went with my gut. If she said everything was fine, then I had to trust her. "How was your day?"

Something akin to disbelief mingled with joy in her pretty eyes, making them sparkle like emeralds in the bright light. "I have something to tell you."

"Okay." My tone held a trace of impatience, and a tinkling laugh fell from her lips.

"Don't look at me like that. It's nothing bad," she assured me as she slipped her arms up my torso and linked them around my neck.

I pulled her infinitesimally closer and locked my fingers together behind her lower back. "I'm all ears."

Her gaze darted away for a second, and she licked her lips before speaking. "Mia and Jack asked me to join them for a meeting today. While I was gone, they finished the spa and it's almost ready to open."

"That's great," I said softly. I knew how much work she'd put in and how proud of it she was.

"Well…" She drew the word out. "They offered to sell it to me, and… I bought it."

I blinked at her. "What?"

"I know it's a big decision, and I should have consulted you first, but they made me such a great offer and—"

I released her waist and framed her face in my hands, halting her rambling. "You're serious?"

She bit her lip and nodded, her eyes wide with worry.

"God, Jules." A smile tugged at my lips as I swept my thumbs over her cheeks. "I'm so happy for you."

"You're not upset?"

"That you're a successful business owner? Hell, no." I dipped my head and kissed her, long and slow.

She broke away and pressed one hand against my chest as she rolled her eyes playfully. "It's not successful yet; We're not even open."

I covered her hand with my own. "There's no doubt in my mind that you can make it work."

She eyed me. "You're not upset I didn't ask you first?"

I'd be lying if I said I didn't feel a zing of jealousy. As a man, I was supposed to be the provider—but no way in hell was I going to quash her dream because of my masculine pride. I cupped her face in my hands once more and made sure she was looking at me before I spoke. "I would have been happy if you'd consulted me, if only to give you my opinion—which, if you want it, I wholeheartedly agree with you. I think it's a great investment, especially with Jack and Mia behind you."

She smiled widely, and I continued. "I want to give you the world, Jules. But I'm not rolling in money—I never will be."

She opened her mouth, but I brushed a finger over her lips to silence her. "But I'm still a man, babe. I want to be the rock, the provider. It's in my DNA." I shrugged. "You're mine, and I want to take care of you, give you what you deserve."

She lifted a brow. "Can I speak now?"

"Only if you agree with me."

"Egotistical much?"

I shrugged unapologetically. "I never want to rely on a woman to put a roof over my head."

"We're a team now." She pinned me with that brilliant green stare. "You can provide as much as you want if it makes you feel better, but if we can have a better life with both our incomes, why not?"

"Because—"

"It was a rhetorical question, you idiot," she said, punching my chest.

Her tiny fist connecting with the hard plate of my vest didn't hurt me in the least, but she let out a little "ow!" and yanked her hand back, shaking her fingers.

I let out a little laugh when her face screwed up in dismay.

"I know what you meant." I took her hand in mine, then brushed a kiss over her knuckles. "I just want to make sure you know that money is yours. Reinvest it in the business; keep it for your future."

"In fact," I said before she could disagree, "we need to get you a prenup."

She flicked me an irritated glare. "No, we don't."

"Don't be stubborn. I want—"

She held up a hand. "The lawyers already explained it to me. First of all, I retain any assets obtained prior to the marriage. Second, we are not getting divorced. Ever." She poked me in the chest as if to stress her point.

"No, baby. We're not." I captured her hand once more and looped it around the back of my neck as I pulled her close again. "You've been mine since the second I laid eyes on you, and I'm never letting you go. Ever."

EPILOGUE

ERIC

Tiny white lights twinkled in the gauzy canopy overhead, their soft glow spilling over the otherwise dimly lit room. Dark fabric stretched across the ceiling, making them look like stars in the night sky we'd stood under months ago.

A tiny smile curved my lips. I'd felt something for her the moment she showed up, but that night cemented it for me. I'd fallen hard and fast and loved every minute of it.

My family had flown in from Illinois a couple of days ago, and my parents were both enamored of Jules. No surprise there. They, along with my men, crowded the chairs on my side of the room, while Briarleigh's employees and half the town residents took up all of Jules's side.

Soft strains of music fell from the speakers overhead, and I watched as Joey walked down the aisle, bouquet in hand. She'd ordered dresses for Jules and the girls through her shop, and I'd heard that she was considering expanding into bridal wear.

Mia came next, a huge smile lighting her face. I'd heard the expression before that expectant women glowed; never had I believed it until I saw Mia. Her pregnancy had become much more pronounced over the past couple of months, and she'd never looked happier or more beautiful.

At least one of the Prescotts was here. I resisted the urge to tug at my tie as I glanced behind me. Carter Reed stood just a few feet away, but Jack was nowhere in sight.

"I swear to God," I growled. "If he misses my wedding…"

"Don't worry, he'll be here," Carter assured me with a grin.

"Then where the hell is he?"

Carter tipped his head. "Right where he's supposed to be."

I followed his gaze to the large double doors at the entrance of the room. What I found there took my breath away. Jules glowed like an angel, lit from behind by the soft lighting of the hallway. Her hand was tucked into the crook of Jack's arm as he prepared to walk her down the aisle. The music changed, and all around the room people climbed to their feet. I didn't notice any of it. All I saw was her.

Green eyes met mine, and a shy smile curved her lips. God, she was gorgeous. Her long, glossy hair fell around her shoulders in those sexy waves I loved so much, and her dress was stunningly simple yet incredibly elegant. No embellishment at all, the exquisiteness was in the cut. It fit her perfectly, showcasing every curve, highlighting her beautiful body rather than detracting from it.

Unable to stop myself, I hopped off the small dais at the front of the room and strode toward them. Jules's eyes widened first with surprise, then pleasure as I approached. I met them halfway down the aisle and reached for Jules just as she extracted herself from Jack's grip.

Wrapping my arms around her waist, I lifted her into the air and spun her around. Her arms looped around my neck, and she threw back her head on a little laugh before meeting my gaze, her cheeks flushed pink with embarrassment.

"I don't think this is how it's supposed to work."

I slowly let her slide down my body until she was steady on her feet. "I couldn't wait any longer," I rasped out, emotion clogging my throat as I stared down at her. "You're so damn beautiful."

Her eyes turned dreamily soft. "Thank you."

Suddenly even this small amount of distance between us was too much. Needing to taste her, to feel her lips beneath mine, I bent my head and kissed her. Hoots and catcalls filled the air, along with the occasional "aww", and I grinned against her lips before pulling away with heroic effort. Nose to nose, I rested my forehead against hers and breathed her in. "I have no idea how I got so lucky to find you, but I swear I'll do everything in my power to make you happy and treat you the way you deserve. I can't imagine a single moment without you in my life."

She peered up at me, her emerald eyes misty with tears. "I love you."

Jack nudged me with his elbow. "Go make it official, Donahue."

I ripped my gaze from Jules and threw a grateful glance his way. "Thank you for this. For everything."

"Just repaying the favor." He tipped his head and strode toward the front of the church to take his place.

I grabbed Jules's hand and gave her a gentle squeeze. "Ready?"

She grinned back. "Absolutely."

I stared down at her for a long moment, completely awestruck. I loved her more than anything in the world. She was mine, and I was never letting her go. I bent and stole one more kiss, then together we walked down the aisle, ready to start the rest of our lives.

You won't want to miss Johnny's story, Hidden Truth! Their distrust of one another runs deep, but when Josi captures the attention of a stranger with a dark secret, John might be the only person who can keep her safe…

Turn the page for a sneak peek!

HIDDEN TRUTH

JOSEPHINE

The place was a disaster. For a moment, I could only stare, shock and anger bubbling in my veins. Clothes had been pulled from the racks and strewn around the room, shoes and accessories littered the floor, and shelves hung haphazardly where they'd been ripped from the walls.

I stood just inside the doorway, frozen in place as my gaze skimmed the room. Everywhere I looked, it seemed to get worse by the second. Tears pricked my eyes, blurring the sight of the ravaged store my grandfather had passed down to me. Who the hell would do something like this? And why?

It seemed like life lately had been delivering hit after hit, and I was about at the end of my rope. I managed to dig my cell phone from the depths of my purse, then dialed the Pine Ridge Sheriff's Department. A familiar voice answered on the second ring. "Sheriff's Department, Riley speaking. How can I help you?"

"Hey, Riley." My voice cracked, and I cleared my throat. "It's Joey from the Emporium."

"Hey, Jo. Everything okay?"

A couple months ago, I'd helped Riley math a partial footprint from a scene to a pair of boots we'd traced to the store. He was a nice guy, and I knew he would be able to help. I drew in a shaky breath. "Someone broke into the Emporium."

I heard a low curse on the other end. "Are you okay?"

"I'm fine." As good as I could be, anyway.

"I just dispatched a deputy. Is this the perp gone?"

My eyes widened as I flicked my gaze toward the back of the store. It hadn't even occurred to me to check. "I... I think so? I don't hear anyone."

"I'm going to stay on the line with you until they get there," he said. "Can you tell me what you see?"

I snorted before I could stop myself. "It's a mess. The entire place looks like it's been tossed. They threw clothes everywhere, broke some of the display cases and shelves..." My voice cracked again, and tears stung my eyes.

"It's okay, Jo," he said quietly. "We'll figure it out. Are you sure you're okay?"

I nodded even though he couldn't see me. "It must've happened sometime last night."

"We didn't get an alert," he said, his tone tinged with concern. "How did they bypass the alarm?"

"Um..." I bit my lip. "I don't have a security system anymore." I couldn't afford it.

There was a heavy silence on the other end, and I could practically feel Riley's disappointment rolling through the earpiece. "Do you have insurance?"

His words were low, just barely loud enough for me to hear, and I swallowed hard. Thank God, that was the one bright spot in all of this. I still had insurance to fall back on. "Yeah. They should help cover some of the damage."

He absorbed that for a second. "Okay."

Through the large display window that overlooked Main Street, I watched a cruiser approach, red and blue lights pulsing. I pushed open the front door just as Sheriff Eric Donahue climbed from the front seat. "Donahue's here."

"Good," came Riley's reply. "Let me know if you need anything."

"Thanks." I disconnected the call then offered a little wave to Eric as he crossed the sidewalk.

He lifted his chin in greeting. "Joey. What's going on?"

"Take a look."

He scowled as he peered inside. "Damn."

"Yeah. Someone had a good time last night."

He slid a look my way. "You okay?"

I lifted one shoulder. "Fine, physically."

He nodded a little, like he understood. "Let me take a look around."

I moved off to the side and waited as he checked the office and storage rooms. When he finally returned, a grim frown pulled at his lips. "Whoever it was came in through the back."

We received deliveries through the back door, but it was steel with no handle on the outside. "What the hell?"

Eric shook his head. "Sorry. Looks like the catch was jammed, so it never closed the whole way."

How the hell had I not noticed that? Damn it, I'd been so preoccupied recently with everything going on that I must not have checked the back door last night before I left.

"Can you check the safe and registers for me?" he asked gently.

That jolted me into action. If they'd taken the money, I was screwed. I wouldn't have to worry about insurance or the security system because I wouldn't be able to afford to stay here.

Carefully skirting the items littering the floor I crossed the room toward the counter. The register sat with its drawer open, a handful of coins inside. I shook my head. "I never leave cash in the register. Only coins. Looks like they didn't even bother with those."

He dipped his chin, then followed me toward the office. The safe was a small one, located behind a panel of wainscoting. I pressed the upper corner and the cleverly concealed latch released, revealing the safe.

Behind me Eric grunted appreciatively. "Herb always was a wily one."

He was. My grandfather had been incredibly attentive when it came to security. I just wished he'd applied the same diligence to the accounting books. I held my breath as the panel swung open, revealing the safe inside. The door was still locked, and I shot a quick look at Eric before spinning the dial to enter the code. The mechanism released and the door popped open, revealing a satchel of documents inside, along with a stack of cash.

"Thank God," I said on a relieved breath. It wouldn't amount to much, but it would hopefully get me by until insurance could cut me a check for the damages. I relocked the safe then pushed to my feet.

Eric gazed around, brows lifted slightly as he took in the disheveled office. "I know it's a dumb question, but does it seem like anything's missing?"

Biting my lip, I glanced at the paraphernalia scattered across the desk and over the floor. "I don't think so? Once I get everything back in place I should be able to tell."

He nodded a little. "My best guess is that someone was looking for easy money. The register was empty, so they came looking for the safe." He gestured over his shoulder. "When they didn't find it in here, they tore the store apart hoping to find it."

I nodded glumly. It made sense. Damn. My shoulders hunched inward as I looked around. This was going to take forever to clean up.

"Do you want me to ask Jules to come down?"

I sent a smile his way. "No, thanks. She's busy enough as it is."

"If you change your mind, let me know. I'm sure she'd be happy to help."

I knew she wouldn't hesitate to drop everything and come help, which was precisely why I didn't want to ask. "I'm good. But thank you. I've been slowly trying to get things organized. This just gave me more incentive, I guess."

He made a little face. "If you need help, you know where to find us."

"Thanks." I followed him to the door and watched as he climbed into the police cruiser. I flipped the sign on the door to closed, then surveyed the room. It was going to be a long day.

Don't miss Hidden Truth, now available everywhere!

ALSO BY MORGAN JAMES

RETRIBUTION SERIES

Unrequited Love – Jack and Mia, Book One

Unbreakable Love – Jack and Mia, Book Two

Pretty Little Lies – Eric and Jules, Book One

Beautiful Deception – Eric and Jules, Book Two

Hidden Truth – John and Josi

Sinful Illusions – Fox and Eva, Book One

Sinful Sacrament – Fox and Eva, Book Two

Retribution Series Box Set 1

Retribution Series Box Set 2

Retribution Series Box Set 3

The Complete Retribution Series

Thrillers and Mysteries

SECRETS OF BROOKHAVEN

Out of Sight

Out of Breath

Out of Time

STANDALONES

Dead of Winter

ABOUT THE AUTHOR

Morgan James is a USA Today bestselling author of contemporary and romantic suspense novels. She spent most of her childhood with her nose buried in a book, and she loves all things romantic, dark, and dirty. She currently resides in Ohio and is living happily ever after with her own alpha hero and their two kids.

Keep up with Morgan and stay up to date on sales and new releases at authormorganjames.com

www.ingramcontent.com/pod-product-compliance
Lightning Source LLC
Chambersburg PA
CBHW021124190726
48288CB00008B/2489